ROMAN ROULETTE

ROMAN ROULETTE

A Daria Vinci Investigation

MURDER IN THE CATACOMBS

DAVID DOWNIE

Alan Squire Publishing
Bethesda, Maryland

Alan Squire Publishing

Roman Roulette is published by Alan Squire Publishing, Bethesda, MD, an imprint of the Santa Fe Writers Project.

Printed in the United States of America.
ISBN (print): 978-1-942892-32-8
ISBN (epub): 978-1-942892-33-5
Library of Congress Control Number: 2022938587

Jacket design and cover art by Randy Stanard, Dewitt Designs.
Author photo © Alison Harris, www.alisonharris.com.
Copy editing and interior design by Nita Congress.
Printing consultant: Steven Waxman.
Printed by Carter Printing Company.

First Edition
Ordo Vagorum

Un'altra Parigi

The Irreverent Guide to Amsterdam

Enchanted Liguria

La Tour de l'Immonde

Cooking the Roman Way

Paris City of Night

Food Wine Rome

Food Wine Genoa & the Italian Riviera

Food Wine Burgundy

Quiet Corners of Rome

Paris, Paris: Journey into the City of Light

Paris to the Pyrenees

A Passion for Paris

A Taste of Paris

The Gardener of Eden

Red Riviera: Murder on the Italian Riviera

Four of Clubs: Murder in the High Sierra

Red Riviera *is one of the most high-spirited, well-informed, and exuberantly written thrillers I've read in a long time, plus it's funny as all get out. Downie, an Italian-American like his protagonist, takes the reader on an informative and unforgettable whirlwind tour of Genoa, its cityscape and monuments and history, architecture and politics, and manners and mores. A gem.*
—Harriet Welty Rochefort, author of *French Toast, French Fried, Joie de Vivre,* and *Final Transgression*

Red Riviera *had me in its clutches from the start—and refused to let go. A shocking premise, a stunning locale, and a complex web of history, politics, and crime that made perfect sense in the end. The pacing is flawless, the engaging characters leave you curious for more. Another, please!*
—Matthew Félix, literary podcaster, author of *A Voice Beyond Reason* and *Porcelain Travels*

Marvelous! Red Riviera *is so well plotted, so sensitive to present and past Italian history, so deep in characterization that I want to see more of Daria Vinci. What a cast. A grand, unputdownable read until the lights go out.*
—Ronald C. Rosbottom, author of *When Paris Went Dark: The City of Light Under German Occupation*

A delightful romp that sparkles like sunshine on the Mediterranean.
—Ellen Crosby, author of *The Angels' Share*

Gripping, with a plot as intricate as a Da Vinci maze, Red Riviera *is wonderfully atmospheric, showcasing author David Downie's intimate knowledge of things Italian—the landscapes, cityscapes, and social mores, all drawn with the lightest of touches. I particularly loved Commissioner Daria Vinci's escape disguised as a corpse, and the dark humor throughout this masterful crime novel. Bravo, bravissimo!*
—Anton Gill, author of *The Sacred Scroll* and *City of Gold*

For Alison, the perfect partner in crime;
and
in memory of my mother,
Romana L. Anzi,
the archetypal mercurial Roman matriarch, a woman of remarkable
talent, strength, and baroque sensibility, stranded in San Francisco

Mille grazie to my editor and publishers Rose Solari and James J. Patterson for their encouragement and enthusiasm; and to book designer and copy editor extraordinaire Nita Congress for all the hard, precise work.

"Enemies are an indication of character."

—Mary Roberts Rinehart, *The Bat*

One

An air-raid siren wailed. Cymbals clashed. The gangling, rawboned contralto center stage flung out her arms, shouting an operatic recitativo. First the words pealed out in German, then English, Russian, and French. Enunciating alternate notes in a shrill falsetto, she followed each shriek with a vibrating baritone bark. One down, one up, one down, one up.

Commissioner Daria Vinci's facial muscles had a will of their own. They followed the singer's contrapuntal lament and pumping, flailing arms. The commissioner's remarkably handsome face was transformed from a study in mature Mediterranean majesty into a twitching mask of martyred human agony.

Daria could not recall the exact words Maestro Katzenbaum had used to describe his *Symphony for a Brave New World*. A teeter-totter of contrapuntal sounds and cacophony of emphatic polyglot words meant to evoke postmodern superabundance in the superheated run-up to climate Armageddon?

During the intermezzo, she had chatted with the maestro, her brother Mario Vinci, and her aged godfather, Ambassador Willem Bremach. That seemed a lifetime ago. She longed for the concert to be over. Kicking herself for accepting her brother's invitation, she knew she had agreed to appease him and honor the memory of their long-dead father. Dr. Mario Vinci, MD, PhD, et cetera, et cetera, was a trustee of the Institute of America in Rome and the host of the annual midsummer fundraising gala. Their father Roberto had also been a trustee, decades ago.

Her thoughts were interrupted by a ball-peen hammer ringing a gong and a pneumatic hand-drill whizzing a wire brush against a towering silver samovar. Groaning out loud, Daria glanced furtively around and rose to her feet. Calculating how long it would take to scoot sideways then disappear among the fragrant box hedges, the leafy acanthus, and topiary laurels bordering the villa's outdoor theater, she guesstimated five embarrassing seconds. A small price to pay. She would incur her brother's wrath. So be it.

Ducking and moving along, the cymbals clashed again a few feet from her head. Glancing at her older brother, Daria wondered if Mario had gone deaf. He appeared imperturbable. The semi-retired Manhattan cardiologist, a part-time Rome resident, was eighteen years her senior, making him nearly seventy. He sat as bolt upright as the electrified upright piano not five yards in front of them on the stage. His large black eyes glowed in the Roman sunset. They remained fixed on the musicians. So did the set of his thick, sensual, but unsmiling lips.

With a jolt and a violent squeal, the piano shook the front rows of the concert hall just as Daria was slipping by. A trombone and tuba blared as a kettle drum rumbled. It was then that Daria heard the muffled but unmistakable report of a firearm. She froze, dropping into an empty front-row seat as if she herself had been shot. A large-bore handgun, she guessed. Listening for the sound of a second gunshot, watching the faces of those seated nearby, she realized no one else had heard anything over the music. Could she be mistaken? Was the shot a car backfiring?

Watching now as several ghostly figures wearing white smocks appeared from below ground, among the shrubbery twenty or thirty feet away, she shook her head and wondered if this were part of the performance. But these apparitions rushed away toward Villa Nerone, one of them stumbling as it ran. Daria checked her watch. Precisely three minutes had gone by since the sound of the gunshot.

Up again and moving swiftly sideways, Daria had almost reached the side aisle when the false soprano shrieked again. The piercing cry seemed to amplify another strident sound— the sound of a woman screaming in real, honest-to-god, unbearable pain. Daria ducked past the clashing cymbals, her ears ringing. As if on cue, half the audience leaped to their feet, thundering out applause as they pushed toward the stage.

"Bravo, bravissimo!" someone cried. Other cheers followed. "Encore!" "*Bis, bis!*" "More, more!"

Trapped, Daria could not free herself.

On the stage in front of her, Maestro Katzenbaum spun on his heels, bowing. Paroxysms of pleasure contorted his shaggy, sweaty head. Before he could take a second bow, a showily dressed, sequin-spangled, heavily made-up woman of middle years teetered forward on high heels and began tapping a microphone with one long, polished red fingernail.

"Please, *attenzione*, is there a doctor in the house?" She spoke breathlessly in a strong Roman accent. "I apologize. There has been a slight accident."

Still seated, Dr. Mario Vinci stood to his full height of six foot three, nodded decisively at the woman behind the mike, glanced around with fiery black eyes, and made his way through the throng. He saw Daria and beckoned. She fell in behind. They were joined by another, younger man.

"Ah, Dr. Vinci," exclaimed the woman who had spoken into the microphone, clasping her manicured hands. "I should have come straight to you. Please follow me."

"I am an internist," said the younger man hurriedly, bustling alongside the others. "May I be of assistance?"

The woman glanced from one to the other, then asked both doctors to accompany her to the villa's infirmary. She glared at Daria, seemed to recognize her, hesitated, then strode ahead.

"I am Commissioner Vinci," Daria volunteered.

"My younger sister," Mario explained. It sounded like an apology.

"Of course, Commissioner," said the woman. "We have met before. I am Patrizia Pizzicato, the Rome director of the Institute."

As the four crossed the villa's marble threshold, Pizzicato added, "I have called an ambulance, but not the police. The burn and wound do not appear to be serious. However, the victim is hysterical. I am unable to understand her. I think what she is repeating is 'Dead, he is dead.'"

Two

Precisely seven minutes after Daria, Mario, and the internist had stepped into the infirmary, the president of the Institute, Taylor Chatwin Paine, arrived at a trot, rushing in through the open doorway. He was short of breath and looked as if he had jumped off the dusty running board of a prewar Bentley. Loose-jointed and boyish despite his almost eighty years, the president of the Institute of America in Rome wore his signature black tails, de rigueur for the annual midsummer fundraising gala and other public events at which he was a notable participant. The superannuated tuxedo made a striking match with Chatwin-Paine's long, silvery, almost white hair slicked back from his forehead like a ghoul's. Several strands of this remarkable head of hair and a snowlike dusting of dandruff on the president's shoulders caught Daria's beady hazel eyes, causing her eyebrows to rise into a Gothic arch.

"There you are," said Mario Vinci in his gruff basso voice to Chatwin-Paine, raising a pair of obsidian eyes from the woman on the examination table in the center of the infirmary's spartan room. "Dr. Giolitti has almost finished dressing her wounds."

"Adele!" ejaculated Chatwin-Paine, leaning forward. His voice was a fluty tenor. "Adele Selmer. What on earth has happened to you?"

Adele stuttered, unable to speak. Her bulbous blue eyes full of tears rolled backward into Adele's small head like the glass eyes of a ventriloquist's dummy.

"She has burns on her right shoulder, chest, and arm," intoned Mario Vinci.

"Much more worrisome," added Dr. Giolitti in a crisp, professional tone, "she has a deep gash in her right temple, apparently produced by a flying chip of tufa stone or a projectile. It appears not to have struck an artery. However, there may be a foreign object lodged deeper. We have patched her up and staunched the bleeding. She should be hospitalized immediately. There may be a degree of fracturing of the skull and potential brain trauma, and the burns require treatment. There is also clear psychological trauma."

"She is in shock," said Mario.

"Yes, clearly," mumbled Chatwin-Paine with a show of empathy, "how tragic, how terrible."

"Dead," cried Adele, sobbing and catching her breath.

Daria left the wall where she had been leaning. Squatting so that her head was level with Adele's, she spoke softly. "I am a police officer. Can you tell us what happened?"

Adele gasped. "Dead," she spluttered again, the tears streaming down. They dropped onto her unnaturally red cheeks and the long blond tresses that spread across her bloodstained white long-sleeved smock. The garment looked like something a ham actor might wear in a costume drama, a peplum filmed at Cinecittà. A toga or perhaps a tunic? Daria was not sure of the proper name, or whether togas and tunics had sleeves like this smock.

"Where did it happen?" Daria asked.

"The catacomb," blubbered Adele.

Daria heard the suffocated bleating of an ambulance siren set at its lowest volume—the setting usually reserved for the dead. Glancing through the open door, she could see the vehicle lumbering up the villa's coiling driveway.

Drs. Vinci and Giolitti glanced at one another. They turned to the president. Before either could speak, Daria stood up.

"There are catacombs on the grounds?"

Taylor Chatwin-Paine seemed surprised by her question. "Yes, of course, the Catacombs of Emperor Nero—or, I should say, a small offshoot from them. The official name is Catacombe di San Calogero dei Campi, named for the medieval church that is now in ruins in the public park flanking the Institute. Our grounds are riddled with abandoned quarries and catacombs." He spoke with a patrician, mid-Atlantic accent and clearly enjoyed the sound of his own voice. Chatwin-Paine seemed as cool as a gravedigger, as imperturbable as Dr. Mario Vinci.

"There," Adele blurted, waving her left hand toward the door. "Underground. Under...the lookout tower..."

The ambulance crew pushed through the infirmary door. Mario Vinci and Dr. Giolitti helped Adele onto a stretcher, then walked alongside it. Daria drew Chatwin-Paine out of earshot.

"Is it normal for Rome Award winners to wear togas and frequent the catacombs?" she asked. "And for what purpose?"

"As a matter of fact," he said, "it's a tunic, not a toga." He smiled around his long, bleached teeth, finally noticed the dandruff and stray hairs on his shoulders, and patted them off. "How fortunate that you are here, Daria," he added good-naturedly. "Your father would be proud." He paused significantly and stared into her eyes. "What a strange sight Adele makes. I wonder what might have happened."

Daria studied Taylor Chatwin-Paine in the half light, trying to recall the last time she had seen him. It must have been five years ago. More. The president of the Institute had not changed. He never changed. Ageless, unflappable, he was as eternal as the Eternal City and its myriad ghosts. "Forgive me for insisting," Daria said. "I am unfamiliar with the catacombs you mentioned or the lookout tower. Might you be good enough to show me the way?"

Chatwin-Paine added to the wrinkles on his remarkable brow. "Colonel Vinci," he said deferentially, "I will gladly accompany you, but I wonder, given your state of dress and specifically your very handsome designer shoes, whether it is advisable for you to attempt to enter the catacombs now? Perhaps we should summon your fellow officers? There is a carabinieri station two blocks away, as I am sure you know. I assume Patrizia Pizzicato, our local director of operations, has already called the authorities, unless she called your people at the Polizia di Stato instead?"

Daria shook her head, "Neither has been called," she said. "Just so you know, I am a major, not a colonel."

"Ah, you mean, you are not *yet* a colonel," Chatwin-Paine murmured.

Daria turned to her brother. "Mario, are you coming with us? We might need a doctor."

It was not a question. Mario Vinci left Giolitti as the ambulance pulled away, walking ponderously, leaning forward, as if his feet could not keep up with his outsize head and long upper body.

"Are there electric lights in the catacombs?" Daria asked as they crossed the grounds.

Chatwin-Paine grimaced in mock pain before answering. "That would not be allowed, Daria. The site is a national monument though it is private and off limits to visitors. I will get flashlights from the gardener's shed." He paused. "Wait for me here."

"That won't be necessary," Daria interrupted. "We have our smartphones. There's no time to lose."

"Someone else may be injured," Mario added in his thunderous voice.

"As you wish," said Chatwin-Paine.

Leading the way through a boxwood labyrinth on the far side of an ornate, glassed-in greenhouse, Chatwin-Paine detoured around the gala crowds mingling by the outdoor theater. A dozen or more candlelit, linen-draped large round tables each set for twelve awaited diners along the panoramic terrace near the rose garden. Champagne corks flew. Pontificating voices and laughter filled the air.

At a thousand dollars a plate, Daria thought as they strode past, Mumm or Veuve Clicquot and beluga caviar were the least the paying guests should expect.

She also happened to know from her brother that each of the fifty-member board currently gave twenty-five thousand dollars per year to the Institute's endowment fund. It had been created a century ago and had topped the two hundred million-dollar mark. The fund allowed the Institute to offer a dozen Rome Awards per year, each worth a hundred and fifty thousand dollars in cash, lodging, food, and travel, and to host a handful of residents, pay local Roman and New York–based staff, and maintain the lavish villa and grounds.

It took just over four minutes for Daria, Mario, and Chatwin-Paine to reach the base of a gape-eyed brickwork lookout tower rising above the ancient Roman city walls girding the villa's grounds and the abutting public park.

"This is one of the entrances to the catacombs," Chatwin-Paine explained, pushing open a low wooden gate. Daria noticed the gate was not locked. "The most practicable of them," he added.

"How many entrances are there?" she asked, following him through a stone doorway and down a steep, narrow staircase hewn out of bedrock. "Are they all open?" She paused halfway, braced herself against the walls, and took off her ridiculous, hateful shoes, clutching them in one hand. The light from her smartphone caught the glossy pink polish of her toenails.

Chatwin-Paine stared at her bare feet in what appeared to be a state of rapture. He seemed about to make a remark, cleared his throat, licked his lips, waited another beat, then said, "Three. Three entrances that I am familiar with. I suspect there are others that are inaccessible. None of them are locked, per se, but the grounds of the villa are secure. It is impossible to enter without being detected. This way," he added, holding up his smartphone to shine a light on the cramped passage that stretched ahead. "I do wish we could have picked up a lantern or flashlight."

"There appears to be a faint light burning ahead and to the right," said Mario as he shuffled forward. "Several lights." Daria glanced at her brother. He was bent double to keep from hitting his head on the rough-hewn whitish stone walls.

"Flickering lights," Daria remarked as they approached a circular chamber at the end of the long, dank tunnel. The walls were scarred on both sides by carved funerary niches. They looked like bunk beds.

"Candles," said Mario.

"Votive lamps," corrected Chatwin-Paine. "There are hundreds of them. We have left many in place by orders of the Ministry of Fine Arts and the Office of the Superintendent of Archeology."

"Oil lamps?" It was Mario again.

"Yes, olive oil lamps," said Chatwin-Paine. "Late imperial period, you know. They were made in the same way for over a thousand years."

"That explains the burns," Mario remarked, "on the young woman's shoulder and arm."

Daria's bare feet sank into the thick tufa dust on the catacomb's unpaved floor. She chased away fears of what might be lurking underfoot and peered at the constellation of twinkling oil lamps. The scent of burning wicks and oil blended with the acrid stench of the powdery tufa and the mildew of nearly two thousand years. There was something else in the air. Daria sniffed, recognizing the cloying scent of smoldering hashish or marijuana and the flinty tang of burned gunpowder.

"My, my," muttered Chatwin-Paine as he crept forward. "What in heaven's name has been going on here?"

A score of terra-cotta lamps shaped vaguely like Aladdin's slippers twinkled along the walls, producing tiny pools of dim, shuddering light. Beyond was utter, impenetrable darkness. On a stone bench carved from the living rock stood a hookah, still smoking, a straw-wrapped flask of chianti tipped on its side, and five wineglasses, two of them shattered, the other three partly filled with red liquid. A broken oil lamp lay on the ground.

"Over there," blurted Daria, holding up her phone. The light fell upon the curving form of a recumbent human body. A man. He was remarkably short, blond, apparently young, and curled in the fetal position. Mario strode over. He felt for a pulse at wrist and neck, and, frowning, shook his head. Then he turned to face his sister and Chatwin-Paine. "It is not a pleasant sight. The right cheek, maxilla, and mandible have been shot away," Mario said grimly, shining the light on the man's gory head then on the wall in front of him. "Brain matter and bone have been projected several feet. The bullet appears to have taken a chip off the wall, there, then struck and shattered the lamp next to it, knocking the lamp down there." The light followed the assumed trajectories of the bullet and fallen lamp.

"Charles Wraithwhite," the president gasped. He reached down to pick up the handgun lying near the body. "Why, it's Jefferson Page's old service revolver," he said incredulously. "How in God's name..."

"Drop it," Daria barked. The revolver clattered to the floor. "Don't touch anything. Don't move, either of you. Not an inch. Wait until the forensic team gets here before you take another step."

Fingertipping her phone, Daria tried to place a call. There was no connectivity. Of course. They were underground. Wordlessly she pivoted, retracing her barefoot tracks to the entrance. Feeling the filthy dust enveloping her feet and puffing upward between her toes, she prayed she would not encounter a rat, or step on a fragment of maxilla or mandible— or fibula and tibia.

At the top of the staircase, pausing, she inhaled deeply and cursed Chatwin-Paine under her breath. Why had he picked up that revolver? Was he going senile? Wiggling her toes and dusting off her ankles and feet, she slipped on her uncomfortable dress shoes. "Filippo?" she snapped when the DIGOS night duty officer answered her call. "Can you see my GPS coordinates? Good. Yes, the Institute. Get our guys over here before I can count to ten. No sirens. No uniforms. Bring headlamps and dust masks. Get anyone who knows anything about catacombs or caves and sewers. Get Canova. Tell him to bring me my running shoes. The red ones. They're in my locker."

Three

Midnight came and went with a clanging of bronze bells from the villa's private chapel. The gala was not over yet.

Daria knew it was going to be an interminable night, with no dinner and little sleep. She and the DIGOS team had taken over a ground-floor reception hall in the Institute's main building, the vast Renaissance Villa Nerone. The room was the size and shape—and also had the airy volume of—a tennis court, though the words "papal court" seemed more fitting to Daria's increasingly fraught mind. The thirty-foot coffered ceiling sparkled with gilded lilies and other armorial decorations. A triple set of tall mullioned windows formed what looked like stone crucifixes and had, presumably, been snatched from a cathedral. They glittered with expanses of small diamond-paned stained glass artfully backlit from outside.

Halfway along the wall of the reception hall, a manorial marble fireplace was large enough to have been conceived for roasting oxen whole. Daria recalled vaguely that the villa had become the headquarters of the Institute of America in Rome over a century ago. Before that, it had belonged for four hundred years to a famous or perhaps infamous Roman dynasty that had produced a dozen cardinals, several popes, and countless other unconsecrated rascals and rogues.

Peering out through double doors flung wide to the warm night, Daria observed the goings-on. Most of the lavish gardens of Villa Nerone had been cordoned off since the discovery of Charles Wraithwhite's body, leaving only a narrow access route from the parking lot to the terrace. Half a dozen plainclothes operatives wearing headlamps searched silently amid the shrubbery while the gala dinner proceeded with a buzz of voices on the panoramic terrace nearby. The scene seemed to have been lifted from a film by Fellini.

It was also breathtakingly beautiful. The luxuriant pine-stippled grounds of Villa Nerone had been the site of countless historic dramas since the days of the Roman Republic. The view beyond the east terrace's marble balustrade beggared belief. In the gloaming, the zigzagging silhouette of the skyline suggested infinite timeless grandeur and startling natural majesty combined. Splashed with orange and purple, the summertime evening colors quivered, melding into each other as the minutes passed. Swallows darted, chirping overhead, unbothered by the absurdity of human activity. The dissolving outlines of ancient temples, cupola-topped churches, and medieval towers—framed by parasol pines—were spotlit like jewels in a boutique on Via Condotti. Scattered across the city's celebrated hills, jets of illuminated water frothing in Baroque fountains danced in the afterglow of a late June evening, mesmerizing Daria's tired eyes.

Yes, she told herself, observing the scene, she could still be dazzled by the magic of her native city. She was proud not to be world weary.

Beyond its beauty, the surreal, seductive scene was also disconcerting. Earlier, the deputy minister of the Interior and the vice questor of the Province of Rome had skipped the music but rolled up to the gala in time to hobnob, feed, and imbibe French champagne. Seated at the best table on the terrace, they were hedged in from behind by half a dozen bulletproof bodyguards. Herded out of the villa by her brother, Daria had been made to stand by Mario's side when he and a dozen other pooh-bah trustees lined up to greet these Roman dignitaries. In the arcane hierarchy of Italian law enforcement, both paunchy, aging Lotharios were Daria's immediate superiors. She drew back as if bee-stung when the deputy minister had taken her hand and with a lubricious squeeze and a twinkle in his eye had murmured *"Mi raccomando."*

Mi raccomando?

The seemingly innocent, encouraging phrase meant everything and nothing. Though she was bilingual and bicultural, the offspring of a Roman father and a Bostonian mother, Daria could not find in her overburdened mind a precise translation of mi raccomando into standard American English. Surging upon her came a phalanx of subtly menacing phrases such as *Make sure you do the right thing* or *I'm telling you, step carefully*, and *Take care, watch out! Be warned.*

Clearly, special treatment was required. Special treatment of what or whom?

As Daria passed along the crowded terrace on her way back to her operational headquarters in the villa after the encounter, table talk had reached her ears. The gem-encrusted ladies and epaulet-hung gentlemen were not discussing Maestro Katzenbaum's *Symphony for a Brave New World* or the urgently needed renovations to the Institute's library. The names of Adele Selmer—the burn victim wrapped in a bloody tunic—and Charles Wraithwhite—whose cerebral convolutions hung like stalactites from the catacomb's walls—were on every wagging tongue.

Like alternating pendulum weights, President Taylor Chatwin-Paine and Director Patrizia Pizzicato continued to come and go from the reception room, repeatedly interrupting their debriefings with Daria to give thanks or bid farewell to someone. An endless stream of donors and dignitaries rose and moved with excruciating slowness toward the chauffeur-driven limousines and luxury cars waiting by the porter's lodge. Chatwin-Paine's and Pizzicato's behavior was highly irregular. Daria would not have tolerated it had it not been for Mario's stern admonitions to be patient—and the kindly reassurance of her godfather, Ambassador Bremach.

We were all equal before the law, were we not? Daria had asked herself and Bremach earnestly. Or was that a convenient fiction to keep the hoi polloi under control? A man was dead, still lying below ground in the claustrophobic circular burial chamber, apparently killed by a self-inflicted gunshot wound during a bizarre ritual Daria was still attempting to understand. For the sake of propriety, his body would only be removed once the last guests had left the grounds. Then the hard work by the ballistics experts and cavers would begin.

Meanwhile, an unknown number of unidentified tunic-clad conspirators, presumably present at the shooting, were still at large. Theoretically they were either Rome Award winners, visiting artists or writers, or infiltrators from outside the Institute. The only participant in the underground ritual who had been identified was in the hospital with serious burns and a head wound. Adele Selmer had been placed in an artificial coma. No information from her would be forthcoming for at least twenty-four and more likely thirty-six hours.

At Mario's insistence, the DIGOS team had so far been extraordinarily discreet, working in silence, methodically and politely checking the network of catacombs, the villa's five acres of landscaped gardens, its two dozen art spaces and writing rooms, the recording studio and indoor concert hall, the research library, chapel, computer room and study lab, the vast dining room and multiple recreation areas, half a dozen outbuildings, including greenhouses and winter conservatories, four maintenance sheds and a porter's lodge, as well as the thirty bedrooms occupied by the Institute's twelve Rome Award winners, ten visiting artists and scholars, and eight resident faculty. Each interview had been conducted with utmost circumspection. So far, nothing unusual or suspicious had been found. The award winners, artists, writers, scholars, and teachers questioned denied knowing anything about the catacomb incident.

Daria ran through the numbers. Of the Institute's thirty official inhabitants and their dozen spouses, wives, husbands, partners, or companions, ten were unaccounted for. Why? Easy. It was June 21st, the end of the spring term. Several award winners had already returned to the United States to take up their busy careers. Two others were known to be traveling in Europe. The remaining five might be out and about, living it up on the town, at a late dinner, or otherwise occupied. That was no one's business but their own. They were perfectly free to come and go as they wished, said the sequin-spangled director, the preening Patrizia Pizzicato, with a tone verging on the indignant.

Daria had to remind Lieutenant Canova, her deputy, and his subordinates, that there was no guarantee that the fugitives wearing tunics who had presumably fled the catacombs were associated with the Institute. They might have come in as guests of Adele Selmer or the dead man, Charles Wraithwhite, or of some other Institute occupant. A list of names of visitors who had registered with the doorman that afternoon and evening had been drawn up, with the help of the security desk at the porter's lodge. These individuals would be traced, contacted, and interviewed. For the time being, the investigation would move forward on the assumption that Wraithwhite had accidentally killed himself playing Russian roulette with an antique yet deadly Smith & Wesson revolver. The gun had been the property of Jefferson Page, a former president of the Institute. There was no indication so far of foul play, meaning homicide or suicide.

At approximately 12:30 a.m., the nonagenarian Ambassador Bremach was still full of vigorous banter. He seemed unwilling to leave Daria's side. Bremach had been a Spitfire fighter pilot during World War Two. He was nearly six and a half feet tall, still played singles tennis and flew his own private twin-engine aircraft. Teetering only slightly from his great height and from the champagne he had drunk, he used his carved wooden cane like a baton. Bremach was eager to reminisce with Daria about the coup attempt the two had helped thwart in Genoa some fourteen months earlier. But a few minutes after the chapel's bronze bells had rung 12:30 a.m., Bremach had been discovered by his yawning wife Priscilla, a woman nearly forty years his junior, and unceremoniously marched away.

"To be continued," Bremach had said to Daria, then whispered conspiratorially, "mi raccomando."

Mi raccomando? Again? Daria felt a chill.

Between 12:30 and 1:00 a.m., most of the gala's remaining guests reluctantly took their leave, rubbernecking as they sauntered out, doubtless hoping to see the body raised from the catacombs, then removed in the ambulance that was standing by.

Alone or in company, Daria had forced herself to return to the scene of the incident twice over the course of the evening. She had followed the special police caver crew back and forth through the maze of seemingly interminable underground corridors and rooms. With her running shoes on her slender, pedicured feet, Daria felt safe not only from bones, rodents, and virulent spores on the floor of the catacombs, but also from prying, prurient eyes. The toenail polish was her one concession to femininity. It always remained hidden from view during working hours. She regretted taking off her pumps earlier in the presence of Chatwin-Paine. He was an unrepentant skirt-chaser of known ambiguous and ambidextrous sexual inclinations, still active despite his long teeth and official marital status. The president's omnivorous satyriasis was the worst-kept secret in the city. His wife was also voracious though nearing eighty, and had swung from bi to lesbian all her life, but was rarely to be seen in Rome with her husband. She preferred the limelight of London and Manhattan, where her sometimes-successful plays were performed off and occasionally on Broadway. Why the couple bothered to maintain the fiction of heterosexual "normality" in the 2020s was an issue no one in America could fathom. But Daria knew why: Italy was still hidebound, a bastion of machismo and the seat of the Catholic Church.

Though she pretended not to suffer from claustrophobia when underground, Daria was secretly relieved to concentrate her investigative efforts above. The narrowness of the subterranean tunnels, the dust and stifling air, and the fear of rodent-borne diseases such as leptospirosis had induced her to allow the forensic team to wrap things up without her. They had promised to bring the revolver, the empty cartridge, and the projectile, when found, to her improvised headquarters in the reception room. The trouble was twofold. First, the fingerprints on the revolver had been smudged, and, second, the actual bullet continued to elude detection. The dust on the floor was one to two inches deep. A metal detector had been requested. So far it had not arrived.

Daria had finally been able to unravel one curious mystery tangentially related to the gunshot and the decibel volume of its blast. The solution to the riddle explained why she had heard the shot fired deep underground but no one else had. Patrizia Pizzicato had explained. The circular burial chamber was roofed by a thin, uneven vault. The chamber sat directly underneath the five front rows of the outdoor theater. That was where Daria and Mario had been seated. The floating plank flooring of the theater—constructed a century or more ago—had been conceived to protect the natural tufa vault and keep that fragile section of the catacombs from collapsing.

The acoustics in the tunnel network were remarkable, added Pizzicato. In certain spots in the gardens or outside the thick city walls encircling the grounds, you could hear word for word what was said deep inside the catacombs. If you stepped a yard to one side, the voices became inaudible.

Many parts of the tunnel network had been reinforced when the villa was remodeled and extended around the turn of the nineteenth century, the director had added. The reconstruction process was described in exhaustive detail in a history book in the Institute's library. The outlying, dangerous underground areas had been sealed off at that time or in ensuing decades with reinforcing walls of brick. Iron gates closed off half a dozen tunnels that once linked the Institute's grounds to the main catacomb network in the park abutting the property. Judged unsafe, those public catacombs had been off limits to visitors since the 1950s.

After the director had finished her narrative and stepped aside, Lieutenant Massimo Canova strode into the hall. Sitting at a long carved oaken table, a relic from centuries past,

Daria glanced up at him. Strewn around her were blueprints of the villa and grounds, a map of the catacombs, and piles of antiquated, printed documentation about the Institute, its location and history.

"We have checked everything except one room on the third floor of the annex to the main building down a service corridor that's locked," Canova said.

"Is the door locked or is the corridor locked?" Daria asked distractedly, concentrating on the material on the table. "Dangling modifiers are not an effective arm against crime, lieutenant."

"Both are locked," said Canova stolidly. "The custodian no longer has the key. To the room, I mean."

Lieutenant Canova was in his early thirties, well built, black haired, dark eyed, of limited intellect and bereft of a sense of humor, as far as Daria could tell. He would go far. "Find the director, Signora Pizzicato," she said.

Canova shook his head. "She does not have the key."

"Then find President Chatwin-Paine," Daria suggested, glancing up from a folder containing biographical information on the year's Rome Award winners and the Institute's other current occupants. "He'll have the keys. Ask him what the room is used for."

"Sì, commissario," said Canova. He waited, hovering until she looked up again. "Please, also note that a gentleman in the porter's lodge insists on seeing you. He will not divulge his name. He says you know him from the Province of Genoa and he has just arrived with important, fresh material."

"*Material?*" Daria pursed her fleshy lips, then swallowed hard. She blushed. "From Genoa proper or Rapallo?"

"Genoa, I think, though maybe he said Rapallo. Aren't they in the same province?"

"Tall, dark, and handsome—and young?"

Sergeant Gianni Giannini had promised to visit her. Their enforced separation caused by her transfer to Rome was becoming painful. She dared not hope.

"The opposite," said Canova. "Short, heavyset, not to say obese, balding, and about your age, perhaps older—mid-fifties."

Daria's face fell. It could not be Gianni. "Well, if the gentleman won't give his name, tell him I can't see him." She began to stand up. Then she froze, glancing toward the entrance. A vast, pneumatic figure filled the wide doorway. "Lieutenant Morbido!" she shouted, jumping to her feet.

"*Captain* Osvaldo Morbido," he croaked in his rough deep voice, stepping forward with outstretched hands and a foot-wide smile. Daria noticed crumbs in the corners of his amphibian mouth. Clutched in one thick fist was an oily paper bag.

"Promoted?"

"Same as you," he said, giving her a hug. "It's only fair. It took a little longer, that's all. I have an appointment to see the deputy minister tomorrow. In the meantime, a guy on the night desk named Filippo said I'd find you here and that you might need a helping hand." Morbido paused and gauged her, looking up from his under-average perspective. "You're taller and skinnier than ever. I brought you some focaccia from Genoa, the very best, it's still practically warm."

"The *material*," Daria laughed, making room for Inspector Morbido at the end of the table. She hoped the antique bench would hold his weight. Despite herself, she licked her lips and salivated. She loved Ligurian focaccia. How sweet of him to remember. She was about to accept a slice when she heard footfalls and looked up. "Too late," she muttered. "No time for explanations." She stood and spoke with her hands. "President Chatwin-Paine, this is my colleague, Captain Morbido, from DIGOS Genoa. He will be assisting my team."

The two men shook hands, eyeing each other warily. Seconds later, Daria saw Chatwin-Paine stealthily slide his right hand into his pocket. She knew the germophobic dandy was wiping the focaccia oil and microbes off, using one of the alcohol-soaked handkerchiefs he always kept folded up in the pockets of his pants.

It was hard to imagine the pair of men belonged to the same species. One was a willowy sallow vampire, the other a giant brown toad crossed with a Churchillian bulldog about half his height.

"Yes," Chatwin-Paine said, sibilating slowly, "Morbido... I am sure Ambassador Bremach has spoken to me about you and, yes, about your father, long ago. Yours is not a surname one easily forgets. Valerio Morbido. A union organizer at the Ansaldo steel plant, was he not, your father?"

"Likewise," Morbido croaked nodding his neckless head, "about the surname, I mean, Sir Chatterton-Paine, is it?"

"Chatwin-Paine," he corrected.

"Descended, I assume, from Thomas Paine?"

"As a matter of fact," Chatwin-Paine muttered, thrown momentarily by Morbido's manner and his wide, fly-catching grin, "it is."

They decided to postpone a further tour of the underground maze until the body of Wraithwhite had been removed and the weapon analyzed. At Mario Vinci's prompting, Chatwin-Paine piped up and agreed that in the meantime, it would be a good idea to take a look at the last unexplored room on the property, the one Canova had referred to. The president of the Institute seemed slightly disoriented as he listened and nodded his head for longer than might be considered normal. Again, Daria wondered. Had he made one toast too many? Or was he physically exhausted—understandable given the hour, the events of the night, and his age?

"Yes," said the president as he often did, starting his sentences with a distracted, single, double, or triple affirmative. "Yes, right you are. That must be the museum room. That's where Wraithwhite would have found Jefferson Page's revolver, which I so thoughtlessly picked up, I don't know why. Yes, of course."

The prewar staff elevator to the third floor's service area had enough capacity for four average passengers. Daria and Canova stood aside and watched as Taylor Chatwin-Paine, Patrizia Pizzicato, Mario Vinci, Osvaldo Morbido, and a captain named Rocco Foscolo squeezed into the cab. Daria had met Foscolo upon his arrival, in the company of the deputy minister and vice questor, at about 10 o'clock. She had not exchanged more than a greeting with him and was not sure why he had stayed behind.

A whispered word from Canova informed her that Foscolo had been detached to DIGOS a week earlier on special assignment from SISMI, the Italian military intelligence service. Foscolo's specialty was political cybercrime. He was training members of the DIGOS anti-cyber blackmail squad.

Why had he had come to the gala and why was he sticking around?

Prepossessing was not a term Daria could use to describe Captain Foscolo. He had the pockmarked, grizzled look of an aging heavy, a rectangular hunk of mustachioed masculinity seemingly incapable of using a keyboard or smartphone with his bearish fingers. Cybercrime? Foscolo's manner and physique made towering Mario Vinci and massive Osvaldo Morbido look and sound like Boy Scout tenderfoots.

The SISMI officer seemed familiar with the Institute. He also appeared to know Chatwin-Paine. Neither fact surprised Daria. Everyone in Roman officialdom, particularly those in the armed forces and the more sensitive ministries, knew and generally admired the president and the Institute. Beyond Chatwin-Paine's gallantry and flawless Italian, he had been a fixture in Rome since the kaleidoscopic 1970s, when Cinecittà had still rivaled Hollywood, the Cold War had burned like dry ice, and failed coups, successful kidnappings, and bloody kneecappings had been as commonplace as swinging, swapping couples, LSD Kool-Aid cocktails, and Euro-Communist Catholic social club singalongs in the Baths of Caracalla. Chatwin-Paine sat on a dozen Italian-American boards, and was the honorary president of the Protestant Cemetery Association and a regular guest at the dinners hosted by the figurehead president of Italy in his Quirinal Palace. No Roman social occasion was complete without Chatwin-Paine's tony, preternaturally old-money American presence.

The elevator seemed to be taking an eternity. "We're climbing," Daria said, beckoning Canova and the custodian, who was waiting with them. They found the back stairway and started up. Daria could not help noticing the contrast with the villa's formal reception areas, as if the stairway had been grafted onto the building from a hospital or high school. The explanation for this architectural oddity was provided by the custodian, Signor Giuseppe Verdi. He had the same name as the composer and even looked vaguely like him. Verdi recounted laboriously how a "modern" neoclassical annex had been added to the rear of the Renaissance villa around 1900 by a noted American architectural firm whose name Verdi could not pronounce despite decades in the Institute's employ and repeated attempts at proper enunciation.

Daria had visited the Institute many times over the years. But she had never penetrated beyond the gardens and reception hall or dining rooms. It felt strange to her now to peer behind the scenes at what was a thoroughly banal piece of reinforced concrete parading as a masterpiece by Michelangelo.

Adorning the walls of the stairwell were dozens, possibly hundreds, of murky oil paintings, framed sketches of architectural oddments and perspective drawings, or posters from decades past—many decades past. Daria squinted at them. The light was abysmal. Most of the artworks were all but invisible.

"We ran out of display and storage space long ago," wheezed the custodian, apparently reading Daria's mind.

Puffing while pulling himself up using the banisters, the well-fed, tobacco-stained, past-retirement-age Roman followed slowly, pausing to catch his bronchial breath at each landing.

Canova spoke up. "There is one curious thing I haven't had the opportunity to mention yet, commissario," he said as they reached the second floor and paused, waiting for Verdi to catch up. "Please allow me to show you what the custodian showed me earlier." Canova spoke stiffly, with stilted precision. Stepping up to a huge, garish canvas hanging forlorn in the semi-darkness, he lifted the bottom away from the wall and shined a flashlight on it. Daria glanced at it hurriedly, then frowned in bafflement.

Glued to the back of the canvas were three decals. One showed a comb or hairbrush, the second a Cheshire cat, and the third a baseball bat or club. Next to them were the capital letters "CC" painted using a stencil in bright glossy red.

"What does it mean?" Daria asked, her interest piqued. She snapped several photos from a variety of angles.

Canova shrugged. "Signor Verdi says the stickers and CCs have been found on a dozen or more paintings in recent weeks and also in very unusual and sometimes difficult-to-access places."

"Such as?"

"Well, for example, in the sub-basement, in a crawl space, a kind of tunnel that has been blocked up since before the custodian was hired."

"When was that?"

"You mean, when was he hired?" Canova asked cautiously. "Forty-two years ago, same as Signor Chatwin-Paine. Verdi thinks this tunnel may lead into the catacombs or the waterworks conduit through the public park, but he is not sure. He wonders if it has not been unblocked by someone recently. On several occasions he has found dusty footprints in the sub-basement in front of the entrance. Also, these symbols have been found on the wall above this stairwell, by the rungs of a fire escape or perhaps it's an access ladder leading to a trap door in the roof, the trap giving access to the electric motor that operates the elevator. We also discovered them on the backs of paintings hanging in both Signor Wraithwhite's and Signorina Selmer's bedrooms."

Daria tapped her half-open lips with her index finger, puzzling before she spoke. "What do the president or director think?" she asked.

"We have not had time to ask them."

"Very well," Daria said, glancing again at the decals and the double-Cs. "Brush, Cheshire cat, club or baseball bat, two hundred in Roman numerals..."

"*Gatto, pettine, bastone*," muttered Canova in Italian, repeating the words softly like an incantation. "There is one more thing," he added as if suddenly remembering. "Another curiosity."

"Well?"

"The custodian and several other occupants of the Institute report that dozens of small transparent plastic bags containing an American candy known as jelly beans have been left in public rooms and again in strange places."

"Go on."

"They have been found in the laundry, in the pockets of freshly laundered clothing, and also in the director's and the president's incoming mailboxes."

"Jelly beans?" Daria shook her head. "Does not compute," she muttered. "Someone who loves Ronald Reagan?"

"Sorry, commissario, I do not understand."

"Never mind," Daria said. "You were not born yet and I was a mere child when the sainted Ronald Reagan popularized jelly beans. Actually, I stand corrected. I wasn't born either— Reagan was governor of California in 1966."

"May I ask why you know so much about jelly beans?" Canova inquired earnestly.

Daria smirked and said, "Like Ronald Reagan, I used them to quit smoking, about twenty years ago, and I also became addicted. I put on so much weight that I started running for exercise. I finally kicked the bean habit."

"But you still run?"

"Yes," she said. "Hyperactivity has a downside, but it happens to help in our profession, don't you agree?"

Verdi, the custodian, caught up with them and together they climbed the last two flights of stairs. "Masterpieces," he wheezed sardonically. "At least they're better than what the award winners produce nowadays."

"Jelly beans," she mused aloud, shaking her head. "What could it mean?"

"Installation art," said the custodian. "Street art, conceptual art. *Nonfunctional tokens*. NFTs. That is what I have been told. These are things I do not understand."

"Non*fungible* tokens, I think it is," remarked Daria.

"Functional or fungible, it's all the same to me," harrumphed the custodian. "This is not the first time it has happened. In 2009 or 2010 there was a group of highly cultivated, well-mannered Rome Award winners who thoroughly vandalized the Institute with graffiti in a similar way. They took photos of the vandalism and turned them into an art show. Now with the nonfungible nonsense, they *sell* the pictures on the Internet or something like that."

"Charming," remarked Daria mirthlessly. "So, this is some kind of copycat action?"

"Possibly," muttered Verdi scowling and visibly disgusted with the inmates of the Institute.

Crowded together on the narrow, uncarpeted landing outside the third floor's mysterious locked room stood Morbido, Foscolo, Pizzicato, Mario Vinci, and Chatwin-Paine. They had not entered yet and seemed frustrated and impatient. The door to the room was armor-plated. It looked like a premodern bank vault. The president had clearly been struggling but failing to get it open. He tried a key, failed again and fumbled, then searched through the many other keys on his key ring, muttering as he went. "It must be this one," he said, slipping an old-fashioned multiple-pronged steel cylinder into what had been a burglar-proof lock in the 1920s or '30s.

Groaning, the door swung open. Chatwin-Paine rotated a vintage porcelain light switch to the right of the door on the outside wall in the corridor. The switch clicked loudly and sparked. Hanging from the ceiling in the center of the room, a dim, dusty incandescent lightbulb glowed. The shutters were closed. The dust in the room was almost as thick and suffocating as in the catacombs. It billowed out into the corridor, causing several of those present to cough or sneeze.

"Tutankhamun's tomb," Morbido spluttered.

"Major Vinci," Chatwin-Paine said, motioning, "after you."

Stepping in, Daria turned on her heels and said, "Please, all of you, stay on the landing, come in one at a time if called, and refrain from touching anything—anything at all."

Four

The Institute of America in Rome had been founded in the late 1800s as a finishing school for American artists and architects in need of classical training. They studied the Coliseum, the Pantheon, and the aqueducts, then moved onto Michelangelo and Neoclassicism, shunning the art and architecture of the Middle Ages, the Baroque, and the Rococo—all decadent, perverse, and anti-utilitarian periods, according to the American arbiters of the day.

Skipping over the founder and several distinguished successors, the Institute's most revered president was unquestionably Jefferson Page, the scion of a prosperous clan of New Englanders whose Pilgrim ancestors had landed in the wake of the Mayflower. Page's claims to fame were too many to enumerate. Only a consummate hagiographer and fundraiser such as Chatwin-Paine could fit them neatly into a nutshell, which he did as they stood inhaling the acrid dust of the third-floor room.

Daria listened attentively as Chatwin-Paine extracted the nut of proud history.

In 1944, while World War Two still raged, Page had been appointed by the board of trustees in New York to occupy and defend, and then repair and revive, the shuttered, shattered Institute. With a knife clenched between his teeth and a revolver in each hand, Page had parachuted into Italy shortly after Allied troops had begun the liberation of Rome. He had fought his way across the rubble-strewn, occupied city and up the steep hill to the Institute's hallowed site, dodging sniper fire and the last desperate Gestapo-killing patrols.

Finding Villa Nerone in the hands of the enemy, Page had entered the grounds surreptitiously, then used his fluent German and peerless diplomatic skills to negotiate a surrender with the kommandant. At the last minute, before the Nazis could capitulate, shots rang out. Narrowly escaping death, Page picked his way through the maze of booby traps inside Villa Nerone and onto the roof, then used his service revolvers to shoot dead the last Nazi holdout. The fanatic sharpshooter had hunkered down with a telescopic rifle in a machine gun nest atop the Institute's main building. The nest was still there, complete with weathered sandbags, though naturally the machine gun had been removed long ago.

The strangest thing of all, added Chatwin-Paine, was that throughout the Nazi occupation, a secret radio transmitter hidden not thirty paces across the rooftop from the machine gun nest, in a cubby hole above the elevator shaft, had been able to broadcast vital information to the Allies. Sadly, the transmitter had been removed and the cubby hole sealed up in the postwar period.

Jefferson Page's tenure had lasted a quarter century, through famine and feast, boom and bust, the end of Fascism and rise of the Soviet and Italian Reds. Vintage photos displayed on the walls of the third-floor room showed a tall, slim, stylish Clark Gable look-alike. Dashing, heroic, fearless, witty, and charming, Jefferson Page had been married atop the Capitoline Hill at Rome's City Hall in 1948. His beaming blond bride was the adoring and beautiful American heiress Caroline Brinton, also of Pilgrim stock. They had met while on duty in Latin America working for the United States government.

There was no mystery, said Taylor Chatwin-Paine. The third-floor room had housed Page's back office and personal archives since the 1940s, though some of his correspondence was in the reserve room of the library. Page's successors, each short-lived until the arrival of Chatwin-Paine, had meant to transform the dusty cache into a museum of the history of the Institute, as Jefferson Page had requested upon his res ignation in the mid-1960s. The job had been left undone. Chatwin-Paine himself had on two occasions in the 1990s and early 2010s hired researchers and detached an assistant librarian from the Institute to complete the project. Budgetary restrictions, thorny personnel issues, entropy, and the passing of time had sidelined Jefferson Page's dreamed-of museum until recently.

That was when a benefactor had left the Institute a seven-figure legacy with the proviso that the museum be created and Jefferson Page be honored. The unexpurgated history of the institution was to be written and published as a hardback coffee table book complete with full-color illustrations and photographs, suitable for gift giving and fundraising purposes.

The board had duly instructed the book committee to take charge. In New York, a candidate was vetted, hired by board chairman Roy Heiffermann, and sent to Rome. Research work in the Institute's library, with forays into the third-floor room, had begun some months ago.

"Yes, you see," said Chatwin-Paine, "that's why we hired Charles Wraithwhite, to put together an up-to-date history of the Institute and help us transform this sadly neglected trove into a small museum." The president paused and glanced from face to face, scrutinizing in particular Daria and Mario Vinci's expressions.

"Wraithwhite was a contributor to *The New York Review of Reviews*," explained Mario. "He is, or was, the author of several well-received volumes of cultural history, and had some training in library science."

"And IT," added Patrizia Pizzicato.

"Yes, he appeared to be the ideal candidate," Chatwin-Paine remarked distractedly. "He was so innocent looking, a blond Rococo cherub. Little did we know..."

Pizzicato spoke vehemently now in her yard-thick Roman accent, teetering forward and waving her sequined arms. "The delay in completing the restoration work was not our fault, we had to wait for the building permit and the construction workers, who were not immediately available, as you can imagine, Major Vinci, this being Rome. Evacuation of objects and remodeling of the room was to begin next week. Now we will have to start all over again."

Stepping in behind the director, Canova spoke up, turning to Daria and pointing. "Commissario, please take note: the same kind of key used by the president to open the door of this room a few moments ago was found in the front pocket of the victim, Signor Wraithwhite," Canova said.

"Which pocket?" Daria interrupted.

"The left pocket," answered Canova. "Does it matter?"

"Everything matters," Daria answered.

"Yes," said Chatwin-Paine, chiming in, "yes, of course, Wraithwhite had the only other key, you see, it is impossible to have copies made, we really must change the lock and the door, and do something about the dust and lighting..."

Daria tapped her lips then drummed them, an unconscious nervous tic that alarmed her whenever she realized she was indulging it. "The dust has a story to tell," she said. "Please refrain from removing it or doing anything in this room until you are given the go-ahead." Indicating an empty glass display case mounted high on the opposite wall, she asked what it was supposed to hold.

"Of course, the case, yes, that is where Jefferson Page's revolver was displayed," said Chatwin-Paine. "Pardon, I should say, where *one* of Page's revolvers, plural, was on display."

"How many are there?" Daria queried.

"Two that we know of," said Mario Vinci from his position by the armored door. "I have seen them and handled them several times over the years."

"And where was the second one kept?" Daria asked.

Mario and Chatwin-Paine pointed simultaneously to the top drawer of a heavy wooden chest standing against the wall under the display case. Daria stepped up to it, eyed the hanging bronze loop handles, asked Morbido and Mario if they would each loan her a pen, then used the borrowed pens to lift and pull the handles without touching them. She peered inside.

"Jelly beans," she muttered.

In a corner of the deep, wide drawer nestled a transparent plastic bag stuffed with brightly colored candies. The bag was tied with a thick black ribbon. Leaning against it was a tiny plastic sword. She stared, frowning and shaking her head. Her attention shifted from the beans and sword to a rectangular object in the center of the drawer.

A velvet-lined mahogany pistol box lay open, another Smith & Wesson revolver inside it. Flanking the wooden box were several faded, battered cardboard cartridge containers. One of them was puckered and had clearly been torn open. Daria could see the bullets gleaming dully inside. "Identical?" she asked, glancing around again at the display case, the wooden chest, and several pieces of forlorn furniture including a wooden chair standing nearby. She stepped closer and studied the furniture without touching it, then turned, still waiting for an answer.

"Yes, identical to the gun in the catacombs, you mean?" Chatwin-Paine spoke at last, sounding solicitous. "Yes, well, I think so, .45 caliber, though I am not an expert. I always assumed they were the same, they certainly look very much alike and feel alike when you hold them."

Mario nodded gravely. "I agree," he said. "I have held them. We sometimes show them to special guests or board members."

"The behind-the-scenes tour," added Pizzicato. "Jefferson Page used one of these guns to shoot the Nazi sniper."

Daria raised an eyebrow. "Evidently, others have taken the tour, so to speak, and left behind jelly beans and a toy sword." The president and director glanced at each other but said nothing.

Piping up, Verdi, the custodian, remarked that in Wraithwhite's room, in addition to a cache of jelly beans, he had also found a large plastic shopping bag stuffed full of tiny toy plastic swords. "The kind the crusaders used," Verdi added, "or Caesar. You know what I mean. A short-bladed gladiator sword."

A baffled silence returned.

"May I?" asked Morbido not waiting for an answer. He stepped to Daria's side and glanced into the drawer, grinning. "A Smith & Wesson M1917," he said. "Standard-issue service revolver used by the United States military for over half a century, also used by other armies and issued to ranking U.S. Army personnel stationed in Italy through the 1950s. Last seen in Italy in the arms caches created by NATO for the anti-Communist insurgency contingency scheme known as 'Stay Behind.'"

"And by the Borghese Coup plotters and the P2 secret Masonic lodge?" Daria asked.

Morbido nodded. He was about to elaborate but fell silent. From the corridor, Captain Foscolo moved swiftly toward them, a juggernaut of brawn. Daria and Morbido made way. With his bright black bird eyes, the SISMI officer looked down into the drawer, took out his smartphone, made a short video, then clicked several stills, the camera flashing. "Captain Morbido's identification is at least partly correct," he said in a gravelly, rasping voice, turning to speak to Daria. "However, I am quite certain this is a special model manufactured in 1937 for the Brazilian military." He tapped the photo gallery icon and used his thick fingers to zoom. "You can see very clearly the crest of the Brazilian armed forces. Technically, we refer to this as a Modelo M1937. There was no similar crest on the M1917 I saw earlier by the body of the victim in the catacombs."

"You were allowed in?" Daria was unable to hide her indignation. Foscolo assented in silence. She was about to ask, *To what do we owe the honor of your presence?* But she restrained herself. "Well, I'm glad cybersecurity expertise includes ballistics. What is the significance of this interesting, speculative analysis, for which I thank you, captain?"

Foscolo shrugged. "Possibly nothing," he admitted. "Both revolvers could fire the same ammunition, those bullets you see in the boxes in the drawer. For reasons having to do with the machining of the barrel, and the extractor and firing mechanisms, one particular type of cartridge worked more reliably in the M1917. In the newer M1937 it didn't matter which of the two types of bullet—rimmed or rimless—was used.

"If, as Signor President Chatwin-Paine explained earlier, Mr. Jefferson Page did his military service in the war somewhere in Latin America, it makes sense he might have been issued the Brazilian model."

"He said nothing about military service," Morbido interrupted. "President Chatwin-Paine spoke of working for the United States government, that is all."

"I stand corrected," said Foscolo, inclining his head.

"Fascinating," Daria murmured. "What else, Captain Foscolo?"

Pulling a pair of ultrathin latex gloves over his huge hands, Foscolo produced two eraser-tipped yellow pencils from an inner pocket. With them he lifted the revolver gingerly, turning and flipping it with acrobatic ease. Peering down the barrel, he used the eraser tip of one pencil to spin the empty cylinder, clicked it out, and spun it again deftly, looked down the barrel from the opposite end, stared into the chambers one by one, clicked the cylinder back in place, and, like a prestidigitator, managed to pull the trigger several times without touching the gun with his fingers, all the while tilting his head to right and left to observe the action of the hammer and other moving parts. He laid the gun down, took off the gloves, and put them back in his pocket.

"Well?" Daria asked.

"The gun should be thoroughly analyzed by ballistics, needless to say. I am guessing it has not been fired or cleaned in a very long time. It is also extremely dusty. If I am not mistaken, the bulk of the dust is from the catacombs. It has been wiped off hurriedly or clumsily, in the process removing most if not all of the fingerprints either intentionally or unintentionally, it is impossible to tell." Foscolo now pulled a jeweler's loupe from another inside pocket, bent over the gun, and examined it again. "No prints are visible but the whitish-yellow dust is, there, there, and there," he pointed. "Would you care to look for yourself, major?"

Daria took the loupe. She studied the surface of the gun. The silence was oppressive. "Anything else?" she asked.

"Possibly. From a cursory examination, I would further guess the chambers have been loaded and unloaded more than once recently—not with all six bullets, more probably with one bullet at a time. With the loupe you can see the traces—the minute disturbance of the two types of dust—the catacomb dust on top and the lower layer of grayish gritty dust accumulated over a period of many years, I am assuming. So, the bullet would have been loaded into one chamber, removed, then reloaded randomly into the same or another of the chambers."

"But never fired?"

"Correct. Not in a very long time. This gun may have been fired a year or fifty years ago, thoroughly cleaned afterwards, and then displayed or placed in its box and never fired since."

"Would that be consistent with the surmise that the revolver had been used to play Russian roulette in the catacombs?" she asked.

Foscolo inclined his head in the affirmative. "Played with and possibly laid down on the dusty floor or in one of the burial niches, where it came into direct contact with a thick layer of tufa dust," he clarified. "That dust was, as mentioned, wiped off recently before the gun was replaced in its box."

"Anything more?"

Foscolo's eyes sparkled as an ironic smile flashed across his lips then disappeared under his moustache. "As you will also have surmised, Major Vinci," he said, "Signor Wraithwhite had very bad luck."

"Clearly," Daria agreed. "What exactly do you mean?"

"The probability of a six-chamber revolver firing a round when only one chamber has a bullet in it is one in six; I think that's self-evident. That probability does not change each time the cylinder is spun and the trigger pulled. That is slightly over a sixteen percent chance. Except that in reality, the probability is infinitely less than one in six, for reasons you are certainly already familiar with or can guess."

"Enlighten us," Daria said, her impatience bringing out an unintended edge.

"Gladly. The cylinder is perfectly balanced when empty and if properly maintained, cleaned, and lubricated it spins freely. If empty, the probability of one chamber aligning with the firing mechanism and barrel is exactly one in six, as mentioned. But if one of the chambers is loaded, the weight of the bullet in that chamber causes the cylinder when spun to stop with the bullet at the lowest or the near-lowest position. In other words, the chances of actually killing yourself playing Russian roulette are extremely small—negligible, in statistical terms. You can, as a general rule, click the trigger two or even three times without much risk. Many players of Russian roulette are known to do this. A single pull of the trigger is not much of a dare."

"It is, apparently, if you're playing *Roman* roulette," Morbido grunted. His contorted, glowering expression turned a mottled shade of purple as he stared at Foscolo.

Daria glanced from him to the SISMI officer. She nodded, thrusting out her lips for emphasis. "That makes perfect sense," she said softly. "When playing Russian roulette, if I have understood you, there is always a dare involved?"

"That is the usual practice," said Foscolo. "A dare, a wager, a challenge of some kind."

Daria thought an extra beat before continuing. "Speaking of dares, since you seem to have formulated a variety of theories, Captain Foscolo, have you any ideas about the nature of the dares this group of young people were formulating?"

Foscolo seemed surprised by the question and eager to hide his uncertainty. He hesitated. "With all due respect, that seems to me to be a question for those representing the

Institute. Given the number of decals and bags of jelly beans and swords and so forth, it could be something do with that, wouldn't you think, Major Vinci?"

"It might," she said. "Do you have anything more to add, captain?"

"That is all for the time being."

"Thank you," she said coolly. "Please give my regards to Colonel Rossi and thank him for the profile of Joseph Garibaldi and the assistance SISMI provided to us in Genoa."

"Brigadier General Paolo Rossi?" corrected Foscolo. "I will give him your regards."

Swiveling, Daria looked Chatwin-Paine in the eye. He did not blink. He did not flinch, blanch, or twitch. "Has anyone checked behind the paintings and photographs on the walls of this room or opened the other drawers in this desk?" she asked.

Chatwin-Paine glanced at the director, who looked at Verdi, the custodian. All three shook their heads. The president said, "Not to my knowledge."

"Or mine." It was Pizzicato.

"Or mine," Verdi wheezed.

Daria turned back to Chatwin-Paine. "You say there are only two keys to this room?"

"Yes."

"Charles Wraithwhite had one of them?"

"Yes."

"This is the other one?" She indicated the key in his hand.

"Yes."

"Please, may I have it?" Chatwin-Paine complied. "This room is now closed. It is a crime scene, like the catacombs and the rest of the Institute and grounds. With the exception of Captains Foscolo and Morbido, Dr. Mario Vinci, me and my operatives, and the other three of you standing in this room, meaning President Taylor Chatwin-Paine, Director Patrizia Pizzicato, and Signor Giuseppe Verdi, no one comes into the Institute, no one goes out, until further notice. I would like to point out that Mario Vinci was sitting in the front row of the theater when the shot was fired. Therefore, he is not a suspect and is free to move around as he wishes."

Daria tipped her head meaningfully at the door. The others turned and stepped out, still in dead silence. She slipped the key into the lock, using it to drag the heavy door shut. Then she turned the locking mechanism twice to the right, glanced once again at the unusual key, and, realizing she had no pockets in her slinky silk dress, handed it to Morbido for safekeeping.

"As Ambassador Bremach said earlier this evening," she remarked, "to be continued. It is now 2 in the morning. All of us need sleep, except Lieutenant Canova. Pick four of your freshest men to guard the catacombs, the villa, the porter's lodge, and the grounds, one each. You shuttle between them. I'll be back at first light."

"*We'll* be back," growled Morbido. He glanced dangerously at Foscolo as the group moved down the corridor, some taking turns riding the elevator to the ground floor, others opting for the backstairs.

Catching a nod from Daria, Canova stayed behind with her and Morbido. They waited silently. When the empty elevator had returned to the landing for the second time, she directed Canova to step inside. He did. She and Morbido did not. Before the doors could close, Daria held them back with one foot. She said softly, "First of all, other than the key, was there anything else in Wraithwhite's left front pocket?"

Canova glanced around, then whispered conspiratorially, "Yes, several other keys, a billfold with about forty-five euros in it and the victim's U.S. driver's license, plus some receipts.

Also, two small aluminum foil packages, one with hashish resin in it, the other containing four Quaaludes."

Daria grimaced. "No flash drive?" Canova shook his head. "What about the right front pocket?"

"A cloth handkerchief, somewhat soiled, nothing else."

"Good," Daria said.

"Forgive me for interjecting," Canova interrupted. "You asked only about the pockets. We did find something else, but it was not in the victim's pockets."

"Well?"

"A cheap plastic refillable gas cigarette lighter was uncovered lying to the side of the body, buried in almost two inches of dust."

"Near which hand and which side of the body?" Daria interrupted. "Please, Canova, be precise."

"Yes, commissario. The left hand and left side."

"Good, go on."

"It is impossible to determine when the lighter was dropped or by whom, but the coroner said it was reasonable to conjecture that the victim had been holding it when he fell forward and to the side after the shot. The left side. His and others' fingerprints were on the lighter."

"What others?"

"We have not had time to identify them yet."

Daria nodded and took a deep breath. "All right. Now for the second thing, lieutenant. When you're alone with Verdi, get him to show you where the crawl space or tunnel comes into the sub-basement under the stairwell. Post a man there. Unless I am gravely mistaken, tonight you will catch a mouse or a rat or perhaps a stray cat."

"And what if no one appears?"

"Then follow the dusty footprints up the staircase to the second floor and turn left. Did no one else notice them?" She saluted and let the elevator door shut.

Morbido counted to five under his breath. Then he said, "My dear Major Vinci, I would like to report that I have dust in my eyes."

"Wait until you get into the catacombs."

"That's not what I mean." He stared at her. She raised a skillfully plucked eyebrow but did not speak. "It's as if someone had powdered me," Morbido added. He made a flicking motion with his fingertips and winced. "You know, Twinkle Toes and Angel Dust."

Daria laughed. "Tinker Bell showering Fairy Dust?"

"Same thing."

She raised an eyebrow again. "Who's the fairy?"

"I'm not sure," he growled, "and neither are you. Not yet."

Five

Declining her brother's invitation to drive them to their respective destinations, Daria announced she would make her own way home. She preferred for Mario to drop Morbido at his budget hotel by Termini Station sooner rather than later. The stubbly cheeked, feral-smelling captain-to-be needed rest and cleansing before presenting himself for the early morning ceremonial with the deputy minister. After dropping him, Mario could easily circle back to the Vinci family apartment, where he and Daria were staying. Rome might be a nightmare to navigate during daylight hours, she remarked offhandedly, glancing at her wristwatch. There would be no traffic at 2:15 in the morning.

In the meantime, she added, she could walk undisturbed down the storied hill crowned by the Institute of America, then traverse the center of Rome at a diagonal, heading north by northwest through the Piazza del Popolo and its city gate, then down Via Flaminia, following the Triumphal Way of antiquity. She was too keyed up to sleep and too tired to talk. Walking was the best and only way she knew to relax and think straight.

"Are you not concerned about safety?" Mario asked, perpetually irked by what he called his sister's "willful stubbornness."

Morbido interjected a strategic laugh. "We could call the police for an escort," he remarked, handing Daria the heavy pronged key from the third-floor room.

"I can outrun any mugger," Daria said, raising and wagging one of her red shoes. She handed her brother the ludicrously expensive leather designer pumps that had given her blisters earlier that evening in less than an hour. "If I can't outrun them, I'll immobilize them." She chuckled mirthlessly.

"Or shoot them dead," Morbido added before she could go on. "Does your brother know you're not only a kickboxer and black belt but also a deadly shot? There's a lump in your silk purse from that key and another, bigger lump from your handgun. It's smaller than an M1917 but just as lethal."

"More lethal," she said.

Mario Vinci glowered. He sat at the wheel of his electric SUV and shook his hoary patrician head, aware it was pointless to argue with his unbending little sister. "Mi raccomando," he muttered, not waiting for her to answer. The vehicle sped away. Osvaldo Morbido waved jovially. His bulk filled the front passenger seat, one of his beefy arms spilling out of the window.

Feeling her face flush at the sound of that two-word, maddeningly familiar, utterly ambiguous expression, Daria tightened her shoelaces and set off downhill. Bouncing along the empty sidewalks and streets laid out between the hilltop neighborhood's dark, sprawling villas and their riotous, leafy, shadowy gardens, she breathed freely and began to relax for the first time in hours. The branches of the perpetually fruit-laden bitter orange trees of Rome reached like outstretched arms across the tall stone garden walls that prickled and bristled with shards of broken glass or coils of barbed wire. Bright waxy mouth-puckering orange fruits dangled overhead, glinting in the wavering glow of the streetlights, most of them smothered by tropical vegetation.

Morning glory, passion flower, trumpet vine, and other, unknown tangled creepers climbed and twisted into the towering palms and black-leaved laurels, then grasped and blanketed the old-fashioned lamps. To many pedestrians, the gloom might have seemed threatening. But Daria felt absolutely safe. Central Rome, though seedy and filthy and infested by pickpockets and petty criminals in certain areas, was not New York, Nairobi, or Naples, either.

There was a further prosaic reality that infused her with quiet confidence. Hundreds of high-definition security cameras had been installed by the authorities in recent years along most of the arteries she would be taking. She knew precisely where they were located. Naturally cautious, Daria had also alerted Filippo at headquarters, spelling out her route. If he wished, the night duty officer at DIGOS could track her step by step from the Institute to the Vinci's apartment, a forty-minute walk at her habitual fast pace. Daria wasn't sure she liked the reality of the new surveillance society, but reality it remained. There was always that secret hope she and millions of others harbored that nature and entropy and vegetable chaos would prevail, tangling human civilization in creepers so thick the gaze of the cameras could not penetrate it.

Daria had grown up in what had been until a century ago one of Rome's outlying neighborhoods—a reclaimed Tiberside swamp and ancient battleground. The blood of Etruscans, Carthaginians, Romans, and barbarians had soaked the soil and streets for three thousand years. That history was now invisible. The solidly middle-class apartment houses covered entire city blocks, like citadels. They had been erected after Italian unification, starting in the last decades of the 1800s, right up to World War One. There was something of the grand old-fashioned European hotel about them. Many were surprising to look at, renowned among architects everywhere for their weighty eclecticism.

Instead of the wooden water towers of New York City, for instance, on the roofs of these massive Roman stone piles perched faux medieval turrets, one at each corner. Small rooftop terraces climbing in tiers formed bizarre Machu Picchu hanging gardens, some planted with tall flame cypresses. Nowadays the turrets and terraces were multimillion-euro loft spaces or glassed-in penthouse garden apartments. During Daria's increasingly distant youth, in the late 1970s to early '90s, the rambling, upper-floor flats had been disdained by the bourgeoisie and used primarily for storage or as children's and maids' rooms.

Trotting past a granite obelisk looted from Egypt at the instigation of a sainted pope, and, next to it, an indigenous ornate Roman marble fountain commissioned by another pope, Daria savored the nighttime splendors of the higgledy-piggledy cityscape. It was a layer cake, a mille-feuille of styles and periods, a vast, open-air bric-a-brac shop. She soon realized she was on automatic pilot, striding down memory lane. This was the same route her father had walked a thousand times to and from the Institute. She had trotted alongside him almost as many times. Until that day in 1995.

That was when Roberto Vinci, a high-ranking government official, sometime-diplomat, and more—mysteriously more—had been murdered and butchered and bundled into bloody suitcases while on assignment in East Asia for the Ministry of Foreign Affairs.

The inscrutable, priestlike pater familias, a pious believer and virulent anti-Communist, Roberto Vinci had been born and lived in the same building his entire, albeit short, life—except during and immediately after World War Two. As a young husband, he had taken over from his parents when they had died from typhoid fever caught, poetically, after swimming in the brackish lagoon of Venice. In what year had her grandparents died? Daria thought perhaps 1947 or '48. Yes, 1948, the year of the American-engineered electoral coup that brought in the Christian Democrats, her father's political party. After the coup, the DC had run Italy for decades, until corruption and the collapse of the Soviet Union in 1989 had transformed the self-righteous center-right party into yet another footnote in the country's millennial Machiavellian history. That clever electoral coup and the death of her grandparents had occurred only twenty years before she was born, the year the blessed Mario Vinci had arrived in a bundle with the storks. That was seventy-odd years ago. A lifetime. Yet, the world of 1948 was another universe, another Italy, another geological epoch.

From the time Roberto Vinci had married, he and his wife, Daria's formidable mother, had never resided anywhere other than the family home, nor had they wished to. Impractical, disjointed, angular, and low-ceilinged, the Vinci rooftop domicile included two terraces on separate stories plus one corner turret, with six small bedrooms tucked under the eaves. Two of her five brothers had shared one of the larger rooms. She and the other three princelings had each had their own closet-sized kingdom under the magical eyrie's red-tiled roof.

As Daria continued down the echoing cobbled streets, drinking in the summery scents of jasmine, linden, and, less pleasantly, the neighborhood's uncollected garbage, she heard the splashing tinkle of the water fountains poised on nearly every corner. The precious spring water ran day and night, brought from the mountains to the thirsty, baking capital by aqueducts, just as it had during the reigns of Claudius,

Agrippa, Nero—or Mussolini for that matter. Eternal the city was, a crazy, suffocating, miasmic, endearing enigmatic mess.

Glancing across at her slumbering neighborhood, her eye followed the meandering Tiber River embankments. She counted the bridges and cross streets and apartment blocks until she caught sight of her own hulking building.

Now, she said to herself, before you get home and face Mario, answer me this: Why would a man as short as Charles Wraithwhite struggle to reach a display cabinet high on the wall, when an almost identical, functioning revolver lay at his fingertips in an unlocked drawer that also held the ammunition he would need for his game of Russian roulette?

Why would Wraithwhite keep his billfold and cash and keys in his left pocket, and hold a lighter in his left hand, and then, given the position of the fatal wound, presumably play Russian roulette and shoot himself from the right using his right hand?

Guilty as charged: I have no answers to any of the above. Not yet. As a matter of fact, I have no answer to why Taylor Chatwin-Paine failed to immediately mention the third-floor room, the unusual key, and the revolvers, or why Wraithwhite, Adele Selmer, and their unidentified confederates had not attended the gala concert either. Was not the musical orgy one of the year's signal events? According to several of their cohort interviewed by Lieutenant Canova, both Wraithwhite and Selmer were on the friendliest terms with Maestro Curtis Katzenbaum, winner of the year's coveted Rome Award for Contemporary Music. Why wouldn't they be there for him?

While we were at it, why would the tunic-clad coven of conspirators or innocuous club members—whatever they were—hold a session or ritual meeting on such a busy evening, when dozens of donors and hundreds of other guests would be swarming over the grounds of Villa Nerone? It made no sense. Would not a secret society, meeting in the catacombs, want to remain secret?

Clattering across a bridge above the pungent, frothing Tiber, she experienced a minor epiphany. A bright copper euro-penny piece dropped into Daria's mental slot. A bell rang, a light snapped on. *Club or coven? Catacombs?* Yes. Perhaps. That would explain the "CC." The *Catacomb Club* or the *Catacomb Coven*?

The image of the decals applied to the backs of artworks swam to mind. Pulling out her smartphone, she glanced at the photo gallery and laughed out loud. Cat and comb and club, not brush and baseball bat. How dense and dim and dull could she be?

Club? The word sent her mind whirling. As Daria strode the last block home, she reflected on the further ambiguous reality that her mother would not be waiting up to chide or scold her. Barbara Vinci had reached the venerable age of ninety two months earlier, and had promptly passed away in her sleep, after a final celebratory champagne birthday soiree at the Circolo dei Cacciatori—a celebrated Roman club. In keeping with her elevated, starched, constipated, conventional tastes, the Circolo was one of the city's oldest, most exclusive, snobbish, and charmless dinner societies—*her* club, the *only* club in Rome worth belonging to.

Naturally, Barbie had not keeled over at a linen-draped dinner table. Nothing that vulgar. She had died in bed, though not peacefully by the looks of her. It was the Vinci family housekeeper, Barbie's longtime companion, who had found the body, cold and lifeless, the eyes wide and mouth grinning—a grin of victory and malice. Daria had arrived half an hour later, following one of her usual fourteen-hour shifts. She had studied her mother's face at length before tugging down the stiff eyelids. But the malicious expression had lingered on the bloodless lips until the coffin had been closed several days later. The monstrous triumphal grin had burned itself into Daria's visual cortex. She shook her head now, batting her tired eyes, trying but failing to dislodge the image.

Barbara Henderson Vinci, aka Barbie the Barracuda, a widow for over a quarter-century, had repeatedly vowed she would only leave the family flat feet first. Nursing homes and hospitals were for the sick. She'd never been sick in her long, tenacious life. Her six thankless children would have to get used to seeing her around for a long, long time, possibly forever, she had chortled time and again, reminding them that they had failed her, all of them. Not a one could measure up to their father, Roberto.

Daria scoffed out loud, then recoiled when she realized she was sounding like her mother. She had her mother's steely determination, resonant deep voice, and hazel—some would swear they were green—eyes. Would she, Daria, the runt, the youngest, live as long as the fearsome Barbie? Compared to Ambassador Willem Bremach, Barbara Vinci had died a whippersnapper. Bremach had said as much in his condolence letter and in his numerous follow-up phone calls. *Whippersnapper* was one of his favorite words. Dear old jocular Willem, her mysterious godfather, even more mysterious than her father had been. It was only natural for him to be solicitous about Barbie and much else. Mi raccomando? Yes, Willem Bremach had used the ambiguous phrase, too.

Counting the streetlights below, imagining the dots of light as glowing pearls in a luminescent necklace, Daria thought of another kind of dot. The phrase "connect the dots" rose to mind and buzzed around her, not a gentle moth but an enraged hornet zooming furiously from dot to luminous dot.

Mi raccomando. Roberto Vinci had been a spy and a trustee of the Institute.

Mi raccomando. Willem Bremach was a spy and a trustee of the Institute.

Who else? Was Dr. Mario Vinci, MD, PhD, et cetera, a spy and a trustee of the Institute? What about Taylor Chatwin-Paine and Jefferson Page and God only knew how many others?

The Italian Communist Party had claimed for decades that the Institute of America in Rome was a nest of spies. No one but the party faithful and other cranks had believed them. They were nutty conspiracy theorists of a low order, though they could not compare in lunacy to their current American counterparts. The good old commies saw American spies under every Roman couch and behind every carved Baroque Roman marble curtain. The Institute was not about spying, of that much Daria was sure. It was about soft power. That was why it had been so successful and had lasted so long. That, in any case, was the mantra she had heard time and again from its boosters.

She wondered with sudden clarity if Willem Bremach had bothered to express his condolences about Barbie to each of her five brothers. They had grown long ago from spoiled-brat princes into gray-haired kings or white-haired emperors of their own haughty domains. She doubted Bremach would have given himself the trouble to reach out to them. The proud, prickly males of the Vinci clan were scattered across the globe. Only Mario had cultivated an attachment to Rome and to Willem Bremach and only because of the Institute—not because of their mother. None of Daria's siblings had shown the least affection for her, had never paid her the attention she craved, or helped Daria take care of the practicalities of helping Barbie through widowhood and old age. They had fled lickety-split, as fast and as far as they could, leaving the lone daughter to mind the Roman nest and watch over the domineering, predatory, dangerous mother bird.

She scoffed again, then regretted her own disloyalty. Had Barbie really been a barracuda or a pterodactyl? Daria had used both nicknames when describing her mother to others. The recollection did not fill her with pride. On the contrary. She was chiding herself now for her wanton lack of respect as she unlocked and opened the front door, eager to get to bed. No such luck was to be hers.

Mario Vinci sat in their mother's favorite armchair in the living room. The spotlit white cupola of the Vatican was framed behind him in a picture window. His grasshopper legs were crossed, the upper one bouncing from nervousness as he gesticulated with one hand and spoke somberly into the old-fashioned landline telephone clutched in the other. She waved and walked past him toward the upstairs bathrooms and bedrooms, relieved to avoid a confrontation.

But before she could escape, Mario cradled the phone and unfolded himself to his full domineering height, then stooped forward as he always did. "I was talking just now to Roy Heiffermann in New York," he said too loudly for comfort. "He's the chairman of the board, as you know." Mario's sub-basso voice made the windowpanes vibrate. He stalked slowly toward Daria, his stoop even more pronounced than it had been earlier, in the catacombs. "Ten senior board members were at the gala tonight. After what happened, while you were poking around underground or in the shrubbery, we held an impromptu meeting. The board in New York called an emergency session via Zoom, shortly afterwards. It is unanimous: we trustees feel the time has come for Taylor to retire. He is nearly eighty and has held his position for over forty years. The Institute needs to innovate, it needs younger, fresher blood, it needs to reflect America and our increasing diversity."

Daria turned to face her brother. "What you're saying is you think Taylor is going senile and this is the perfect opportunity to ask for his resignation?"

Mario stiffened. "Senile is your term, not mine, though you may be right."

Daria snorted. "He's not much older than you and no more senile than you or the president of the United States of America."

Mario ignored her remark, waving his hands as if she were a pesky horsefly. "We have drafted a letter recalling Taylor to New York. I will accompany him as soon as possible. We might leave later today, seeing that it is nearly 3 a.m., or tomorrow, if I can book a flight. His wife will just have to get used to having him with her year round, though I'm sure he will in future be a frequent guest of the Institute."

Daria felt the heat mount to her cheeks. "Taylor Chatwin-Paine will not be leaving Rome until the investigation has been completed," she said coolly. "Neither shall you." She faced away, strode down the hall, climbed two flights of wooden stairs, and locked her bedroom door behind her.

Six

"**C**ongratulations, Captain Morbido!" Daria exclaimed, looking up from the cluttered wooden tabletop in the reception hall of Villa Nerone. She beamed with a genuine smile. Sunshine poured through the open windows. Daria clapped her hands quietly as Morbido ambled in and bowed in the manner of a Shakespearean actor.

"Congratulations? To me? 'Tis nothing!" declaimed Osvaldo Morbido, agitating his fists. One of them clutched a plump, greasy paper wrapper. "I hope you like cuttlefish ink and risotto and polenta," he added in his usual guttural voice, grunting with pleasure as he peeled the wrapper back and steered the business end of a long sandwich into his mouth. "Give me porchetta any day of the week. Best thing about Rome if you ask me," he continued, chewing with delight, "though I do like those milk-filled braised lamb's intestines with tomato sauce—"

"Please, you're making me ill," Daria cut him off. "How can you think of braised entrails so early in the morning? And what do you mean, cuttlefish and polenta?"

"Ink," he said, "it's the squid ink, they put it everywhere, even in the sweets."

"Who?"

"The Venetians," he said, finishing the porchetta sandwich with three ogreish bites.

Daria shook her head. "Is this some kind of riddle? Are you trying to imitate Ambassador Bremach?"

"Not at all," Morbido said, wiping his mouth. "What your Sergeant Gianni *Adonis* Giannini will think when he hears the news I can't imagine. Love conquers all, but Venice is even farther from Rapallo than Rome."

"Osvaldo!"

"Well, don't tell me you haven't heard?"

"Heard what? I went to bed at 3 a.m., got up at 6, and have been here for the last two hours, trying to put the pieces together and keep the fires from burning Rome to the ground again."

"Aha! Emperor Nero's fire brigade? Well done! This *is* the Villa Nerone. It was Nero and not Caligula who burned Rome, wasn't it?"

"Can you cut to the chase?" she asked. "What does Venice have to do with anything?"

He stared at her. "This morning, at the ministry, when the deputy minister and vice questor gave me the commendation and confirmed my paltry little promotion to captaincy, the buzz in the corridors was not about me or the coup in Genoa we thwarted or the cleverness of Ambassador Bremach in outing the conspirators and so forth. It was about the death in Venice—and you."

"Me?"

"You!"

"What death?"

"It's said you're to replace the tragically deceased vice

questor of the Province of Venice. He burst his gut two days ago from a surfeit of squid ink, like that English king I read about in my lessons. Henri the something..."

"That was eels, Osvaldo, lampreys, nine hundred years ago."

"Eels or squid, same difference. They say I will never rise above captain if I don't improve my English."

Daria stared incredulously. Then the light clicked on. "When?" The word came out like a gunshot. "When did they say I would be sent to Venice?"

"Today, tomorrow, the next day, I'm not sure," he answered. "The transfer and promotion were to be immediate, *urgentissimo*. It's incredible you don't know. Surely..."

Daria smiled bitterly. "I get it."

"Get what?"

"I'll tell you one day," she said, "when you grow up or wake up. I'll bet you can figure it out yourself, once you've digested the porchetta and had another espresso."

Morbido grunted in bafflement. Disposing of the empty wrapper, he extracted what looked like an ancient papyrus scroll from one of his capacious pockets, flipped through, showing her three dog-eared pages, holding them up one by one. "Look familiar?"

"Now what?" she asked, peering at the wrinkled, smudged sheets. It was a children's coloring book, in English, with illustrations of objects and words spelled out in big boldface type. "Cat," she read aloud, glancing at the first image he showed her. Morbido flipped forward. "Comb," she said. "Club."

Morbido's smile ran from lobe to lobe as he mouthed the garbled words along with her. The smile shrank to a tiny pink hole when Daria said, "I figured that one out last night. The CC isn't for two hundred in Roman numerals. It's for Catacomb Club."

Shaking his head, Morbido muttered an incomprehensible imprecation. He folded away the book. "What are these people anyway, thankless dogs lifting their legs on the Institute that feeds them? They get a hundred and fifty thousand dollars each and behave like this?" He gestured at no place in particular. "What in God's name can it mean? Are they foolish adolescents with their decals and red letters hidden behind paintings? And jelly beans and swords?"

"I don't think so," Daria said. She pursed her lips. "More important, you must realize that someone wants to take me off the case."

"By kicking you upstairs and sideways halfway across the country to Venice?" He grimaced. "Yes, it is apparent now even to an overweight clod with a working-class Genoese accent."

"We don't have much time, Osvaldo, and none for self-pity. When do you need to be back in Genoa?"

"Yesterday."

"Impossible. I need you here."

"It can't be done."

"It will be done." She opened her lips halfway and tapped them. "Wait until this afternoon, then call in and say you have the flu. No. Say you've been poisoned by a tainted porchetta sandwich and lamb entrails in tomato sauce and you can't travel yet. I will follow suit if need be. Now come with me. Lieutenant Canova is waiting upstairs. I'll brief you as we go."

It took Daria exactly seven minutes—the time required to walk from the reception hall to the annex and wait for the elevator to the second story—to bring Morbido up to date.

First of all, she said in rapid-fire Italian, at 6:28 a.m. Lieutenant Canova and Sergeant Pompelmo had grabbed a man wearing a tunic as he crawled out of a tunnel in the sub-basement of the annex. They had immediately run a wand over him and detected gunpowder. He identified himself as one

Hugh R. L. Fowler, a visual artist and Rome Award winner. In his room, watched over by Pompelmo, Fowler was made to remove the tunic and his outer clothing, including a pair of black and white polka dot sneakers. He was then placed under house arrest. The garments were sent to the lab. The results had come back about three hours later.

Fowler's tunic was flecked with blood and brain matter, as were his blue jeans and tennis shoes. The blood type corresponded to that of the victim, Wraithwhite. Yet Fowler maintained he was not present at the shooting, having left the circular chamber before it occurred.

Second, DIGOS had conducted blanket interviews with nearly all the current occupants of the Institute. The interrogations and the security camera footage confirmed that all but half a dozen suspects had attended the gala concert. Therefore, the six individuals in question might have been in the catacombs at the time of the incident—or they might have been off campus.

Third and finally, as Morbido may have discovered by reading the Institute's Wikipedia page, the existence of the crawl space or tunnel where Fowler had been apprehended was easily explained. It had nothing to do with Emperor Nero's celebrated Domus Aurea across Rome on another hill—the Villa Nerone had been built atop the foundations of one of the emperor's many unfinished summer villas, hence the name. A short section of underground aqueduct branching off one of Rome's main ancient aqueducts was known to traverse the grounds, presumably to feed Nero's villa. A variety of tunnels from antiquity to the modern age made use of former quarry passageways dug nearly two thousand years ago to extract stones for the building. The excavations were extensive. In them, the early Christians, fearing persecution and the desecration of their tombs, had created the catacombs in the second and third centuries AD. A complete archeological history including a detailed map of the site above and below ground was in the Institute's library. Daria had asked the librarian to bring the volume to her half an hour earlier. So far, the librarian had not shown herself.

"Have you asked your brother about this? Or the director and president?" Morbido inquired. "Surely they know the history backwards and forwards?"

Daria pursed her lips, explaining that the three were closeted and unavailable. "Zoom meetings with other trustees and the Institute's lawyers in New York and Rome," she said. "Chatwin-Paine is on the way out. Like me."

As they stood waiting for the elevator, the librarian appeared, clutching a slim leather-bound volume. She apologized for taking so long. Carla Tomaselli was a remarkably handsome older woman fashionably dressed in a summery floral-patterned dress and high heels. She did not correspond to received notions of what a librarian should look like, especially one who seemed closer to seventy than sixty. She smiled amicably as she proffered the archeological history of the Institute's site to Daria.

"There is one caveat," Tomaselli said politely. "Please do not remove the book from the grounds, and please treat it with utmost care. It is the only copy in existence. I brought it to you from the reserve—our treasure room—which is strictly against protocol. But given the circumstances..."

Daria thanked her, glancing at the book and its faded black-and-white engravings and photographs of the grounds of Villa Nerone circa 1890. "Signora Tomaselli, I am sorry to trouble you with this further request but, given that the book is quite short and very precious, might you be able to scan it into a PDF and email me the PDF this morning? I do not want to damage or lose the volume, and I don't have the time to study it this instant."

Tomaselli frowned, clearly not pleased. But she nodded, smiled ruefully, and agreed that, yes, it was not a bad idea. She had been meaning to digitalize the book. She would do it herself right away. Noting down Daria's personal email address—it was more reliable, Daria explained, than the official DIGOS address—Carla Tomaselli said goodbye, turned, and began to walk to the library. Daria called her back.

"One other thing, please, before you go, signora. Last night, President Chatwin-Paine mentioned that several attempts had been made to compile a modern history of the Institute, and a certain assistant librarian had been involved in the undertaking something like a decade ago. Might you give me the name of this assistant and let me know how to reach her or him?"

The librarian smiled again but shook her head. "I regret to say that she no longer works for us," Tomaselli answered, glancing over her shoulder. She stiffened slightly. "Officially, I have been overseeing the current research project. The fact is, Mr. Wraithwhite was a self-starter and entirely independent. He did not consult me, other than to familiarize himself with the layout of the library, the online catalogue and various card catalogues, the scanner and photocopiers, and so forth."

Daria seemed taken aback. "He never sought your advice or had questions for you? Surely you know a great deal about the history of the institution?"

"Never," she said. "I will admit, I was astonished. It was as if Charles Wraithwhite already knew most of what he needed to know, in terms of official resources. He did ask me, at the outset, as you just have, to be put in touch with Johanna Harrison, the former assistant librarian. I had to explain to him that when Johanna left our employ, she, like all departing Institute employees, signed a nondisclosure agreement." Tomaselli paused and seemed to be waiting.

Daria remained expressionless. Then she said, "Johanna Harrison is the name? Does she still reside in Rome?"

The librarian hesitated again, glanced around one more time, then nodded. "I believe she does. I have not been in touch with her since, well, since she left."

Daria tapped her lips, recalling Chatwin-Paine's words from last night. *Thorny personnel issues.* "I think I see what you're trying to say, Signora Tomaselli. My guess is Mr. Wraithwhite managed to track down this former employee despite the NDA and I shall be forced to do the same."

"She won't talk to you," the librarian answered decisively. "It would be pointless."

Daria looked the librarian in the eye. "Signora Tomaselli, you have lived in Rome some time, I am guessing. You are doubtless familiar with some elements of Italian law and police procedure. To be brief, if you do not know this already, you need to know that a privately signed NDA, particularly an NDA concerning a foreign entity such as the Institute, cannot be invoked in Italy in cases of murder or conspiracy investigations. Therefore, in order to save all of us time and trouble, I would ask you to give me the contact information for this former assistant at your earliest convenience. I thank you for it in advance and for the scan of the history book. This is an extremely urgent matter and very serious." Daria watched Tomaselli color slightly, nod her graying head, then tiptoe away in her high heels toward the library.

Morbido had been listening with shaggy eyebrows raised. Now he shrugged, cleared his throat, and said, "All in a day's work, eh? It is startling how secretive and cultish a place like this can be. I'll wager you that librarian has been here as long as the president and is just as fiercely loyal."

"Ferocious loyalty," Daria mused as they rode the elevator up, "is not always a good thing. People make mistakes, institutions head in the wrong direction—stuff happens."

Pacing up and down a long institutional corridor on the second floor, Lieutenant Canova was unshaved and looked seedy after his fifteen-hour shift. Saluting, he strode up to Daria. Without being asked, he began talking in a tense, angry voice.

"He is like a caged animal, this Hugh Fowler," Canova said, revealing his own agitation. "Impolite, unrepentant, arrogant. If he were not an American citizen and a guest of this institution, I would have arrested him and put him in the lockup downtown for round-the-clock interrogation."

Daria smiled wickedly. "You may get a chance to do that yet," she remarked. "Let's see what develops. Captain Morbido will assist me for now. Knock off, lieutenant. Get some rest. How soon can you be back?"

Canova blinked. Then he hung his head and looked away. "Commissario, I assumed you had been told. They have reassigned me. I am joining the team at the Vatican."

"The Vatican? Since when do we have jurisdiction at the Vatican?"

"The pope has personally requested us to intervene in the pedophilia child-smuggling ring investigation."

Daria flushed. "Which one? There are dozens."

"The new one, involving the cardinal and the ambassador..."

She turned away and tapped her grimacing lips. "I see," she muttered. "Very well, lieutenant. Do you have anything else to report before you leave?"

"Only that we have found another of the fugitives."

"*Only?* When?"

"Twenty-eight minutes ago," he said, checking his watch. "She is being detained in the upstairs apartment in the outbuilding flanking the greenhouse, near the outdoor theater. It was Dr. Giolitti who phoned an hour ago to inquire about Signorina Adele Selmer's condition. He took the opportunity to mention that he had seen some person last night wearing a white smock run through the garden after the concert and climb the stairs to the apartment. That apartment was locked and no one answered last night when we tried to check it. She must have been hiding inside in the dark. She was one of those we did not see on the security camera tape. Her name is Aisha Williams. She is a poet, age twenty-six, from Cincinnati, Ohio, female but wishes to be identified as 'other' and addressed as 'they.' We are encountering certain difficulties interrogating her."

"Why was I not informed immediately?"

"I assumed you had been informed, commissario. Perhaps you were on the phone or otherwise engaged? Your telephone does not appear to be working—at least I have not been able to get through to you."

Daria frowned. She had turned the phone off to avoid seeing the inevitable summons from headquarters. "Have them confiscate the clothing this Williams has been wearing, including the tunic and her shoes, and then get them to the lab."

"That is being done as we speak."

"Good. Have they run a wand over her?"

"Yes."

"Well?"

"There was nothing on her body—she showered last night she admits. But on her hair, they found traces of gunpowder."

"Strange," Daria remarked. "What woman showers after witnessing a horrific event like that and fails to wash her hair?"

"She cannot wash her hair in its current state," said Canova uneasily. "She has a peculiar kind of hairstyle, it is matted in places and braided in others, with beads, and very difficult to undo, she says."

"Dreadlocks," snorted Morbido. "She must be a Rastafarian."

"That is what we thought," said Canova. "She says she is not officially Rastafarian but empathizes with them and that the hairstyle is called cornrows."

"I'm astonished you had the perspicacity to inquire," Daria remarked.

"I did not, commissario, others did, including an officer much younger than myself."

"All right," Daria grumbled. "You may go. But expect a call from me at the Vatican soon. I want to get to the bottom of this, this," she looked for the word, "this obfuscation and obstructionism." Daria saluted and pivoted and marched down the hallway to another plainclothes operative. It was Sergeant Eugenio Pompelmo, a swarthy swain with bulging, close-set dark eyes, a blue-cheeked, permanently unshaved complexion, and an equally permanent wolfish grin that made him appear even stupider than he actually was. Pompelmo had just topped fifty and would rise no higher. Saluting, he stood stiffly in front of a tall, narrow white wooden door, baring entry or exit. On the door was the number 12 and the name "Hugh Fowler" on a plastic doorplate. Daria nodded. Pompelmo knocked loudly, then pushed open the door, standing aside for her, his grin widening.

Taking a step forward across the threshold, the air in the room hit Daria and Morbido like a filthy wet rag thrown in the face. The stench was nauseating—overripe body odors, stale ale, tobacco, and unwashed, overheated bed linens. They glanced around before proceeding.

Like the door leading into it, the studio was narrow, long, and painted white, with a surprisingly high ceiling and a series of many-paned windows reaching from wall to wall and floor to ceiling. It had an industrial feel. Apparently, this was one of the ateliers designed over a century ago for painters, sculptors, and architects. It faced north. On the far end of the room, another narrow door stood open. Beyond it stretched an out-door terrace. Daria glimpsed a spectacular view of Rome through the waving large, thick, branches of a parasol pine standing at least eighty feet tall, she reckoned. On a marble balustrade sat an antique marble mortar overflowing with cigarette butts. Crumpled beer cans and fast-food wrappers littered the floor of the terrace and the inside of the studio.

A gangling white male in his late twenties or early thir-ties sat near the windows holding a paintbrush in his left hand. He stared fixedly at a sheet of heavy white paper pinned to the wall in front of him. Around the paper the wall was stained and scratched and marked with daubs or slashes of red paint. Hugh Fowler barely turned to glance at his guests. His thin lips curled when he spoke.

"Now what?" he snapped. "I've said what I had to say. You people are keeping me from my work."

Daria could feel Morbido's weight pressing from behind her, his hands raised and ready to pull Fowler to his feet. "Well, Mr. Fowler, now you will say it again, and say more," Daria almost whispered. "Unless you would prefer me to place you under formal arrest and have my colleague here take you to the sta-tion to be questioned. At the very least this is a manslaughter and criminal conspiracy investigation. You may be held incom-municado for up to a week. It is up to you, Mr. Fowler. Do not be deceived, this is not the United States of America, this is Italy; there is no Miranda, you cannot call a lawyer or anyone else. You are in serious trouble."

Fowler turned the rest of the way around, hacking and coughing. He sneered. "So, now the pigs sic an American cop on me? For what?"

"My nationality is not your business. Your business, Mr. Fowler, is to cooperate. Immediately. Or be arrested. Immediately."

As she waited for him to respond, Daria could not help glancing up and pivoting around, her nose twitching, her eyes watering and sinuses closing down from the acrid nicotine emanating from Fowler and his clothes. According to the Institute's biographical sketch, Hugh Fowler was a visual artist, meaning a painter, she assumed, born in 1992, in Dallas, Texas, winner of one of the three annual awards for the Non-Dematerialized Visual Arts. His social media pages showed him scaling skyscrapers, exploring caves and subterranean spaces, and using specialized telescopic ladders, poles, suction cups, and other mountaineering or caving equipment to apply paint and tiles to otherwise unreachable places. He certainly did not look athletic, Daria mused. But you never knew.

On the wall high above the entrance door, Daria now recognized the cat, comb, and club decals and the letters CC painted in red. On Fowler's workbench was a can of red spray paint and a stencil. He was making no effort to hide his handiwork. Her eyes returned to the painter. He wore a pair of ragged, filthy artist's overalls. Rangy, craggy, long haired, self-adoring, snide, neurotic, an angry spoiled scofflaw—these were the words that sprang to Daria's mind. She was unable to summon other words to describe his artworks. She did not possess the vocabulary. The splashes and globs of glossy primary colors, and the roughly stitched slashes in the canvases, like sutures on fresh wounds or badly healed scars, could only be described with the precise terminology of the art critic.

Fowler threw his brush down on the cluttered tabletop and stood, yawning and stretching, managing to communicate extreme annoyance, brashness, and belligerence in this simple, innocent gesture. "They put up signs everywhere telling us we can't smoke or play loud music or act and breathe and talk the way we want to. But nowhere does it say we can't go into the catacombs or explore or *embellish* the grounds and the godawful crap they call *art* on the walls of this ridiculous, pretentious place." He had a Texas drawl Daria struggled at first to understand. "No one said we couldn't borrow those guns or play Russian roulette. It isn't illegal where I come from. A little wine and song, a bong or some smoke underground, it never hurt anyone, no signs down there, no one telling us what we can and can't do." He paused, snorted, and ran his fingers through his lank, greasy hair, slouching forward and leaning on the workbench as if he were still hungover. "I guess I must've fallen asleep in the tunnel. I wasn't there when it happened."

"When what happened?" Daria asked.

"You know, the accident."

"Then how do you know it was an accident?"

"I can hear, can't I? I hear people talking. Besides, the place is crawling with cops. I'm guessing Charlie blew his brains out. Serves him right. He and his stupid jelly beans and those tiny plastic swords and the Russian roulette—and that smirking roundhead asshole in a carnival mask."

"Tell me about it."

"I can't, I wasn't there."

"Lying to the police is a serious offense," growled Morbido. "You were there, Fowler. We know it."

"Prove it."

Patiently and quietly, Daria read from a printout, translating into English. "Analysis of garments worn by Mr. Hugh Fowler... gunpowder, blood, brain matter..."

"You don't get gunpowder, blood, and brains on your clothes by sleeping off a hangover in a tunnel," Morbido said in roughshod English, astonishing Daria by the progress he had made. "So, you were there. Did you pull the trigger? Who says it was Russian roulette? You might have killed him. You were drunk and high. You hold up the revolver. You click and you laugh and you click and you click and you point it at Wraithwhite and you laugh and bang!" Morbido stamped his foot to emphasize the sound of the gunshot, then turned to Daria. He was purple in the face. "Let's take him in, lock him up, he'll talk, this is a waste of time." Pulling a pair of hand-cuffs from his back pocket, with one huge hand he reached up and grabbed the slouching Fowler by the shoulder, spun him around, yanked Fowler's long, sinewy arms behind him, and clamped on the cuffs. "Now you can stand up straight and answer respectfully when Major Vinci asks you a question."

"Okay, okay," the painter bleated, his face as red as his paintings. "I didn't do it, Charlie shot himself, at least, I think he did. He had the gun. It was his turn. It was so dark down there and I was on the far side of the damn grotto near Adele, so I couldn't see anything on his side, plus we'd smoked some heavy-duty hash and had some wine, we shared a couple of Quaaludes cut into other things."

"Yes?" Daria asked encouragingly.

"The club was my idea from when I got here and realized this was some kind of boot camp and bullshit phony vacation spot for Ivy League jerks. I wanted some privacy and a place we could do what the fuck we wanted when we wanted, then Charlie joined and started crashing our catacomb parties a couple of months ago, bringing this other guy with him..."

"Keep going," Daria said. "Who is the person you referred to as wearing a carnival mask?"

"Take the cuffs off," Fowler complained, "and give me another cup of coffee and some food. I didn't get dinner and didn't even get breakfast this morning."

"You'll get coffee and breakfast at the station plus plenty more unless you keep talking," growled Morbido.

Daria tapped her lips. "Remove the handcuffs, Captain Morbido," she said quietly. Leaning out into the hallway, she asked Sergeant Pompelmo to have three espressos and some brioches sent up.

"The kind with apricot jelly in them," Fowler shouted past her, "two of them for me, and make mine a double cappuccino with chocolate on top, I can't take that bitter espresso shit." He rubbed his wrists and glared at Morbido. "I fucking hate it that we all have to sit at long tables at the same time every day and eat the same Italian stuff every day for lunch and dinner. We asked them why they don't just have a food court with some Tex-Mex and maybe Hunan or bagels, anything but the damn pasta, and let us eat when we want, or have the food sent up to our rooms when we want so we can keep working and don't have to sit around bullshitting with these bullshit academic types or Mr. President Taylor What-the-Fuck, you ever heard a name like that? Fucking Pilgrim Protestant type, old white man, super-WASP. We call him the Black Widower or the Vampire, looks like a fucking bloodsucker and such a total hypocrite, fucking hypocrite asshole. Can't even bring him-self to say LGBTQ but he's always laying his hands on anyone he can and feeling you up, pretends he's Mr. Morality and Mr. Culture but everyone knows he's a fucking molester and rapist and his wife's a lesbian who won't give it to him anymore and you know what?"

Daria shook her head, letting Fowler blow off steam.

"No one could care less, no one gives a fuck about his little lie, it's, like, wake up, dude, you can sleep with whatever you want, including cats and dogs for all we care, just don't pretend you're something you aren't and refuse to recognize reality."

Morbido and Daria looked at each other in silence. "So," she said when Fowler had calmed down, "I gather you have a variety of gripes with the establishment and its administrators. It isn't our job to interfere in that sphere. What we need is for you to tell us about the Catacomb Club and its members, its operations, Wraithwhite, and this man who wears a mask."

Fowler blinked at her tiredly and seemed deflated. "You might as well sit down," he grumbled, yawning again and making space on his rumpled, pungent bed. There was nowhere else to sit. "This could take a while."

Seven

A t 10:22 a.m., Daria, Hugh Fowler, and Sergeant Eugenio Pompelmo approached the second locked iron gate of the morning in the underground labyrinth of the catacombs. Pausing and looking down, their headlamps and flashlights shone on the thick terra-cotta conduit of the ancient Roman aqueduct, then picked out the glinting brass padlock on the gate. Identical to the first padlock on the first rusty gate they had passed through, closest to the Institute's sub-basement, this second padlock had a long shackle that fitted around the corroded, heavy black metal bars closing off the tunnel.

Daria could not help thinking of *The Count of Monte Cristo* and the many dungeons she had read about or seen with her own eyes over the course of her twenty-odd years at DIGOS. Though dry, the air in the catacombs was dank and musty. Wherever the aqueduct ran, the walls were puckered, flaky, and covered with spores and mildew. The gnawed bones and dismembered bodies of bats, birds, rodents, and other unidentifiable creatures—scorpions and giant spiders and centipedes, presumably—lay strewn underfoot. Daria shivered with horror remembering how she had walked barefoot last night through the dust. It was a layered biomass of filth composed not only of powdered tufa stone but also of living, dying, or dead creatures and their fecal matter, mixed and mingled with the powdery bodies of early Christians decomposed nearly two thousand years ago.

As Fowler fiddled with the padlock, Daria reflected on what she had learned so far from their morning conversations and excursion underground. They had spent the last forty-five minutes exploring the tunnel from its inception, revisiting the circular burial chamber and the three official entrances to the catacombs that Taylor Chatwin-Paine had referred to the previous evening. The first of them Daria knew. The second entrance was narrow, not much wider than a large porthole at each end—meaning only cats, rodents, and slender humans could get through. The tunnel to it straggled up and down across the grounds, coming out behind the porter's lodge. Thankfully, before organizing the expedition, she had sent Osvaldo Morbido away to question Aisha Williams above ground. Otherwise, he might have become lodged in one of the narrower passageways.

A wooden hut the size of a large doghouse had been built around the second entrance about a century ago, according to Fowler. It was meant to disguise the porthole and keep out heavy rainfall, but also to discourage impromptu visits by the area's many feral felines. There was definitely an anti-cat faction. Opposition to the colony came mainly from those who were not animal lovers or did not appreciate the numerous half-eaten rat and mouse carcasses left almost daily around the Institute's grounds. According to Fowler, President Chatwin-Paine was bent on destroying the creatures, another reason the cat-loving members of the Catacomb Club wanted to attack and undermine him.

The third entrance to the catacombs branched almost directly off the circular chamber, on the side where Charles Wraithwhite's body had been found. Access proved difficult. Though it was a shorter route from the surface to the chamber or vice versa, the slippery steepness of the uneven stairs was a good reason why Chatwin-Paine had avoided it for their initial visit the previous evening. The stairway debouched into another shed, this one larger than the first and abutting the greenhouses. At the top of the stairway, a rickety wooden door barred their way. It was locked with a premodern mechanism requiring a heavy black iron key, again, a reminder of *The Count of Monte Cristo*.

Trying the door, Daria had cursed Chatwin-Paine—he had claimed all the entrances were open. She was about to retreat when Fowler had grinned around his large nicotine-stained teeth and extracted a set of keys from his painter's overalls. Wielding a four-inch skeleton key, he had opened the rickety door.

Upon close inspection, the shed proved to be filled with motorized gardening equipment, gardening clothes, and dozens of hand tools hanging from nails or hooks on the walls. While poking around inside, Daria and Pompelmo had been surprised by the unexpected appearance of the Institute's head gardener. Startled in his turn, the gardener had gasped, recoiled and invoked the Madonna, shading his eyes from the bright headlamps the spelunkers wore.

Apologizing, Daria had switched off her light and sent Pompelmo back down the staircase with Fowler, instructing them to wait for her in the burial chamber. Then she had identified herself, flashed her ID badge, and had soon discovered the timid gardener's name—Signor Leopardi. She had asked him a series of pointed questions.

No, Leopardi had replied, he had not been present during the gala. He had hung up his clothes and taken off his overshoes punctually at 6:30 p.m., his usual hour, and gone home to dinner and sleep. No, he had not noticed anything unusual before leaving or since his return.

But then Leopardi had paused and fidgeted and glanced around, frowning as he struggled with a recollection.

"Nothing unusual?" Daria had insisted.

"Well, maybe, but it is really nothing, nothing at all."

"Please explain," she had coaxed.

When he had come on duty that morning—only allowed onto the villa's grounds after a vigorous verbal tussle with Daria's siege force—Leopardi had gone to the gardener's shed as usual and as usual had entered without turning on the lights. The Roman sun was so bright who needed electric light? he asked rhetorically. He had reached out to pick his dark green coveralls off the usual coat hook, but they were not there.

"They were hanging on the next hook over," Leopardi had said, puzzling momentarily. "And my overshoes were not standing side by side but at a ninety-degree angle to each other."

"How unusual is that?" Daria had asked.

"Oh, very unusual. In thirty years working here it has never happened before, or, no, perhaps once, and also, perhaps, at the time of the gala."

Daria had glanced at Leopardi's dark green coveralls, noticing that the garments were clean, pressed, and apparently new. So were the matching dark green rubberized overshoes. Was that also unusual?

"Oh, no, not at all," he had said. "The coveralls are laundered nearly every day, I have five sets of them, as you can see if you look. The boots are also cleaned every day if they get dusty or dirty. Signor Presidente Chatwin-Paine is very strict about appearances. Staff must appear clean every day—clean clothes, clean shoes, and clean boots. All male employees must be clean-shaven and have bleached, white teeth. Before the trustees arrive for the gala each year, we are all sent to the dentist and issued with brand-new uniforms and shoes, or, in my case and those of my under-gardeners, overshoes and gum boots."

Daria had considered this curious tidbit of information and allowed the compact Leopardi to scratch his balding head and elaborate. "I suppose the housekeepers when they returned my coveralls this morning very early hung them on the wrong hook, and tripped on the overshoes or inadvertently pushed one out of place. There is a new girl in the laundry. Everyone is especially nervous and flustered when the trustees are present in great numbers for the gala."

"So, in fact, there was nothing unusual in the unusual events you describe?"

"Perhaps not," Leopardi had agreed, blushing.

"One last thing," Daria had said, glancing around the shed. "Are all of these coveralls yours? There seem to be scores of them."

Leopardi had laughed pleasantly. "No, no, no, signora. Those on that wall belong to the under-gardeners of which there are three. They are my assistants. Those in that corner belong to la Dottoressa Pizzicato, the director of the Institute, who is an avid gardener. And the ones next to them belong to the president, Dottor Chatwin-Paine. He is a world-renowned expert on tea roses, as you surely must know."

Nodding noncommittally, Daria had wandered over to Chatwin-Paine's coveralls and studied them in silence. Then she said, "Also new?"

"Yes."

"But they are different from the others."

"That is only natural," Leopardi explained, splaying his hands. "The president is very long in the leg and torso, for a start, and he always wears black, so his coveralls and gloves are also black. He says they stay clean longer, imagine that, what a strange idea!"

Strange idea! The expression returned to Daria's mind again and again as she continued her explorations of the catacombs.

Now, as she, Fowler, and Pompelmo were passing through the second locked gate in the tunnel, she wondered aloud who had keys to the various doors and padlocks and how many keys there were—the DIGOS caver crew had not been able to lay hands on them or explore these sections of tunnel. Fowler grunted. Then he grinned and said, "Until last night, no one has used these tunnels except us. Everyone else goes in and out of that one entrance Taylor showed you. So, I made a pass-key for that one door up there to the gardener's shed and cut the old locks off everywhere else and put on the new padlocks. That was almost a year ago, when I first got to Rome. I had two keys for each of the locks, but I made a few copies just in case."

"In case of what?"

"In case I lost one, or gave one away."

"And that's what you did?"

"Yeah," Fowler said defensively. "I gave one to Charlie. He said he needed it to get in and out without being seen. Then he went and copied the keys again—I could tell he did, because the padlocks started feeling rough when you turned the keys in them. He must've given the extras to his jerk pal."

"The man who always wore a carnival mask," Daria suggested, walking ahead of Fowler down the tunnel. Pompelmo silently brought up the rear.

"Yeah, the asshole who wore the Venetian mask on the upper part of his face and the dust mask below, to hide his roundhead smirk."

"Because, he claimed, he had asthma and couldn't stand the dust in the catacombs?"

"Yeah," said Fowler. "Like I told you back in my studio. That's what he said. It might've been true, I don't know. He looks like some kind of gymnast or acrobat, so it's hard to think he's a wimp with asthma. He only took off that dust mask to take a swig or a puff or a snort. Then he put it back on, though I could still tell he was smirking underneath it. Once, when he was taking off the dust mask, the other mask fell off and I saw his whole big fat face, but just for a second or two."

They were approaching a bend in the tunnel and as they rounded it, Daria could see faint daylight ahead. Soon they would be in the public park, the Giardini Gabriele d'Annunzio. She knew the sunlight and fresh air would change everything. Not wanting to lose her newfound intimacy with Fowler or lose track of what he was saying, she slowed and paused and turned, directing her headlamp away from Fowler's eyes.

"Just to be clear," she asked, "you said earlier in your room that the man's name was Tork or Torp, you don't know the spelling, that he seemed to be around thirty-five years old, was average height but with an athletic build and a remarkably round face, and spoke fluent English and Italian?"

"Yeah, he talked kind of like you—one of those people you can't place, you can't tell where they come from. He could be American or Canadian or Italian or all three. That's about all I know, except Charlie kept telling us how great Tork was and how he had been an Olympic competitor in something or some bullshit story like that, and he was going to help us skewer them, so we had to let him into the club and work with him when the time came."

"Skewer who? The Institute?"

"Yeah, Taylor, the Prez, Mr. Smoothie. For all the reasons I already tried to tell you up in my studio. He's a fucking molester and a cheat and a reactionary fascist. This whole place is a joke, it's, like, a total scam. The artists and writers and architects are crap, totally mediocre shitheads, the only good people are the residents and teachers and they already had their careers. They come here for a vacation. This is a fucking resort gated community for asshole academics, it's a make-work scheme, a boondoggle, a fiddle, and that Taylor dude, he lives high off the hog. I'll bet he pays himself a million a year. Charlie dug up some heavy shit on this place, he said he'd tell us about it and then we'd help him kick the shit out of these bastards."

"Okay," Daria said, walking again toward the light. "Back to the masked man, the man you say is named Tork. Can you describe his face?"

"Well, I *am* a fucking artist," Fowler scoffed. "I did eight years of studio art. You think I'm a phony like the rest of them? I can draw that asshole's face for you once we're out of here and you give me a drawing pad."

"Excellent," she murmured, checking her pockets and extracting a notebook. "In the meantime, please tell me what his face looked like."

Fowler cursed under his breath and spat onto the slimy wall of the tunnel. Then he said Tork had a round full-moon head, black hair, and dark eyes that were widely spaced, a nose that was slightly hooked and had flaring nostrils, and thick black eyebrows.

"Good," Daria said, "very good. Now, before we step out of the tunnel, could you make a quick sketch in my notebook?"

"Here? In the dark?"

"Yes, if you don't mind. We can shine all three headlamps on the notebook. Pompelmo, please lend me your light." The sergeant took off his headlamp and handed it to her. She gave Fowler the notebook and trained the lights on it. Scowling, he began to draw and, in a few minutes, working like a practiced caricature artist, had produced a small portrait sketch from memory. Daria took back the notebook, thanking him, and stared at the face as they walked slowly along.

"It's a pretty good likeness," Fowler said. "Maybe the nose isn't as hooked as that, he isn't a hawk or anything, but it's close."

"Really excellent," Daria said. "Bravo! Now, since you are obviously an unusually observant and intelligent person, please tell me another thing and be frank. Do you think this man Tork shot Charles Wraithwhite, perhaps by accident, while handing him the gun, for instance?"

Fowler stopped dead. He scrunched up his thin lips. "Oh man, I don't know. I don't know why he would. Maybe. By mistake. But like I said up top, I think it was a fuck-up, I think Charlie shot himself. He was always clicking that goddamn trigger more than once, especially if he was high. I always thought the damn bullets were blanks or duds. The fucking guns are like, I don't know, sixty or seventy years old and the ammo looks just as old. Who could think it would actually work and was live?"

"You make a very good point," she murmured. "May I ask you a final favor, a personal favor? If you should think of anything or find anything specific that Charles Wraithwhite told you about the Institute, would you email me or phone and let me know? Here is my personal email address and my mobile number. I will be sure to note in my report that you have been very helpful and cooperative." She finished writing and tore out the page in her notebook.

Fowler took the slip of paper warily. He read the email and phone number twice, his lips moving, then he tore up the slip and dropped the scraps in the tunnel, stamping them into the dust. "Charlie said not to leave behind any traces—no paper trail, no flash drives, nothing in the cloud."

Daria nodded thoughtfully, thanked Fowler once again, and strode the last few feet down the increasingly damp, mossy tunnel to the final iron gate. Beyond it, up a crumbling brick staircase, she could see the hot Roman sunshine pouring down through the branches of trees.

"We're in the park now, correct?" she asked.

"Yeah, right," said Fowler, pulling out another key and opening the final padlock. "Man, it stinks like piss," he scowled. "There's a public toilet twenty feet away, but the assholes and whores are always coming down that staircase anyway and doing their business here, right on the gate, goddamn them..."

Moments later, the gate swung open with a groan and a shriek that reminded Daria of Maestro Katzenbaum's symphony. Ducking, she stepped through, feeling like Dante exiting the Inferno, in this case leading the way, followed not by Dante's guide, the poet Virgil, but by the silent, placid Pompelmo and the snarling Fowler. Before the artist could snap the padlock shut, Daria heard a familiar, deep, rasping voice and glanced up.

"Don't bother to lock it," said Captain Foscolo in accented English, staring down at them. "We were about to go in. Now that we've found you, Mr. Fowler, you can lead the party."

Eight

Daria and Captain Foscolo stood apart from the others, about twenty feet from the tunnel entrance, in the shade of a coppice of fragrant laurel trees. The sun was high. She had begun to perspire. Foscolo, though wearing a preposterous, ill-fitting camel-colored polyester suit and baby blue tie, looked as cool as the spring water flowing through the ancient aqueduct underfoot. The water hiccupped from a dinged and dented turn-of-the-century dark green cast-iron drinking fountain standing nearby.

"We were informed that you had left for Venice," Foscolo said in his raspy voice, his face a stony blank. "We were ordered to take over the case."

"We?"

"Yes, we, SISMI. I am not authorized to discuss the details. That is the purview of the questor—his purview or that of my superiors at the Ministry of Defense. I have no right to offer my opinion, Major Vinci. But I should think you would be relieved to be taken off the case and thereby avoid any perceived conflicts of interest."

"To what do you refer, captain?"

Before speaking, Foscolo glanced to each side, then let his eyes rest on the children who had rushed up and were horsing around in the drinking fountain's splashing water. They leapt and wriggled, squirting each other and squealing. "Your father was a trustee of the Institute," said Foscolo, deadpan, "your brother is a trustee of the Institute, your godfather is a trustee of the Institute, the president of the Institute was a frequent guest at your parents' home long ago. You are an Italian and an American dual national and the Institute is the flagship of the American cultural community in Rome. You were a guest at the gala last night, invited by your brother, who paid for your meal and has contributed approximately a hundred thousand dollars to the Institute this year. Shall I go on?"

Daria shook her head, glancing away. "Isn't it funny, captain, that the term *insabbiare*, 'to sandbag' in English, is actually best rendered in Italian not by metaphorical sand or obstacles or bobby traps but by rubber—*il muro di gomma*, the rubber wall? Everything that hits it bounces off."

"I am unable to comment, and unwilling to speculate," Foscolo said dryly. "Perhaps, had you left your smartphone on, or, if it was on, had you allowed notifications or vibration, you might have realized earlier this morning that your transfer to Venice and your promotion had been decided at the highest levels and you were requested urgently and repeatedly to return to headquarters for a briefing followed by an immediate departure."

"Perhaps you are right," she agreed. "But, as you say, why speculate?"

Foscolo glanced around again, suspicion sparkling in his diamond-tipped eyes. "Best of luck to you in the north, Major Vinci, I am honored to have had the opportunity to work albeit briefly with the future vice questor of the Province of Venice." He clicked his heels, gave a slight bow, saluted, and started to walk away.

"One more thing, Captain Foscolo," Daria said, as if remembering. "Since I am being forced to drop this case, might you tell me for the sake of professional curiosity whether you and ballistics have thoroughly analyzed both revolvers?"

Foscolo thrust out his prominent jaw, then nodded almost imperceptibly. "We have," he admitted.

"Had the gun in the catacombs been fired more than once, by chance?"

Foscolo shook his head. "It was in almost exactly the same condition as the revolver in the drawer in the third-floor room, except that it had been fired. Once. The fact that Wraithwhite dropped it onto the floor of the catacomb after shooting himself explains the large quantities of dust on the inside and the outside of the gun's various parts."

"The spent cartridge? Was it the rimmed or rimless kind?"

Foscolo frowned and seemed about to refuse to answer. Then he said, "It was a .45 Auto Rim."

"So, it was the preferred cartridge for that older M1917 model? It was more likely to fire properly than the rimless cartridge, unless of course the ammo had been loaded into the gun using a moon clip, in which case, a rimless cartridge would work just as well as a rimmed cartridge?"

The captain watched Daria's wry expression. "That is correct, Major Vinci," he said. "I was not aware you were familiar with moon clips."

"You do me an injustice, Captain Foscolo. So, I wonder, would Wraithwhite have chosen a cartridge that was more likely to fire or less likely to fire, do you suppose? Would he not want a cartridge almost guaranteed to fail, unless he meant to commit suicide?"

Foscolo shifted uncomfortably. "The victim would have had to know about such things, as you apparently do, Major Vinci. My compliments. In any case, unless he studied the cartridge boxes and understood the names and numbering, or knew how to recognize one cartridge as opposed to another, the chances of selecting the more efficient cartridge would be fifty-fifty, given that there are equal numbers of each type in that drawer. Presumably, he would simply reach into the drawer and pull out a bullet, any bullet. The luck of the draw."

"Exactly," Daria said. "Unless someone else selected and loaded the bullet for him, one of the other club members, for instance, or the unidentified man who always wore a mask and might know about such things." She took a deep breath through flaring nostrils and stared at Foscolo. He stared back and did not flinch. "You are as aware as I am, Captain Foscolo, that cartridges for that particular handgun are still manufactured today and sold by specialized sites on the Internet. So, the question of freshness or lack of freshness and therefore lethality is moot."

Foscolo opened his mouth then shut it again without speaking. A moment later he cleared his throat and said, "Clearly you know that it is virtually impossible to distinguish a modern, contemporary cartridge from a vintage M1917 cartridge and that, in any case, ammunition does not come with a best-by date. Bombs and mines from World War Two still occasionally explode."

"Very occasionally," Daria agreed. She smiled, adding, "What's the famous old saying? Keep your powder dry and your sword sharpened?"

"Oliver Cromwell," Foscolo murmured.

"Actually, Kaiser Wilhelm," Daria retorted, "in *The Extraordinary Adventures of Arsène Lupin, Gentleman-Burglar*." She laughed. Foscolo maintained his stone face. "The catacombs are dry, are they not?"

"Very dry, except where the aqueduct is above floor level."

"Therefore, ideal hiding places for weaponry?"

Foscolo thrust out his jaw again, blinked, and said, "Perhaps."

"And those little plastic swords, are they sharp?"

Foscolo waited a beat. "One would have to feel them to find out."

Daria smiled wryly again. "Thank you again, captain, and good luck to you with this most baffling case of," she paused and drummed her lips, "of accidental ritual suicide? Or involuntary suicide? Or involuntary manslaughter? Or perhaps murder? A double murder, if Adele Selmer dies, as sounds likely from the reports I have received."

Without another word, Captain Foscolo rejoined Fowler and Sergeant Pompelmo by the tunnel entrance. Pompelmo glanced back helplessly, raised his eyebrows, shrugged, and splayed his hands. A moment later the three disappeared into the darkness, their headlamps flashing. She heard the gate swing shut and the padlock click.

Standing alone under the laurels in the Giardini Gabriele d'Annunzio, listening to the children cavort by the water fountain, Daria checked her wristwatch. It was a few minutes before 11. She wondered how much longer she could tease things out. An hour, two? She could pretend she had inadvertently allowed the battery of her phone to die. But they might be able to verify that. She could legitimately explain that she had been underground most of the morning, with no connectivity. Well, part of the morning. And she had honestly been too busy the rest of the time to respond to new stimuli—of which there were too many.

How was she supposed to know of her sudden promotion and transfer to Venice? What did it matter if she put her departure on hold for a day or even a week? She could not just drop her life in Rome. She was still dealing with the formalities of her mother's will, deciding in consultation with her brothers whether they should keep the apartment for their own use, sublet, or sell it. Her mother's funerary urn had not even been placed in the family tomb at the Protestant Cemetery. It was preposterous, even more preposterous than Foscolo's clashing suit and tie. She could not leave for Venice at the drop of a hat and that was that!

Glancing again at the portrait Fowler had drawn, she marveled at its quality, spurring her tired, anxious brain to concentrate on the masked man's features. There was something familiar about him. But what? Should she snap a photo and share the sketch with headquarters? If they put out an APB, there was a slim chance the masked man could be apprehended, if he hadn't already fled Rome. If she helped find him, would she somehow be playing into Foscolo's hands?

Reluctantly, Daria powered on her phone. Placing the notebook on a park bench, she took several photos of the drawing, hesitated, and in the end did not send them to HQ. A discomforting sense of paranoia began to steal over her. Why should she not help a colleague, whether he was a SISMI operative on loan or one of her own at DIGOS? They were on the same side, weren't they?

Pocketing the phone without looking at the screen, she strode away from the grove of laurel trees toward the perimeter fence twenty-five or thirty feet away. It rose to a height of seven or eight feet, was made of sturdy wrought-iron bars painted black and topped by sharp ornamental spear ends that were in turn crowned by coils of razor wire—no easy barrier to scale. Whoever the masked man is, she told herself, he must be a pole vaulter or have found a way to get through the fence into the park at night, unless he was bribing the park guards or had a passkey to the main gate.

The masked man was clearly not alone in his after-hours comings and goings, judging by the quantities of discarded condoms, wads of dirty toilet paper, empty cigarette packs, and other detritus scattered along a well-beaten path through tall weeds along the perimeter fence.

Daria had never been a hunter, not of animals. She did not like firearms though she knew a great deal about them and was an excellent shot, as Morbido had joked last night. Was it only last night? She shook her head and felt tired, hungry, and dazed. Pressing forward following the fence, she remembered how she had learned the hunter's basic tracking techniques at the police academy and then practiced on the job. Nothing could be easier than following someone in the wild in Italy. For one thing, there was little or no wilderness in the country. For another, all you had to do was follow the beaten path—the omnipresent illegal path in the forbidden spot trodden by countless hurrying feet.

Like it or not—Daria decidedly did not—when it came to illegalities, her fellow citizens everywhere, in the prosperous north and the impoverished south, behaved less like the obedient citizens of a civilized industrial power and more like the proverbial unherdable cats or perhaps a hamper of slithering, slippery eels.

Yes, a creel of eels clawed by kittens and ravenous feral cats, that was it.

Skittering or wriggling over and through and around any barrier real or metaphorical placed before them by the authorities, vast numbers of Italians were ungovernable, undisciplined, unruly, and profoundly disdainful of the law. It was supremely ironic that the codification of law was a Roman invention, and doubly supremely ironic that the unquestionable success of Italians around the globe, from the thuggish mafioso mobster to the proudly elected governor, prefect, or president of a nation—not to mention the myriad super-star Italian CEOs—was due at least in part to their cat-and-eel qualities.

Applying this novel maxim to the case at hand, Daria stalked along the fence with increasing disgust. She recognized the telltale signs of the sex trade. The setting seemed ideal. There was a quiet street at a discreet distance below, a wide, overgrown vacant lot, a public park with a convenient drinking fountain for washing, and an apparently dead-end staircase in the park near the fountain, leading to a locked tunnel, where business could be transacted and, afterwards, nature's call could be answered.

She guessed she would find a way through the fence soon enough, from the park into the strip of garbage-strewn land between it, the coiling street, and the impenetrable towering perimeter wall of the Institute of America in Rome.

Every Rome native knew that famous city wall, visible from far and wide. It had been built of brick and stone at the time of the first barbarian invasions, in the late third century of the so-called Christian era, then patched up and made taller and modified and extended and reduced and repaired time and again over the ensuing one thousand eight hundred years.

As she had expected, the path through the increasingly tall undergrowth climbed a gentle slope. Cloaked by a dense tangle of elderberry, laurel, pine, and cypress, the trail kinked at a ninety-degree angle, ending abruptly at a gaping hole in the fence. Four iron bars had been sawn off, bent or chiseled out of their masonry base. Slipping her willowy body through the gap, Daria wished she still had her headlamp. Amid the vegetation, it was almost as dark as in the catacombs.

After climbing for twenty or thirty feet more, the path split into three, branching to the right, center, and left. Pivoting and glancing back from the intersection, she could see into the park, over the fence she had breached and over the ancient Roman city wall into the groomed grounds of the Institute.

Which way? High ground, she told herself, turning right and following several switchbacks up through scrubby wild fennel and head-high weeds until she reached the top of a dusty barren knoll. From it on one side she could see the red tile roofs and campanili of the city spreading below. On the other side rose the parasol pines and flame cypresses that stippled the public park and the groomed grounds of the Institute, ahead and also slightly below.

Recognizing where she was, she realized she had looked out at this knoll from the terrace last night, during the gala, and had been reminded by Taylor Chatwin-Paine that its existence was a perennial thorn in his flesh. The filthy, cat-infested vacant strip and tatty hilltop, visible from the Institute's pristine garden and the upper stories of Villa Nerone, were allowed to remain a no-man's land, as they had been since the time of the emperors? It was scandalous! For decades, Chatwin-Paine had lobbied the municipal government trying to purchase the land or, short of that, have it securely fenced in and annexed to the Giardini Gabriele d'Annunzio. But the coalitions that had run the city since time immemorial had steadfastly refused.

Laughing quietly at the impotence of the Institute's American potentate when faced by the famous Roman rubber wall, Daria glanced around the knoll at a dozen or more shelters built for resident cats. They had been constructed from cardboard boxes tucked inside large black plastic leaf bags for insulation and waterproofing. Dishes of cat food and water were arranged neatly around the houses. She thought of the hundreds, possibly thousands, of stray cats that haunted the parks, ruins, and vacant lots of Rome, and the brigades of cat-loving locals, usually aging widows or empty-nester mothers, who fed and groomed them. They had a name in Italian: *i gattari* or more accurately, *le gattare*, feminine.

Meanwhile the cat-hating municipal authorities and anti-feline shopkeepers or homeowners did everything they could to exterminate the prolific animals. This colony seemed particularly well groomed and orderly. Daria wondered why the cats needed houses when they could comfortably live in the catacombs. Holes and passageways the size of human heads riddled the crumbling brick city wall. Surely the beasts could squeeze and scramble in and out and feed on the abundant vermin and other urban fauna?

Awakening to the unpleasant realization that her smartphone was simultaneously ringing and pinging and vibrating, she cursed it and herself, knowing that she had taken the wrong path. The masked man would not have come this way, exposing himself to public view on the knoll. Anyone in the Institute would be able to see him. He would have entered and exited the vacant lot and park from the jungle below, climbing up from the coiling street she had glimpsed through the tangle of trees.

Glancing at the smartphone's screen and confirming that it was now 11:09 a.m., Daria decided that triage was the only way forward. Morbido was the priority. She answered his call and asked how he was getting on with Aisha Williams.

"Thank God," Morbido blurted, "I thought you'd never answer. Where are you?"

"I am looking at you right this minute," she said. "You're walking from the greenhouse toward the outdoor theater, passing under a pine tree."

She watched mirthfully as Morbido stopped and whirled around as if searching for spirits. She waved at him but he did not see her. "Where?" he barked.

"It doesn't matter, Osvaldo. I'm on the hilltop, outside the walls. What about Aisha Williams?"

"It's impossible for me to understand her when she speaks, chief. She says 'like' about three times in each sentence, and uses words I have never heard before. When I say 'you' she says 'they, please.' I cannot interrogate her. You must do it. Luckily the officer with us is about eighteen years old and seems able to communicate with her..."

Morbido then provided the rundown. Like Adele Selmer and Hugh Fowler, Aisha Williams had been present at the shooting in the catacombs—she had tried to deny it, but the tunic had been found in her apartment, and the gunpowder detected in her cornrows, as Canova had already reported. She admitted eventually that she had been seated by Adele Selmer's side but had not been burned by the hot oil or hit by flying stone chips. However, the blast had deafened and terrified her and she had fled blindly with the others, groping through the catacombs and out the farther entrance, the narrow one near the porter's lodge. From there she had made her way along a carefully studied route to her apartment above the reconverted greenhouse, where she had showered, run a load of laundry on the hottest setting, with the tunic in it, then taken a sleeping pill and been awakened only when the police pounded on her door the following morning.

"She and Adele have been working on a project," Morbido added. "It's some kind of interactive virtual poem-artwork that maps out the security cameras in the Institute and around Rome. They've figured out how to move through the grounds and the city without being seen." He paused and read something off a sheet of paper. "It's called *The Invisible Visible Freedom Empowerment Poetry Project*."

In the grips of her nervous tic, Daria tapped her lips repeatedly as she considered this information. "All right, I don't have time to hear the details right now. Did she have anything more on Wraithwhite or the masked man? Any opinion about whether it was suicide or murder or just an accident?"

"Negative."

Daria muttered to herself, aware they had hit another dead end. "Hold on a minute, Osvaldo, I'm going to send you a photo of a portrait sketch of the guy. Fowler calls him the asshole, right? Says Wraithwhite called him Tork, something like that. Fowler made the sketch for me half an hour ago. I haven't sent it to HQ or asked for an APB yet."

"Why not?"

"It's too complicated to explain. I'm out of the picture. Foscolo has taken over the investigation. That dust you mentioned is stinging my eyes."

Morbido's breathing became suddenly labored. He growled when he spoke. "So, what do you want me to do with the portrait?"

Daria frowned. She wasn't sure. "Take a look, see if you recognize the guy. He seems familiar to me for some reason, like maybe he was one of ours once upon a time, I don't know. Show it to Aisha and get a confirmation if you can. Ask if she thinks he may have fired the shot instead of Wraithwhite, in theory by mistake. Then I'll decide what to do. And Osvaldo? Make sure you call in sick in Genoa. Get away from the Institute, get off the grounds. Wait for me in a café somewhere. Go over to Monteverde or down to Trastevere. Text me the address." She disconnected, brought up the photo of the portrait sketch, and sent it to Morbido using a proprietary encrypted app.

"Next," she said to herself, scrolling through the messages and checking the call register. HQ, HQ, HQ, Mario, Gianni, HQ, Mario, Bremach, Bremach, Bremach...

It was now 11:20 a.m. Willem Bremach had texted her twice and left a voice message. She hesitated, then decided it must be important. HQ was a rabbit hole straight to Venice. She risked disappearing down it for good. Her beloved Gianni and irksome brother Mario would have to wait. Bremach always knew something no one else could possibly know. She had grown up calling him the Wizard of Oz.

"My dear Da," the message began in Ambassador Bremach's resonant, unmistakable prewar English voice. "Why not meet me at the parapet in Piazzale Garibaldi, overlooking the great Giuseppe's cannon, at two minutes to high noon, precisely, please? We would not want to miss the firing of said armament. Then we can have a bit of jaw-wag. This afternoon Pinky and I must migrate north to our enchanted Riviera, there's no stopping her, the hydrangeas and wisteria are in bloom, the cats are lonely, and she never did care for Rome—too chaotic for her Norwegian sensibilities. Speaking of the north, I understand you are off to the land of no land, the land of water, the dark Lagoon City and et cetera. Don't let me down, Da. You won't regret making the time. Ta-ta."

Nine

Daria performed several quick calculations and began jogging west, replaying Willem Bremach's message as she went. The words purred through her earbud. "...the parapet in Piazzale Garibaldi, overlooking the great Giuseppe's cannon, at two minutes to high noon..."

Several minutes before the appointed hour, Daria slowed her pace and strode into the panoramic plaza on the shoulders of the Janiculum Hill, her eyes scanning the horizon.

Piazzale Garibaldi spreads its unusually wide expanse across a ridge high above labyrinthine Trastevere on the Tiber and the forbidding brick bastions of Vatican City to the east. "Giuseppe Garibaldi again," she said to herself, thinking of the coup attempt in Genoa and the murder of the Italian-American super-rich spy, Joseph Gary Baldi. "The great Italian patriot is a personal obsession of Willem Bremach."

Making her way through the crowds of indigenous gawkers, foreign tourists, and miscellaneous holidaymakers and moochers, she stepped up to the parapet, looking right and left for her elusive godfather.

The parapet teemed with school-age children. They bustled and jostled, their fingers already plugging their ears in delighted anticipation of the daily noontide event. A kaleidoscope of helium balloons tethered to the children's arms jerked up and down as the seething, squirming hamper of human eels squealed, shouted, and shrieked. Whirligigs spun into the air, some crashing into the windup toy parrots in noisy flight overhead. Groups of slow-moving grown-ups watched benignly, ready to be stunned and deafened but too proud to plug their ears like the children. It was only the uninitiated outsiders who seemed oblivious to what was about to happen, and the entwined hormonal adolescents who leaned bodily over the parapet to see the heavy creaking doors of the old gun battery wobble open and the cannon rumble out.

Cupping her hands over her ears, Daria felt a presence pressing in beside her. A mottled hand reached over. It grasped her uplifted right arm. Turning cautiously, she saw it was Willem Bremach, beaming toothily at her. Seconds later, at precisely noon, the bells of Rome's thousand churches began booming, tolling, and ringing wildly. At the height of the peeling paroxysm, Garibaldi's faithful cannon erupted in a tremendous blast—orange sparks flying and gray smoke pouring from the antique fieldpiece's dark iron muzzle.

The children squealed in terrified ecstasy, unplugging their ears. Others grimaced or wept, holding their aching heads.

"Just think, dear Da," said Willem, "what might happen if your temples were down by the barrel of that little old peashooter." Adjusting his hearing aids, he smiled again, then continued. "You would be deafened by the blast, perhaps permanently, and you might even suffer a concussion. You might experience fracturing and hemorrhaging. What a life the artillery men had, not enviable, and that is a small-bore cannon."

Daria listened patiently. "Imagine what might be the effects of a little old service revolver held to the temple and fired?" she asked. "Even if it were loaded with a blank cartridge."

"Oh, clever, clever Daria, that's it, precisely. Bullet or no bullet, even with a blank it could be lethal."

She waited again. It was no good rushing Willem Bremach. His every word was weighed and weighted with multiple meanings. She knew this from a lifetime in his company.

"Leaving aside the toy gladiator swords for now," he said, "what in the world might Wraithwhite have intended with the jelly beans? Let us reflect. Jelly bean, jelly bean, 'jelly belly'? Like your well-fed Communistic friend Morbido, who I am so glad has finally risen from lieutenant to the well-deserved rank of captain. Or perhaps jelly bean, jelly bean, as in candy? 'Candy is dandy, but liquor is quicker'?"

"That's one of those antediluvian ditties you and my father used to say," Daria remarked. "It's totally un-PC if you stop to think about it, Willem, so I prefer not to."

"You mean, tempting virtuous young ladies to do what they absolutely in their heart of hearts do not desire to do, for they are made to be angels and virgins forever and ever amen? Not like the Virgin Mary, naturally, who gave the poor old biblical Giuseppe quite a surprise." He chuckled. "If I told you how many women young and not-so-young tried to seduce me once upon a time, throwing themselves at me with candy or liquor and other tempting things, you would not believe me, because you cannot imagine this teetering wreck of a man as a strapping young devil nearly six and a half feet tall and idiotically unafraid of anything, particularly death." He paused and smiled. "You do know that it takes two to tango, don't you? Since when have you become a prude, Daria?"

"You know I'm not," she retorted. "It's just…"

"I see, it's *just*, as in justice? Never mind, never mind. Let us think about candy and cats," he said, pausing again to eye her. "Might our Zorro, our masked man of the catacombs—should we confirm his existence and identity—might he have been the Candy Man referred to in the conversations and messages exchanged by Charles Wraithwhite and others, intercepted by a certain intelligence organization with which you are familiar and which has theoretically taken over this investigation, leaving you free to seek new adventures?"

Daria glanced at him. "You're at it again, Willem. Didn't you retire about thirty years ago?"

"Of course, but I keep a paw in. I can't resist playing cat's cradle, you know. It's astonishing how the cats of Rome seem to be everywhere, even in the catacombs, which is only right, *n'est-ce-pas*? They are the proverbial household gods of the diaspora, are they not? The poets sing of them. *Splendido lare della tua dispersa famiglia*, I believe the line runs. The household gods of old, all that's left after the Diaspora. The cat in the hat box, the poem, I mean. Eugenio Montale, Nobel Prize, 1975. You've heard of him?"

"Willem, I beg of you—"

"Think, Daria, if cats could speak, what they might tell us about the Candy Man and so much else." He paused and, still leaning on the parapet, faced her. "You're not saying much, Da. Cat got your tongue?" Daria raised an eyebrow but could not help rolling her eyes and groaning. Before she could speak, Bremach held up a small plastic bag of brined lupini. "Care for one of these lupin beans?" he asked. "What a shame we don't have time for the Punch and Judy show. I remember when you were a toddler, how your father loved to bring you up here to gobble lupins and watch the performance. That would have been right around 1975, when Montale won the Nobel. Of course, back then it was a real live performance, not something prerecorded and blasted out of speakers. Knock, knock, knock, Punch's stick comes down on Judy's head, again and again. Enough knocks on the head and Judy stops? No, indeed, never!" Bremach laughed a full-throated laugh.

"Will you never grow up?"

"Never! Remember the famous words of Madame la Marquise Augusti-Contini di Mandrella, spoken when we last saw each other on the Riviera. The key to longevity, she said, goes beyond the whisky and egoism. It is being childlike."

"Childlike or childish?"

"Both," he said, his eyes twinkling. "Now, I promised no Latin conundrums, puzzlers, or enigmas this time, after all those mottoes and old chestnuts in Genoa. So, I have limited myself to trying to understand the double entendre or hidden meanings of the cat in *catacomb*, and consulting via the Ouija board the keepers of the cats who might be able to interpret what the nasty little beasts have seen and heard inside and above the catacombs, the way the oracles of old were interpreted. Your investigations might fruitfully lead you in that direction, as your courageous Captain Morbido appears to have found only moments ago, if my sources are reliable. But I do think you might also turn your attention to the jelly beans and the little plastic swords."

Pondering, Bremach began muttering under his breath again. "Jelly, jelly, jelly, jelly... sounds like... no, that's not quite right... in English there is no stress on the double consonants. Get a real Italian to pronounce it, a real Roman, you, for instance, or a southern Italian. What if 'jelly' was somehow a reference to someone's name? And the sword? It must be symbolic of something, don't you agree? Your Mr. Wraithwhite seems to have had a wicked sense of humor and a devious mind, methinks."

Daria felt momentarily mesmerized by the flow of Bremach's words. "Willem, I think the Institute is in for a very rough ride, one way or the other," she said at last. "Not even the coddled Rome Award winners think much of it these days. It seems like they were conspiring with Wraithwhite to bring it down and break Taylor's stranglehold."

Bremach made a *tsk* sound and pretended to be taken aback. "Admittedly, the Institute may not be what it was once upon a time. How to charitably characterize its current incarnation under our good president Chatwin-Paine? A way station or perhaps a pit stop for the gravy train along the MFA corporate highway? The deliciously cynical and profitable Way of Prosperity? The road to fortune that links universities and publishers and the big-league art dealers, collectors, and museums, et cetera? Along it, all creative merchandise becomes overwrought, like the artisans who produce it. Do you read much these days, Daria? No? Well, pick up the leading magazines and literary journals or buy a bestselling, award-winning novel. Everything wins awards now. Let's see what you find. In fiction, a *window* in winter is no longer *frosted*, it is *etched*. The boulder is frosted—with lichen. Metaphor metamorphosis and simile-*osis* are rife. Everything is over-written, overemphatic, overplayed, or the opposite—entirely flat, bland, and colorless. Every dialogue must contain several ejaculatory 'yeahs' and nonsensical 'likes,' because that is the way the people speak, particularly the young—if speaking is what they are doing. Every scene must be set in dreary council housing—what you call 'housing projects' in America—or even drearier suburbs, where nothing but 'yeah' and 'like' are repeated ad nauseam while the heroes of the drama get drunk or take drugs, indulge in something akin to a mating ritual, and, of course, curse nonstop and whine about the inherent unfairness of life. As it goes with the writing, so it goes with the visual arts, and the so-called music. My God! Katzenbaum! He wins awards? And people applaud? But you see, Daria, I am becoming an antique reactionary; it is time I resigned as a trustee."

"*Becoming?*" she laughed. "You just did a fine job of—what did you call it? Metaphor metamorphosis?"

Bremach smiled his toothiest smile and laughed. "Touché," he said. Then before she could speak, he added, thoughtfully, "That said, let us not throw the proverbial *bébé* out with the bathwater. We need reform, not revolution or destruction. It would be such a pity to see the Institute undone for perceived sins committed so long ago that only those of us headed to the elephant boneyard or the saber tooth tar pit can remember or understand the context, the goals, and the results. Just remember, young Daria, there was a method to the madness, a reason for what was done. Sometimes failure is success. Remember that! If our world looks the way it does today, and miraculously resists turning into Putin's Russia or America's Trump Land—with or without the Orange Baboon in the Oval Office—it is in part because of what we—meaning your father, Jefferson Page, I, and countless others—what *we* did when everyone was clamoring for our heads and calling us unpleasant names. I refer to how the Committees of Public Safety accused us of everything and its opposite. The self-styled Revolutionaries. The Reds who were as black as they were red. The clever Communists managed to get entire generations of humanity to slander the anti-Communists with the label of Fascist while they themselves, the Reds, were the stooges of Communist Fascism. You know who I mean. The creators of the original Big Lie. Captain Morbido's trade union father et al., the Communist sympathizers, funded then as now by Mother Russia or China or the Mafia or all three. They wanted Stalin and Mao or, at the very least, Khrushchev and Berlinguer. We wanted Churchill and FDR and JFK and LBJ. None of them perfect. Life is messy. The world did wind up with the clumsy authoritarian Trump, it's true, but it was temporary, an aberration. We, the Western World, tossed out the stooge of the Russian Mafia, the system purged itself. The West did not go under. You do see what I mean?"

Daria waited a beat longer, wrinkling her brow. "What about Taylor Chatwin-Paine? He's not on your roster of the heroes. That's what I was supposed to notice, isn't it?"

Bremach snorted, stepping aside to allow a pair of shrieking young girls to clamber onto the parapet and teeter perilously away. "A whippersnapper," Bremach said, guiding Daria by the elbow. "Taylor is not of our generation. He is, I believe, turning eighty soon, therefore fourteen years my junior. He would then be, what, twenty-five years younger than your father and the great Jefferson Page? He's an able administrator. Taylor, I mean. Who else could devise a board with fifty trustees, all of them handpicked, trussed, hamstrung, and at his beck and call, except me? Oh, Taylor is still beloved. He has always been the life of any party, very amusing, as long as his moist attentions are not focused on your wife, husband, son, or daughter. Beyond the moral considerations, the man is just not made of the same stuff as Page or your father or even me, if I must say so myself."

"What you mean," Daria said, "is he did not fly a Spitfire and win dogfights or become a double agent with three passports, like you, or dodge Nazi sniper fire, like Page, or help arrest Mussolini, like my father?"

"Oh, Taylor fought in Vietnam and did creditable service, don't underestimate him, he killed plenty of Vietcong as a young lieutenant. Whether or not he really was in the employ of the Company when he took over the Institute remains an open question. It is a question I cannot, and in any case would not be willing to, answer. That's not what I mean."

"Then what do you mean?"

"What I mean," Bremach said, shaking his huge, jowly head, "is this. Taylor Chatwin-Paine has transformed the Institute into his profitable, personal fief. He is venal and rather vicious and vainglorious and liquor-loving where we were quietly patriotic, morbidly private and self-effacing, retiring and secretive, dedicated to our countries, our families, and our cause, and able to resist the temptations of Bacchus and Priapus, at least in public."

"Which cause?"

"The defeat of Fascism and Communism, cost what it might."

"The heroic generation," Daria sighed. "Imagine, Willem, how hard it has been for all of us to grow up in the shadow of Olympus."

"Tut-tut," he said. "Most of us are no longer here to fling thunderbolts at you. I shall be joining Roberto and Jefferson soon, somewhere out there," he waved a bony, age-spotted hand at the fluffy clouds floating over Rome in a summery Tiepolo sky. "In gaseous form, no doubt," he added, "since I have become a terrible antique gasbag and the Catholics never would have me."

"Repent," she said, pulling out the notebook and flipping it open to the page with Fowler's sketch. "Here's a good way to start—do a good deed, identify this man." Bremach glanced over, stopped walking, pocketed the lupins, and took the notebook in one large, surprisingly steady hand. He studied it a full minute.

"Well, well, well," he murmured. "Well done, Daria. I will not ask how you got this—never reveal sources and all that." Holding it up to the sunlight, he pored over the drawing again. "What a charming fellow, he usually hides behind a close-cropped beard, doesn't he? But I still recognize him. When clean-shaven, this young gentleman looks remarkably like the former prime minister of Italy, Romano Prodi, many decades ago. But of course, it could not be Prodi because he is now almost as old as Chatwin-Paine and, like Captain Morbido, might get stuck in a catacomb passageway. They called him Mortadella, didn't they? A face like a Bologna sausage."

"Very round," Daria agreed.

Bremach's pupils glinted, the sun catching the artificial lenses of his powder blue eyes. "Hmmmm," he remarked, grinning. "Hmmmm, hmmmm, hmmmm." He handed back the notebook, sucked his lower lip, and said, "Let us get to work and put a name to him. What do you Americans call a cicatrice?" He paused long enough for Daria to frown. "And what are little Italian children's favorite things to eat, so that they ruin their sharp tiny teeth with caries or cavities as you call them? And while we're at it, how do you get a spoiled child anywhere to eat an apple?"

"Oh Willem," Daria exclaimed. "I don't have time for riddles."

"You must *make* time," Bremach teased. "Use your considerable mental abilities that are so often wasted on the trivial. Now I understand why Wraithwhite referred to our masked mystery man as the Candy Man. It wasn't just the cocaine and heroin he supplied to the virtuous members of the Catacomb Club."

"Please," she begged.

"The truth is, I think you would be better off not solving the riddle, not recognizing someone you surely must recognize, and quietly taking your promotion, so to speak, by sliding diagonally north to Venice, as soon as possible."

Daria went suddenly pale. "A cicatrice in England is a scar in America," she said mechanically.

"Good," said Bremach. "Go on."

"Candy, as in caramel or *caramella* in Italian. Apple, caramelized apple, *mela caramellata* in Italian."

"Lovely! Keep going."

"Scaramellata or Scaramellato?"

"Excellent," murmured Bremach, beaming again. *Bravissima!* And now, his first name?"

"I can't remember." She paused and drew breath. "Wraith-white called him Tork or Torp."

Bremach raised both eyebrows and made them dance. "How many names, especially Italian names, let alone Anglo-Saxon Christian or middle names, begin with or can be bastardized into Tork or Torp? Not many. And, my goodness, Daria, do you realize where we are and what once grew and still stands, so to speak, as a rotten stump held up by iron props, what still stands, I say, not a quarter of a mile away from us, on the edge of this panoramic esplanade, a stone's throw from a celebrated convent and the Vatican?"

"Willem!"

"Did you not read poetry at that excellent English school your parents spent a fortune sending you to? What was it, Saint Alban's British School, something like that?"

"Yes, I did read poetry, lots of poetry, mostly English and American but of course all the Italian classics."

"Then pray tell, who lived or rather died in the convent I referred to just now, right over there, and was memorialized by a certain oak tree that he sat under in his dying days, writing poems and letters, across the street from it? Come now, Daria, I know you wanted to be a doctor and wound up a policewoman but really... even an American autocorrect program will not underline his name in red."

"Tasso!" she cried triumphantly. "Torquato Tasso! *Jerusalem Liberated!*"

"Hallelujah!" Bremach shouted, sweeping his fist. "Why would Signor Scaramellato go by the name Torquato—Torq— when his Christian or first name as you say in America is quite different, quite banal?"

"So that no one would figure out his real first name?"

"Precisely! And why Torquato?"

"Because he is Italian and has read Torquato Tasso the way we read Shakespeare or Milton."

"Yes, my dear, and I would also guess Torquato Scaramellato has a fine sense of humor, like Charles Wraithwhite, or a highly developed sense of the grotesque. How far are the Institute and catacombs from Torquato Tasso's oak tree and the convent? A stone's throw."

"If you have a strong arm."

"So, there you have it, Da. The notorious fixer, the messenger of our friends in the Kremlin, the best buddy of Snowden and Assange, not to mention the sometimes-best bud of the personal, private counsel of a certain recently deposed would-be dictator of God's Country, whose acolytes stormed not the Bastille but the Capitol, flying Confederate flags. Everyone's friend, everyone's informant, negotiator, blackmailer, et cetera, et cetera, et cetera."

"Everyone's murderer?"

Bremach shook his head. "I rather think not. He's not the type, though you never know with choice subjects the likes of Torquato Scaramellato. If I'm not mistaken, he's a trained lawyer and still has a license to practice in Italy, though he was once famous, not to say notorious, as a rugby man and athlete with a weakness for hormones and doping and so forth, hence his love for Mother Russia. Since you won't want to raise signal flags on the home front, so to speak, might I suggest you skip your DIGOS people and go freelance? Use Google or Facebook. You'll surely get many responses to a facial recognition search using that sketch. I believe the proper first name, by the way, is Marco. Marco Torquato Scaramellato. But I repeat my injunction. Drop it, Daria. Flee. Get while the getting is good. Take that train, leap into a water taxi, live it up as vice questor of the Lagoon City. How many truly hideous or heinous crimes happen in the Province of Venice these days? You'll have plenty of time to read poetry and ride in gondolas, tossing flowers into the canals with the handsome Signor Giannini, the traffic cop from Rapallo. Perhaps you can arrange for his transfer to Venice? He could hand out mooring tickets instead of parking tickets."

Tapping her lips to hide her consternation, she watched as Bremach raised a hand and waved at a red convertible slowly circling Piazzale Garibaldi with its top down. "Priscilla?" Daria asked, her heart sinking at the thought that Bremach was leaving Rome right when she needed him most.

"Indeed, it is Pinky, sharking around like an anxious teenager, waiting for us to finish the jaw-jaw so she and I can speed north into the afternoon sunshine of our sunset years. The cats command us!"

She laughed at Bremach's silliness but was filled by sudden dread. "Willem, one last thing. Who is Captain Rocco Foscolo and where does he fit in? Why is a cybercrime and ballistics specialist from SISMI pretending to be on loan to us at DIGOS?"

"Cybercrime and *munitions*, actually, it's slightly different from ballistics, but there you are, let's not quibble."

"All right, munitions. How much does Foscolo know that I don't?"

Bremach smiled with satisfaction. "I am so glad you asked, Daria. As a trustee of the Institute, I should not reveal our ongoing trials and tribulations but I shall reveal a few, to help you along, in hopes you will see the futility of your efforts and happily pass the hot spud to Captain Foscolo. Now, you will have guessed or heard, perhaps from the esteemed Dr. Mario Vinci, that the Institute is being blackmailed? Cyber blackmailed. No? Well, now you have heard. Malware was uploaded or downloaded or otherwise inserted into the computer system by someone, we still do not know who or when or how, though we have our suspicions, and if you review the probable date of contamination and the beginning of the sojourn of the cherubic Mr. Wraithwhite, you might be tempted to leap to conclusions. The greedy blackmailers want an even million, otherwise they say they will shut everything down and..." he paused and frowned histrionically.

"And what?"

"Oh, they might also, for instance, threaten to reveal sensitive information there is no need for you or anyone else to know, prehistoric stuff, so old as to need Carbon-14 dating."

"Foscolo knows?"

Bremach shook his head and began walking toward the car. It had pulled up with its emergency flashers on. Priscilla Bremach née Anderson wore a bright pink shawl tied around the masses of blond hair bundled on top of her head. She smiled, blew kisses, and waved at Daria. "Don't forget, sometimes failure is success," Bremach said, getting into the car. "Foscolo is in the proverbial darkness about many things—everyone is, even Mario and Heiffermann, the chair, in New York. Only the shadow knows."

"Meaning Taylor and you?"

Bremach pursed his thick lips and, mimicking his wife, blew Daria a kiss. "Ta-ta," he said. "See you in Venice soon. Pinky can't wait, can you, my dear? Won't it be fun to land a seaplane on the lagoon?"

Ten

Walking swiftly back toward the Institute, Daria felt fatigue and hunger hounding her. Little sleep, less food, and too many confusing details to process— her head had begun to whirl, a kaleidoscopic whirligig like the windup toys flying over Piazzale Garibaldi.

Cats, jelly beans, and plastic swords, cyber blackmail and munitions and crimes committed long ago, and personal failings and candy-is-dandy-but-liquor-is-quicker? What did Willem Bremach mean when he said *failure is success*?

The final salvo Daria had fired at her enigmatic godfather when departing was *Mi raccomando. Take care.* She had meant it. But she had also meant the phrase to be a provocation, a tit-for-tat or quid pro quo for all the other mi raccomandos.

No matter what might transpire, she knew, Willem Bremach would be fine. He would top the century mark. His mother had lived to be one hundred and two and that was before the advent of modern medicine.

No, Daria worried not about the aged spymaster but about herself. She worried about Marco Torquato Scaramellato. She worried about those, who had whispered *mi raccomando* to her in the last thirty-six hours.

Checking her phone, she found a message from Morbido, directing her to a café by an imposing city gate a quarter mile from Piazzale Garibaldi. She was familiar with the scabrous but endearing blue-collar hangout. The cabbies of Rome used it, not to mention the ambulance drivers and orderlies from the medical facility down the street, and the ladies—and gentlemen—of the night, most of them Brazilian transvestites. *De gustibus non est disputandum*, she told herself, reciting the timeless Latin cliché. There is no accounting for taste? A better modern rendition of the original nonjudgmental motto seemed to her to be, "anything goes." If anyone knew how to swing, sexually and otherwise, it was the ancient Romans.

Unsurprisingly, the café teemed with the usual heavy-smoking heterogenous crowd. A dozen small rectangular tables packed with voluble patrons spilled across the disintegrating sidewalk onto the pitted pavement of the traffic circle surrounding the city gate. In a maelstrom of blue-gray exhaust fumes, the endless stream of cars, motorcycles, three-wheeled Ape trucks, and two-stroke Vespas flew past the café's customers, inches from the tables. Osvaldo Morbido's bulk spilled across two folding chairs standing side by side. Daria perched herself opposite and watched him tuck into a plateful of panini. Piled high, they appeared to be stuffed with salami, porchetta, mortadella, and mozzarella *con pomodori*. Nothing green could be seen, other than the single slice of unripe tomato poking out from the sodden bread surrounding the mozzarella.

"Have one," Morbido grunted amiably. "I ordered extra so you wouldn't have to wait."

Hesitantly, Daria chose the mozzarella panino, nibbled at the tomato then took a timid bite, swallowed it, then unceremoniously devoured the rest of the sandwich with unladylike vigor. Gulping down an entire half liter of sparkling mineral water, she blinked, sighed, and waved the waiter over. "Two double espressos," she said, "and another bottle of water. And the bill—we're in a hurry."

"That's all you're going to eat?" Morbido asked incredulously.

Daria eyed the mortadella sandwich, thought of the famously round heads of Romano Prodi and Marco Torquato Scaramellato, and took a tentative bite. The panino was gone before the waiter returned with their coffees and water. "Now," she said, sighing again. "We've got to shift out of first gear. What did the poet, Aisha Williams, say about the sketch?"

Morbido brushed the crumbs off his chest and stomach, gulped his coffee like medicine, and shook his jowls. "She wasn't sure. Said it might be the guy. He always wore the two masks, as Fowler told us. The masks fell off once last week and she caught a glimpse but she isn't sure. It was too dark. She has no idea who fired the shot. She had her eyes closed most of the time, meditating and tuning into the lives of the Paleochristian dead, she claimed." He paused and grunted. "She did say one interesting thing."

"What?"

"She's a poet, right? She has actually read a lot, including Italian poetry, if you can believe that."

"Why not believe it? Dante and Petrarch and Ariosto and Tasso and Leopardi—"

"Exactly," Morbido interrupted. "Tasso. *Torquato* Tasso. Aisha Williams thinks the masked guy's name is Torquato."

Daria nodded. "Okay," she said. "I know that already."

"You know it?"

"Yes, but it's not his first name, it's his middle name."

Morbido glowered. "Right, his first name is Marco," he retorted triumphantly. "Marco Torquato Scaramellato, the fixer thrown out of the professional rugby league ten years ago for doping with the Russians so turned to crime."

"I knew that too, except, didn't he come from a Mafia family and just wind up carrying on the clan tradition?"

Morbido sat up straight, his cheeks flushed purple. "Well, what's the point of me being here? I figure out something that's key to the case and you know it already? Listen, I need to get back to Genoa this evening, they're not buying the indigestion story, they think I'm up to no good, and my wife is furious." Morbido pulled a creased piece of paper from one of his pockets and unfolded it in front of her. "Before I go, I've brought you a treasure map," he chortled. "This is a back-of-the-envelope sketch the poet made of the routes you can follow around the grounds of Villa Nerone without being picked up on the security cameras. Pretty leaky watertight security system if you ask me, if she's right."

Daria studied the map, running her long, elegant index finger over the various camera-free zones. Then she tapped the entrance to the large shed, the one where she had met Leopardi, the head gardener, that morning. "So, you can move from here to here to here and no one will see you on camera?"

"Correct," said Morbido, "at least that's what Aisha Williams claims."

"Very interesting, excellent, Osvaldo, this is good sleuthing. Now I understand."

"What?"

"You'll soon see," she said. "We need to get moving."

"Where to?"

"I'll tell you as we walk. But first we need to find out if he was left-handed or ambidextrous."

"Who?"

Daria stared at Morbido as if he were an idiot. "Wraithwhite, of course, who else?"

"Of course," he said, shaking his head.

"The poet or the painter should know, they spent a lot of time with him. We can divide and conquer. You go back to Fowler and I talk to Aisha this time."

Morbido shook his head and began to flush purple again. "Before we do that or leave the area, there's something else you need to know, something even better than the security camera stuff or the left-handed issue." He paused and gloated. Daria arched her eyebrows impatiently. "When you phoned from that knoll an hour ago, and I turned around and tried to find you, I saw someone walking up through the vacant lot from the other side," Morbido said. "She was one of those crazy old cat ladies, a gattara. So, I leaned over from the terrace of the Institute and shouted at her to ask about you and she said she had seen a woman going down toward the park a minute earlier. Then I asked her if she went up there to the knoll often. She said yes, twice a day, every day, to feed the cats. So, I asked if she had been there last night and she said yes, of course she had. Then I asked if she'd seen anything strange. She said she'd seen lots of things but whether they were strange or not she couldn't say. There was always something going on at the villa or in the park and the vacant lot—lots of "action," as she put it. There was some horrible outdoor concert last night that scared the cats out of their wits, she said. Then she asked me to come down to talk to her because she was tired of shouting—the sound of our voices scared the cats, like the music. I said I'd come back in a couple of hours and could she be there at two? She didn't want to because that's not her usual time to feed them but then she said all right."

Morbido checked his watch, took a deep breath, and used a moistened fingertip to pick up the last crumbs on his plate, then gobbled them lustily. He watched Daria for a reaction to what he had said.

"Brilliant," she exclaimed. "Of course!"

"Of course, what?"

"Of course, Ambassador Bremach! The cats, the cat's cradle, all that nonsense he was blathering at me."

"Bremach?"

"Never mind, I'll tell you as we walk over there. Let's arrive early."

Eleven

Watching anxiously as Morbido struggled through the hole in the park's perimeter fence, dislodging masonry and using his ham-hock hands to yank out one of the loose wrought-iron bars, Daria was glad all over again that she had sent him to talk to Aisha Williams that morning instead of having him follow her into the catacombs. He was surprisingly strong, and as supple as a squid or an eel—he waltzed divinely, like Burt Lancaster in *The Leopard*, a featherweight on his small, leather-shod feet. It was Morbido's spherical shape that precluded him from passing through fences or narrow entrances and exits, a cannonball stuck in the muzzle of a fieldpiece—Garibaldi's cannon, for instance. The thought reminded her of her conversation with Willem Bremach and his plays on words around "cat."

By the time they had clambered up to the three-way intersection edging the woods, then checked for clues, and, finding none, had climbed the switchbacks toward the knoll to meet the cat lady, it was nearly 2 o'clock.

"From here you can see the exit of the tunnel that Fowler

showed me, over there, by the water fountain," Daria said, pointing over the fence into the park. "So, after the shooting last night, Scaramellato would have come out there and hightailed it the way we just came. At the intersection in the woods, I think he would have gone to the left then downhill to the street on the other side, where the prostitutes are. He wouldn't have come up here on the knoll or someone might've seen him."

"If it's a three-way intersection, why not go straight ahead?"

Daria tapped her lips. "Maybe, but I'll bet it's a dead end. The trail is much less worn. To the left, down on the street, he might have parked his car or a motorcycle, or an accomplice may have been waiting. The prostitutes make for perfect cover—he could pretend to be a client."

They stepped out of the undergrowth onto the knoll, glancing west and down slightly into the grounds of Villa Nerone. From the side opposite the villa, the side facing downtown Rome, an elderly woman was beetling along a looping dirt path, carrying a brightly colored shopping bag. She paused long enough to glance up at them, then started climbing again.

"I already told her I was from the police and not to worry," Morbido said. "Was that wrong?"

Daria raised her eyebrows. "I don't know, we'll see, sometimes these quirky characters are wary of the authorities. Can you blame them? Let me put her mind at ease about the cats. That's what she'll be concerned about."

It took several more minutes for the diminutive but vigorous woman to reach the top of the knoll. Without saying anything to Daria or Morbido, she reached into her electric pink shopping bag and began dispensing crunchy nuggets of cat food, using an acid green plastic scoop and calling in a wheedling voice. At the sound of the scoop and her words, several smoky, tiger-striped cats appeared from nowhere, followed by another and another and another cat, some of them calico, others solid black, gray, or white. Soon they were swarming around the woman's short stocky legs in a feeding frenzy, their tails erect in the air, rubbing their heads and necks on the woman's old-fashioned knit stockings. Daria counted ten full-grown cats and half a dozen kittens, but there may have been more. Cats and eels, she said to herself, waiting for the woman to speak.

"See how nice and fat and healthy they are," the cat lady purred with satisfaction. "My darlings, it's not your usual dinner time, it's very early, don't eat it all so fast, wait, or tonight you will be hungry and I might not be coming back. Now, that's enough, you must let me speak to these nice people, don't hiss or scratch, my darlings, they look like nice people, see how nice and fat the man is?"

Morbido listened to her voice as if bewitched, a smile slowly spreading across his face. He guffawed. "I'll bet you're a good cook, signora," he roared. "Do you have anything to feed me?"

The woman laughed amicably. "You have already eaten plenty," she teased. "I can see the crumbs on your face and clothing!" She poked him with her index finger. Daria watched the woman's finger then her whole hand slowly disappearing into Morbido's jelly belly—like the Pillsbury Doughboy in the old advertisements. He stepped back, blushing and laughing as he brushed her hand aside.

Unable to disguise her mirth, Daria held out her hand for the woman to shake. She introduced herself and added, "We are not here about the cats, we are both cat lovers, like you, signora."

The woman eyed them with no apparent fear. Daria noticed that her eyes glinted the same way Bremach's eyes had glinted. She guessed the cat lady had undergone cataract surgery and was about Bremach's age—mid-nineties.

"I could tell that the gentleman likes cats," said the woman, glancing up at Morbido's huge head. "Doesn't he look like a cat himself, like the Cheshire Cat or the lion in that old movie?"

"The Cowardly Lion in *The Wizard of Oz*?" Morbido guffawed again, wiping tears of hilarity from his plump dark eyes. "You're not the first to say so." He jerked his thumb at Daria and spoke to the cat lady, "She is my boss, signora, she is in command. I'm going to let her ask you a few questions about last night, while I have a look around the shrubbery."

"Look down there," the woman said without hesitating, pointing to the path through the woods. "Take the middle path and go to the end. If you look from here," she said, stepping away to the far side of the knoll and dragging Morbido by one sleeve, "you can see the thing you're looking for, the white thing, over there."

Morbido and Daria glanced at each other, then with their eyes followed the woman's pointing finger. They could just make out what looked like a piece of white cloth or clothing wedged behind a dead pine tree below.

"But, signora, how do you know what we're looking for?" Morbido stuttered out.

The woman laughed again, reaching down to stroke her cats as she spoke. "Why else would you be here? Last night I saw the little man come rushing out of the park and run up the hill. He was carrying a duffel bag as he always does and wearing the white smock and the mask, like a Halloween or carnival outfit. He always takes them off very carefully and puts them inside the bag while he's still inside the park, but he was in a terrible rush last night. So, that thing down there is what he peeled off as he ran into the woods. He hid it, then came out of the woods and ran down the hill on the other path, to the left."

Daria was nonplussed. "Captain Morbido," she said pivoting, "please go down and see if you can recover that smock. Be careful how you handle it. Bring it up here so we can take a look."

Morbido nodded, said "Sì commissario," and stepped gingerly down the dusty trail into the woods. Daria turned back to the woman. She was squatting now, petting and grooming the cats with a bright blue plastic brush she had pulled from the shopping bag. "You have excellent vision, signora, my compliments," Daria remarked.

"I see better now than when I was your age," said the cat lady. "I also have very sensitive hearing. Though you are trying to hide it, I can tell by the tone of your voice and the expressions on your pretty face that you think I am an eccentric foolish old lady and perhaps I am," she added amicably, then paused. "But perhaps I am not. I am very old, older than you think. I remember the bombing raids and the roundups during the war. I will let you do the arithmetic. Once upon a time I had a career, a very long career. This is Rome, the mother of all bureaucracy. I was a ministerial functionary for forty-five years. I can recognize a DIGOS officer a mile off, even in plainclothes. That is what you are, major. Not exactly secret service but almost."

"You are correct," Daria said.

"Well, it was an easy guess. You called your colleague *Captain* Morbido and he had already said you were his superior officer. Therefore, you are a major. A colonel would not deign to come here and speak to me in my current state—a crazy old cat lady!"

Daria smiled. "Again, my compliments, signora." She paused until the woman looked up at her, paying attention. "Might I ask how you seem to know this man you referred to as wearing a smock? You mentioned that he always or often comes out and takes off the garment and mask within the boundaries of the park."

"Two or three times a week," she confirmed. "In the last two months, I've seen him a number of times, but I don't know who he is anymore than I know who the people up in that private garden are. The *Institute*, it's called. For a long time, I wondered if it wasn't some kind of luxury hotel. But the gardener set me straight. It is a *cultural* institution, he says."

As casually as she could, Daria showed the woman her notebook, with the sketch of the masked man. "Do you by chance recognize this individual?"

The cat lady did not hesitate. "Oh yes, the human peacock who wears the smock, the muscleman who comes strutting out of the tunnel there wearing a mask. As I said, he takes the smock off and the mask and packs them in his bag and then goes down the path. But last night, he detoured and left the smock behind in the trees. I think the duffle bag was already full. Something was hanging out of it."

"Really?" Daria mused. "What might that have been?"

"Well, it looked like a dark green or perhaps a black outfit of some kind. It was definitely a piece of clothing with a sleeve hanging out."

Daria pondered, wondering. She would have to ask Fowler or Aisha Williams or Adele Selmer—when Adele came out of the coma—about the duffle bag and outfit.

"Here comes your Captain Morbido!" the cat lady exclaimed. "He's carrying the smock in his hands."

Morbido appeared a moment later pinching a dirty white tunic between his right thumb and index finger. "You wouldn't happen to have an empty plastic bag, would you, signora?" Morbido asked, catching his breath.

"Naturally I would," said the cat lady, digging in her shopping bag. She took out a recyclable green plastic grocery bag, shook it inside and out, and handed it over. Watching with obvious amusement, she nodded her approval when Morbido daintily dropped the tunic into the bag and tied the handles together.

Daria searched in an inner pocket of her dark blue DIGOS summer pantsuit, then handed a card to the cat lady. "Would you be willing to testify to what you have just told us, signora?"

The woman took the calling card, read it silently, and laughed. "Given the speed at which the Roman court system works, it's unlikely I will be alive when wanted, but if I am called upon, I will appear," she said. Daria noted down her name, address, and telephone number. She lived nearby and had one of those only-in-Rome monikers—Livia Emilia Aurelia. The paucity of digits in her phone number proclaimed its antiquity. Daria suddenly wondered if Italy was the only country in the world where telephone numbers from the 1950s, '60s, and '70s had remained unchanged, a mere five digits, while numbers from the 1980s onward had grown to seven, eight, or nine digits.

Livia Emilia Aurelia spoke again in her lively, chirruping voice, waving a small, manicured hand at Daria's smartphone. "I do not use email and I do not have one of those phones," she said. "My cats are my full-time occupation." Pausing and pointing to the public park and water fountain, she whispered, "Here comes that stern-looking young man who was here earlier this morning, looking around as if he'd lost something, sticking his head into the holes in the city wall and shouting, then listening to someone inside shouting back at him."

Daria and Morbido turned simultaneously and spotted Captain Foscolo below. He was alone. Making his way slowly toward the hole in the fence, Foscolo paused to prowl around, poking a wooden stick into the weeds as he went. Daria frowned. She took a deep breath. "Signora Aurelia," she said crisply, "we thank you, but we must be off, we are late already. Please do not mention to our stern colleague that we've been here or that we have talked to you already. He is rather jealous and envious, I'm afraid. And, if I might suggest something else?"

"That depends what it is."

"Ask a friend to feed your cats for a while, take a vacation, don't come back here. If you can't find anyone, call me, and I will get one of my officers to do it for you starting tonight."

For the first time, the cat lady seemed displeased. "I see," she said coolly, shaking her head. "Who can be surprised? The mother of all bureaucracy is the mother of all intrigue."

Morbido bowed, then he and Daria scampered down the hill, following the looping trail the cat lady had walked up earlier. When they got to the bottom, they turned and looked back at the knoll, wondering whether Foscolo had seen them. But he did not appear to be on their tracks. Had the cat lady run interference?

"No time to waste," Daria blurted, catching her breath. "Down on Viale di Trastevere we can grab a cab if we're lucky, or the streetcar. Let's run for it."

"Run? Again?" Morbido panted and spluttered when he spoke. "Then what?" They rushed down staircases through alleyways an arm-span wide under lines of flapping laundry, weaving between tumbledown Fascist-era tenements built of brick or stone.

"Then we figure out what to do," Daria said, answering his question while dodging a speeding motor scooter. Moments later she pushed her way onto the streetcar when it stopped on the boulevard and the automatic doors sprang open. Morbido heaved himself inside as the doors began snapping shut. Startled, half a dozen passengers muttered and stared suspiciously. Turning to glance back through the futuristic new streetcar's picture windows, Daria caught sight of a brawny man wearing a camel-colored polyester suit and baby blue tie, running pell-mell toward the streetcar stop. He paused on the corner, his head swiveling.

"Foscolo," Daria whispered, "duck!"

Twelve

Daria had a sensation, an intuition, a gut feeling that she had better get off the streetcar soon—on Via Arenula one stop before the end of the line. The traffic-clogged Piazzale Argentina was famous for its unidentified ruined ancient temple, its colony of feral cats, and busy streetcar terminus. It would be the logical place for Foscolo and his men to expect them to step down.

Piling out with a handful of other riders, they dashed between speeding cars, heading east along a kinking, imperfect diagonal into the maze of the historic Jewish Ghetto. Squeezing bodily toward the Tiber side by side down narrow back alleys, they doubled back past the Ghetto's bustling kosher delicatessens, bakeries, restaurants, souvenir shops, and haberdasheries.

"In here," Daria barked in a hoarse whisper, hustling Morbido into a hole-in-the-wall clothing shop. Seconds later, Captain Foscolo and two undercover operatives clattered by in the cobbled alleyway, shouting to each other as they ran. Smiling at the startled proprietor, Daria flashed her badge, put her finger to her lips, then pointed to a wide-brimmed black hat, a lightweight man's cape, also black, and what looked like a shawl or mantilla, asking for the biggest sizes available. "Cash," she whispered, laying down two large-denomination euro bank notes and scooping up the clothes and change.

"A present," she told Morbido as he gaped at her. Glancing outside, she jerked a thumb toward the streetcar stop on Via Arenula as they stepped back into the alleyway, hurriedly pressing the hat onto Morbido's extra-large head. "Now the cape," she whispered, "and now you bend over like this, because you're feeling your years."

"Ain't that the truth," he wheezed, pretending to hobble.

Wrapping herself in the mantilla, Daria tipped her head down and began walking behind him, slower than her usual pace. "That's a very attractive outfit," she remarked, "we'll give the cape to your wife as a peace offering."

Morbido grunted. "You're still walking too fast for someone wearing that mantilla, and you're not far enough behind me."

"You better hand me the bag with the tunic," she said, realizing that she did not want Morbido to take the heat if Foscolo or his men cornered them.

Cautiously traversing the Ghetto's main street, she pointed to an alleyway even narrower than the others they had taken. "Go up there, keep following the alley until you come out in the little square with the turtle fountain, go right on the wider road, and wait for me in front of the church of Santa Caterina dei Funari, you can ask anyone where it is."

Morbido stopped dead and pivoted. "You mean, the church where they found Aldo Moro's body crammed into the trunk of a parked Renault 4?"

"Exactly," Daria said. "The Red Brigades. May 9, 1978, a day that lives on in infamy. There's a plaque on the sidewall of the building abutting the church. You can't miss it. I thought you might recognize the spot." She paused, racking her brain. "If you see Foscolo or his men, detour into the courtyard across the street from the plaque and wait there; it's open to the public. There are three exits if you need to run. If you get lost and can't find the church and the plaque, circle back here and take the main road through the Ghetto. It's called the Portico d'Ottavia. Go to the other church, Sant'Angelo in Pescheria, the one built into a ruined Roman temple. It's down there, three or four hundred yards away. Go through the archeological park out front and meet me by the mound of marble slabs fronting the theater, the one that looks like a miniature Coliseum."

"You mean," he panted, "the Teatro di Marcello, where the beloved Sophia lives?"

Daria was nonplussed. Why would Morbido, a Genoese who had never lived in Rome, know such insider information? Without further ado, she strode up a different alleyway, this one leading to Piazza Costaguti, taking the longer way around and hoping to throw off Foscolo if he or his team had spotted them. She needed to get clear of the Ghetto. It was too easy to be trapped here.

Peering around corners before continuing at a painfully decorous pace, Daria made it a few minutes later to the street corner and church of Santa Caterina dei Funari. She signaled to Morbido to follow her—at a distance. Keeping fifty to sixty yards ahead, she led him through a tangle of narrow tilting streets and crooked alleys—the back way to the hard-driven pocket-size church of Sant'Angelo in Pescheria, shoehorned into the walls of an ancient Roman temple. They entered but left the church almost immediately, picking their way around half-buried columns and ruined foundation walls to the archeological area facing the Teatro di Marcello.

"Now what?" Morbido asked breathlessly, the sweat making him look like a summertime emoticon. "It's hot under this hat and cape. We can't just keep running all day."

Daria pointed to a tree-clad hill across the curving, multi-lane boulevard bounding the archeological park. Cars and buses and scooters wove between flying trucks and motor tricycles and bicycles and pedestrians trying to get across. "Monte Caprino," she said. "Wild Goat Mountain. The most solitary hill in central Rome."

Joining a clutch of terrified tourists waiting on the sidewalk, Daria and Morbido waved their arms and waded perilously through the slaloming vehicles. A few of the drivers slowed but most swerved or streaked past with homicidal insouciance, horns blaring. On the far side of the roadway, Daria skipped ahead and began climbing a steep stairway up Monte Caprino. The crumbling brick steps zigzagged into a seedy park shaded by moth-eaten laurels and choked with weeds and litter. Morbido clambered up behind her, glancing ahead periodically from under his hat to make sure he was going in the right direction. After climbing in silence for what seemed an hour but was closer to five minutes, they found themselves in a parking area nestled below an administrative office building unaccountably hidden away in the thick vegetation of this strange, sinister corner of the city.

Kicking away the garbage, Daria perched on a collapsing brick wall in the deep shade, waiting for Morbido and catching her breath. When he lumbered up to where she waited, she jerked her thumb and said, "The Capitoline is over there, maybe four hundred yards away. There are probably ten thousand tourists standing on the crest right now, gawking at the Forum from above, or clustering around the equestrian monument to Marcus Aurelius. Plus, there's everyone going to City Hall to bounce off the rubber wall and the bureaucrats who work there, and the police from the station across the street, not to mention the crowds trying to get inside the Capitoline museums. But here, there's never anyone."

"I wonder why," Morbido wheezed sardonically, surveying the surroundings. His face was as purple as the pope's Lenten cape, with rivulets of sweat coursing down it. Panting, he seemed about to expire. Morbido no longer looked leonine—as the cat lady had suggested. He looked canine—like an overheated Saint Bernard. When he finally managed to keep his tongue in his mouth long enough to talk, he said, "No one comes here, as you say, except the highly considerate people who left the garbage and vandalized the staircase and spray-painted tags and graffiti all over the back of this building." He glanced around, wincing in disgust. "Genoa is a mess, I admit, but nothing beats Rome."

"For beauty and blight," Daria admitted philosophically. Using her fingertips, she carefully removed Scaramollato's tunic from the plastic bag, then waited for Morbido to scoot over to her side and examine it with her. She was surprised yet somehow not surprised by what they found. There were no visible bloodstains, no splotches of brain matter, and no telltale gray misting from gunpowder on either the sleeves or the front of the garment. She did spot a few minute traces of something black and dusty, and when she sniffed the tunic, beyond the foul body odor, she thought she could detect a chemical smell. "We've got to get this analyzed," she muttered.

Morbido sniffed at the tunic, made a face, then shrugged. "Why bother? You know as well as I do that whoever was wearing this smock did not shoot the gun that killed Wraithwhite."

Daria nodded. "So, he really did shoot himself?"

Morbido shrugged again, splayed his hands, then took off his cape and hat. He used the hat to fan himself. "Who knows? It looks like it. More to the point, who cares? Honestly, Daria, something sleazy was going on up there. Everyone involved is so unsavory and pernicious. Like that Fowler guy said, maybe Wraithwhite deserved it. Could this be poetic justice? He was blackmailing the Institute with the help of Scaramellato?"

Daria pursed her lips. "You may be right, but I have to know, I need to know for sure." She stood up, pulling her handgun from a holster behind her back. "Quick, catch it or take it from me," she tossed the gun to Morbido before he could answer. Catching it, he clutched the gun, his eyes bulging and veins swelling visibly in consternation. The pistol looked like a toy in his hands. "Now, let's play Russian roulette," she said. "You go first."

Morbido eyed her, worriedly shaking his head. "Thanks a lot. You know we can't play with this kind of gun, there's no cylinder to spin."

"Pretend, Osvaldo, do what you would do if you were playing for real. Just maybe don't pull the trigger?"

With his fat fingers, Morbido passed the gun from his right to his left hand, pretended to flick out the fictional cylinder and spin it using his right-hand fingers, then pretended to click the cylinder back in. He handed the weapon back from left to right, raised it, and pointed it at his right temple. "Bang," he said.

"Perfect," Daria agreed. "Now you hand it to me." She went through the same steps, taking the gun with her right hand, passing it to the left, spinning the cylinder and so on. "Bang," she said, holding the gun with her right hand to her right temple. "Well?"

"Well, what?"

"What side did Wraithwhite shoot himself on?"

"The right side, of course."

"Why *of course*? You saw his handwriting. You heard what he had in his pants pockets. Everything important was in his *left* front pocket. And the cigarette lighter was lying in the dust under the *left* side of the body."

Morbido made a face. "That's why you want to know if he was a lefty?"

"Try playing the game the opposite way around. Go ahead and try it."

Morbido obeyed but fumbled.

"Ever tried to flick a lighter with your left hand if you're right-handed?"

"Okay, okay, I get it. So, he was left-handed but he shot himself from the right?"

Daria tapped her lips and grimaced. "He was shot from the right. It's not exactly the same thing, is it?"

"But if Scaramellato was wearing that tunic, and it wasn't Scaramellato who shot him on the right side, who else could it have been?"

"Excellent point. Either Scaramellato had an extra tunic with him or this tunic exculpates him." She paused and tapped her lips. "Exculpation, exoneration, it makes Scaramellato the perfect witness. He can't be indicted and he can swear it was an accident—he was there, by Wraithwhite's side, Fowler said so."

"So did Aisha Williams." Morbido paused then raised his fingers and snapped them. "That's why he left the tunic up there? To be found?"

"Exactly," Daria said, glancing at the screen of her smartphone.

"Found by whom?"

"You still have dust in your eyes?" she asked.

Morbido limited himself to a growling one-word roar. "Foscolo!"

Daria blinked several times while nodding affirmatively. "That begs the question," she mused, "if it wasn't Scaramellato who shot Wraithwhite in the catacombs, who else was there with them?"

Morbido shook his head. "No idea," he admitted. "Someone hiding in the dark? Someone who came in and went out unseen? They never accounted for about half a dozen people who were at the Institute and didn't show up on the security camera tapes."

Daria frowned and clicked her tongue. "Unless it was the poet with cornrows," she said. "Aisha Williams? She washed her smock so we'll never know if it was spattered with brain matter and blood. Could Fowler be covering for her?" Daria slipped the handgun back into its holster, preparing to move.

Shaking his head, Morbido muttered, "Believe me, Daria, it wasn't the poet. If it turns out to be her, I will hand back my promotion and maybe I'll just go ahead and resign."

Daria waited several long beats, glancing around to make sure the coast was still clear. "You need to get back to Genoa, Osvaldo. That's an order. Otherwise, they'll demote you for real and your wife will kill you. I'll see what else I can figure out before heading to Venice. I don't think I have much choice. If I don't go, they'll put a tail on me and I won't be able to achieve anything."

Morbido laid the hat and cape down on the wall and slumped forward heavily. He used a handkerchief the size of a hand towel to mop his face. "Okay, it's a deal," he said. "If you give up and go to Venice, I'll go back to Genoa this afternoon. I have a ticket on the 6 o'clock Intercity train."

"Done," she said and held out her hand. They shook. "Isn't that the train that's always late or breaks down?"

"The same," he growled.

"In any case, your negotiating skills need improving. You didn't specify *when* I had to go to Venice as part of the deal, so don't expect to see me at the train station with you this evening waiting until kingdom come." She smiled wickedly.

"Trickery!" he muttered. "Treachery! You're staying here and continuing the investigation without me?"

"Now, do me one more favor before we part," she said, gazing out through the branches of the laurel trees at the weather-stained marble arcades of the Teatro di Marcello across the way. "Say the word 'jelly' as in jelly beans three times slowly and clearly, pronouncing it as if it were an Italian word, beginning with a *g* not a *j*."

Morbido watched her warily. Then he enunciated "*Gelli, gelli, gelli*," laying emphasis on the double consonants.

"Licio Gelli," Daria almost whispered.

"Licio Gelli?" Morbido repeated incredulously, sitting up straight.

"Coup-plotter extraordinaire, subversive right-wing fanatic, head of the Propaganda 2 secret Masonic lodge, and so forth, you know the tale as well as I do."

Morbido smacked his forehead with one huge hand. "Oh God, how stupid could we have been? *Jelly beans*. Licio *Gelli* beans. The P2 Masonic lodge, Gladio, the sword, of course, the sword is the symbol of Gladio, *gladius* in Latin, as in gladiator. NATO's nightmare, the bugbear of the Communists, the arms caches, the corruption and links to the Mafia."

"Stay Behind," Daria said, shaking her head. "The failed Borghese coup. That's what Willem Bremach meant when he said failure was success, or success was failure, whatever. The CIA and secret intelligence agencies of Italy *made* it fail. This is what Wraithwhite's message to Chatwin-Paine means—it's a warning. That's the dirt on the Institute Bremach was talking about."

"And it may explain where those revolvers came from," Morbido said. "Not the war but the Stay Behind armaments and munitions caches."

"*Munitions*," Daria repeated, smiling. "Now I get why Foscolo is involved. It's not just the cyber blackmailing. Except it's still not clear to me who shot Wraithwhite."

Morbido stood up and shook himself, splaying his hands as he spoke. "Look, if that's what this is all about—Cold War stuff from the fifties and sixties—then frankly, what's the big deal? It's ancient history, as dead and buried as the gladiators of the Teatro di Marcello."

"The gladiators fought in the Coliseum," she muttered. "Gladio was only shut down in 1990, after the Berlin Wall fell."

"Okay, same difference, it's still a very old story, everyone involved is dead or at least no longer in power or dangerous. Everyone's done their mea culpas, it didn't work then trying to convict them, it won't work now to try to punish them. Gelli got away with it. The weapons were retired and destroyed—at least the ones the Mafia didn't get hold of were. It's finished, *basta*, *finito*. You know what I mean?"

Daria knew what he meant. But she wasn't sure how dead Gladio and Stay Behind really were—or the P2 and Licio Gelli either. In fact, she was very sure they were very much alive, an authentic deep reactionary state within the Italian state. They lived on in different forms, incarnated by different leaders and acolytes not only in Italy but everywhere—from Rome to Paris, Buenos Aires to Washington, D.C. Willem Bremach and Taylor Chatwin-Paine were still alive, after all. The Institute had not really changed since those days, either, and the number of subversive conspiracy theorists and domestic terrorists was on the rise everywhere. Still... There seemed no point dragging Morbido further into the investigation. It required the kind of digging that could take months or years to complete.

"You are so right," she said in her mildest, most mendacious voice, the benign untruth stinging her lips as she spoke it. "Now, if we just mosey on over in that direction on this pretty garden path, we'll wind up in Piazza della Consolazione. We can share a taxi to your hotel, as long as you don't mind making a quick stop along the way so I can drop something off. Then you can check out and walk to the train station early."

"Drop off what? The tunic?"

Daria smiled. "Don't you worry your giant little head about it. I'll figure out something to do with that rag sooner or later. You're on vacation now. You've got a couple of hours to kill, you can stroll around the scenic Termini train station and watch the pickpockets at work, unless we get stuck in traffic, which is almost guaranteed." She tapped the Signal icon on her smartphone. Then she used the unbreakable encrypted app to send a short disappearing message followed by a second, longer one. Both were set to self-destruct five minutes after being opened.

Waiting until Morbido had put his hat and cape back on, she trotted ahead, her mantilla flapping, following a narrow trail that felt underfoot as if it had been hit by a series of landslides and never repaired. They waited under the trees on the edge of the piazza. When the limo she'd called pulled into the square, Daria beckoned with a nod of her head. She slid out from under her mantilla. Holding his hat on his head as he ran, with the cape fluttering behind him like one of the Three Musketeers, Morbido dashed from the park into the blazing Roman sun of late June.

Shaded behind the tinted glass of the air-conditioned car, they sat in silence, watching the scenery go by.

"Venice!" Daria sang out with forced gaiety. "Do come and visit, and bring the wife. Don't you Genoese just love the Venetians?"

Morbido glowered at her. "Like I said, what you're doing is treachery. You're a traitor to me and to Genoa, your adopted city. We whopped Venice so many times in the Middle Ages it's not funny, and now it's the world's worst tourist trap."

"That's ancient history," Daria remarked, "as dead and buried as Gladio and Licio Gelli! You're envious because Venice is more popular than Genoa and you know it!"

Thirteen

The lab was privately owned. DIGOS and other police or intelligence units outsourced to it for chemical, ballistics, and DNA analyses when the in-house and government-affiliated labs were too busy for drop-dead urgent work.

Daria knew the facility near Termini Station as well as she knew the morgue or the Santa Maria della Pietà psychiatric ward in the northern outskirts, and the hulking, bleak Regina Coeli prison edging Trastevere, as terror-inspiring today as it was a century or three centuries ago. *Roma eterna*, she whispered to herself. Nothing was merely old in the capital of Italy. Everything was ancient, timeless, imperishable—eternal.

Daria had shed sentimentality long ago. No one doing her job could afford squishy feelings. By the time she had said a quick goodbye to Osvaldo Morbido at his fleabag hotel, then circled back on foot to the lab, the first round of urgentissimo test results awaited her.

As Morbido and she had expected, no one wearing that smock could reasonably be suspected to have fired the shot point blank that killed Wraithwhite, under the circumstances as currently known. If this was the murderer's outer clothing, he or she would have had to be wearing some other protective clothing on top of the tunic or be standing several yards away from the victim, with the sleeves rolled up, when the shot was fired. There was less blood and brain matter on the fabric of this smock than there had been on Fowler's tunic, and only trace quantities of gunpowder. The coroner had established beyond doubt that the muzzle of the revolver had been within inches of Wraithwhite's temple when the gun went off.

She knew now that it was imperative that she talk to Fowler again and ask him whether Scaramellato or anyone else at the club meeting had been wearing two smocks or had something else on—a pair of coveralls, for instance. Painters' coveralls? What if Fowler had fired the shot and the others were covering for him? That had not occurred to her until now. But it seemed unlikely. Every instinct in her rebelled against the notion.

Carrying the garment away with her in a large white plastic laboratory bag, Daria paused to reread the printed report, then pocketed it and started walking again. She walked past the ruins of an ancient bathhouse. She skirted a square with an elaborate and ridiculous yet endearing carved marble fountain splashing wildly in its center. In the space of a mile, she counted nearly twenty historic churches, one set of imposing city walls, an ancient aqueduct on mile-high arches, and guesstimated she had encountered at least one thousand tour buses, each belching black fumes into the air.

Perching on a worn green wooden bench above Piazza del Popolo, on the panoramic terrace edging the Villa Borghese parklands, Daria made several encrypted phone calls. She contemplated the view of obelisks and fountains. She reviewed the PDF of the archeological history of the Institute, tracing the tunnels and walls and burial chambers with her fingertip.

Then she tried to reach the former assistant librarian whose contact information the current head librarian had finally emailed her. Failing to get an answer to her calls and texts, Daria gave up and yawned violently until her jaw popped and her head shook. With her eyes shut, she decided she needed to change her attitude, relax, and look forward to her new life in the Lagoon City. She tried to meditate, reciting her trusty mantra—*calm, quiet, methodical.* But try as she might, the prospect of moving to Venice nagged at her.

The trouble with the magical city, to her mind, was its flatness and relative newness. Compared to Rome, la Serenissima Repubblica di Venezia had been excogitated and built yesterday. It was only a thousand years old and had no ancient Roman ruins or cypress-topped hills. There was also the minor problem of mosquitoes—she was allergic to their vicious bites. Not to mention the *acqua alta.* The periodic flooding of the city was amusing and romantic to the itinerant tourist, but not to those who had to live with it full time. Worst of all were the obscene, maddening crowds. The crowding she could cope with, maybe. She was almost inured to it from the regularly scheduled seasonal invasions of Rome by neo-barbarians. If DIGOS assigned her a motor launch of her own and provided her with a relatively secluded and quiet apartment, far from the city's hotspots, she might be okay.

So, let's be proactive, she told herself. Let's join the new heroic generation and stop complaining in advance. Before leaving Rome, she would stock up on mosquito repellent, buy a tropical mosquito net, and when in the Lagoon City, wear long sleeves and pants even at the height of the sticky, sweltering Venetian summer.

The real unsolvable problem then was—what? The flatness? Yes. And no. No. Definitely not. It was the distance from Venice to Rapallo, as Morbido had said, needling her. She sighed audibly, surprising herself and wondering again whether this rushed reassignment and promotion to vice questor was in reality a death sentence. It seemed destined to kill her budding intimacy with Gianni Giannini, the municipal policeman whose beat was the small seaside resort of Rapallo, twenty miles from Genoa—hundreds and hundreds of miles from Venice. She had not so secretly hoped to be reassigned to Genoa, a city she had come to love. Who wouldn't love the Italian Riviera?

When in a teasing mood, Osvaldo Morbido called Gianni Giannini "the traffic cop" or "Adonis." It was true: Sergeant Giannini issued traffic and parking citations and he was too good-looking for his own or anyone else's good. Gianni was also nearly ten years Daria's junior. What were the chances a long-distance love affair could last? They'd already been unwillingly separated for over a year because of her transfer to Rome, and had only managed to spend three weekends together, plus the two weeks in Sardinia. Fourteen dreamy days hiking in the windswept barren mountains, and swimming in the warm blue sea, making dangerously delicious love on the sun-warmed, wave-wetted sand of that cove. What was the impossible Sardinian name of that cove?

Daria sighed again, wrote one last time to the unrelenting logistical department at DIGOS headquarters, and then challenged herself to walk the rest of the way home in under forty minutes. How long would it take to pack her bags? No more than a few hours. She had lived in limbo with a half-packed suitcase in her bedroom ever since returning to Rome, having been suspended and demoted in disgrace and not knowing what the future held. When the truth of the Red Riviera coup attempt had come out, she and Morbido were eventually vindicated, then lionized and raised from pariahs to national heroes, their exploits told in a wild, outlandish crime novel. That had taken over a year.

Why then should she have bothered to unpack her bags? First of all, she had been told the transfer to Rome was temporary. Second, if it proved long term, she had planned to find her own apartment and move away from her mother's dinosaur den—Barbie's barracuda-infested territorial waters. Then her mother had died, more swiftly and suddenly than anyone expected. Now Daria had to figure out what to do with the ashes and the urn, the apartment, and the thousand and one things kicking around the place that no one wanted to live with or claim but that no one was willing to actually throw away either. Her brothers expected her to take photos and make videos and send them around the world, then sort and clean and pack and ship the best items to America, Australia, England, Japan, and Germany. When? She worked twelve hours a day, six days a week.

Daria had already prepared her speech to Mario about the funerary urn. She would say, *I'm taking Mother to the cemetery tomorrow morning, early. The questor insists I be driven in an official DIGOS vehicle to Venice. The driver is arriving at 11 a.m. sharp. Goodbye and over to you!*

An epiphany of enraged frustration made her flush purple like Osvaldo Morbido, then tremble and growl. "No!" she shouted out loud. People sitting on nearby benches glanced over to see if something was wrong. They just as quickly looked away. After the fit passed, Daria felt relieved, elated, liberated.

Deciding that for once in her life she was going to let her brothers deal with the mess, that she was going to let them clean and pack up and decide the fate of the family property, and take the urn to the cemetery or leave it in the kitchen until kingdom come, for all she cared, she was suffused by a transformative glow. She had not experienced anything like it in decades, not since the time she had left Rome to study medicine at Yale, thirty years ago.

Upon reflection, she hoped her new start in Venice would be more successful than her earlier, failed attempt at a life of her own in America, including a medical career and a conventional romance with a longtime fiancé heading for nuptials. Everything had been cut short by the brutal, unsolved murder of her father. She wondered now if the death of parents was destined to be a set of bookends bracketing every adult life. Would there be a new life for her now, after the death of her all-consuming mother?

At the hardware store a block from her building, Daria bought enough chemical insect repellent to last five years and kill her ten times over. She found two repellent-impregnated mosquito nets, supposedly tested in the Amazon rainforest. Then she added twenty square yards of white weatherproof insect-screen textile to the pile in her shopping basket. The textiles were woven from some kind of plastic webbing and looked absolutely hideous. With them she would seal off her windows without completely stifling the city's sea breezes—assuming the breezes actually still blew in the new, superheated world of post-climate-change survivalism. She thought of Maestro Katzenbaum's *Symphony for a Brave New World*. Venice would be among the first to drown in the New Flood, submerged by climate Armageddon.

Before checking out, Daria asked an eager young clerk to help her find a powerful headlamp—the kind worn by miners or spelunkers—and a hand tool for gouging out mortar from between bricks. Then she lined up at the checkout stand. The elderly cashier had known Daria for decades and seen her grow up. She wondered out loud with a wry smile where the fearless inspector was going now. To the Amazon to mine gold?

"Who told you?!" Daria snapped indignantly. "My assignment is top secret."

They laughed together as only Romans can, with a deep, ironic, quaking-and-shaking sardonic hilarity distilling the essential absurdity of work, travel, love, life, and death—above all death.

Praying that Mario would be at the Institute and not at home, she slipped the bag containing the tunic into one of the larger shopping bags from the hardware store and walked the rest of the way home suffused with feisty satisfaction, periodically looking over her shoulder to see if she was being followed. Letting herself in, she beelined to the stairs and began climbing to her bedroom, her real priority not packing but figuring out how to speak freely to Hugh Fowler and sew up the case before leaving.

"So, there you are," she heard Mario thunder, sounding aggrieved.

Those were the same words spoken in the same self-righteous tone of voice he had used at the Institute two nights earlier, Daria recalled. When Taylor Chatwin-Paine had blown into the infirmary breezily, as if fresh off the running-board of a prewar Bentley. A dusty running-board, she now recalled. The image and words persisted in her mind.

"Well?" grumbled Mario when she did not answer.

"Later," she said, closing the door in his face before he could step in after her.

Free, she whispered to herself, *remember, you're free at last.*

But later came sooner than hoped. Half an hour slipped by as she packed and rummaged and conceived a predeparture master plan—she would order a burrito for Fowler and lure him away from the Institute, or sneak a message to him, somehow, asking him to meet for a last chat. Mario knocked, then without waiting, pushed open her door and strode in. He had always done that. None of her brothers had shown her the least respect when they were growing up. Why bother? They were the princes. She was their slave, the maid, the family Cinderella, her mother's whipping girl.

Now, with evening upon them and the encounter with Mario several hours behind, she clutched the plastic bag containing the dirty tunic and climbed noiselessly out of her bedroom window. Following the service walkway across the roof, she padded down the backstairs to the courtyard and from there into the twilit street.

Concentration and focus on the task at hand were often made difficult by the complexities of life. In this specific instance, the gorgeous weather and the season seemed to conspire to make the mind wander. It was such a perfect, soft, warm early summer night, a night for a long solitary walk. Daria hesitated, calculating the time she would save if she took a taxi or a streetcar partway to her destination. Either way, she would then hike the last half mile to the storied hilltop crowned by the Institute of America and the Giardini Gabriele d'Annunzio—and the vacant strip of no-man's land outside them. Was time of the essence, she asked herself? Wasn't it always? Tempus fugit.

She answered her own rhetorical question with a fleeting, wry smile. Fourteen hours lay open to her until the arrival of the DIGOS driver assigned to escort her to Venice. HQ had sent her photos via WhatsApp of what awaited. The DIGOS Venezia building she would be occupying appeared to overlook the Venice Port Authority and the busy car bridge from blighted Mestre—the unlovely landlocked city where most Venetians actually lived. The site did not exactly look classy. Why had she imagined a suite in a frescoed Renaissance palazzo on the Grand Canal?

Daria laughed out loud, suddenly making up her mind and stepping into the first streetcar that slid to a stop, its overhead wires sparking and sizzling and dented body swaying on worn springs as if palsied. The vintage streetcars in her neighborhood had not been updated or upgraded like the ones in Trastevere. She was thankful. They worked fine. She hoped they would prove as eternal as the city itself, as long-lasting and beloved as the cable cars of San Francisco, preferably without the tourist mobs who made the Californian conveyances useless to local riders.

As the streetcar jostled and switched tracks and jogged toward the Vatican, Daria reviewed in her mind the tangle of information, misinformation, and disinformation that Dr. Marlo Vinci, MD, PhD, narcissist and bore, had dispensed to her a few hours earlier in his best Olympian style.

The Institute with Mario as spokesman was sticking to its story: Taylor Chatwin-Paine was showing signs of something like incipient senility. The time had come for him to go home and be put out to pasture, Mario had opined, though not in those exact words.

But wasn't Rome Chatwin-Paine's true home?, Daria had objected. He had been at the Institute since her childhood, back when the Cold War still raged, if a conflict inside a minus-seventy centigrade freezer can be said to rage.

Mario had shaken his head with finality. Whether afflicted by dementia or not, Chatwin-Paine was out of touch and no longer an asset to the Institute. The board in New York was already at work recruiting a new president as well as an equity and inclusion officer. Among the EIO's duties—theirs, not his or hers, Daria noted—would be the application of strict pronoun preference guidelines and an ongoing gender-and-race-affirmative-action campaign. Outreach efforts would be made across America to find a more representative selection of Rome Award candidates. The staff would be reshuffled and new blood brought in. Naturally, a 5G network would be installed so everyone could have instantaneous access twenty-four seven to high-speed Internet everywhere inside the Institute's buildings and out of doors, including underground in the catacombs. The tunnel network would be reopened and reborn as a peaceful labyrinth for meditation, with custom lighting and comfortable seating and high-tech ventilation and perhaps a café or snack bar and indoor/outdoor smoking area. Everything would be rewired on the property so everyone could plug in and charge up everywhere, inside and out. Parking areas for recharging electric scooters, bikes, and cars would be installed.

Many helpful suggestions had already been made by current and former award winners about the lack of world foods and vegan options at the Institute's mess hall, continued Mario. The difficulty and slowness of getting takeout deliveries through the security check at the porter's lodge would soon be resolved. Everything would have to change in order to stay the same. No one should be forced to lunch or dine at a given hour in the close company of fellow Institute denizens. The discriminatory prevalence of meat-eaters and omnivores, and middle-aged or elderly visiting scholars, writers, and artists, nearly all of them white, would be redressed by encouraging a careful screening of applicants to include more vegetarians, the young, and the nonwhite.

It was long past time for the Institute to open itself to the totality of Rome, Mario had pronounced, as if Daria might actually be as concerned as he was about the Institute's internal affairs and prospects. In future, its celebrated curated excursions would embrace not only the sites and monuments of ancient Rome and surroundings, including by necessity Christian churches, but also Rome's vibrant, expanding new communities from Africa and Asia. The influence of foreign, non-European cultures, political systems, faiths, and religions on classical Western civilization down the ages, and the history of the contributions of enslaved peoples, would be emphasized.

The real mistake, Mario claimed, striking his most righteously wrathful note, was to have hired Charles Wraithwhite to write the Institute's history. Though he had had the appearance of a Baroque angel as painted by Raphael or perhaps Caravaggio, with blond curls, blue eyes, and a winning puckered smile, he had clearly been in league with forces of darkness bent on dishonoring and discrediting the Institute.

How could anyone reasonably construe this century-old Institution to be an *anachronism*, its very purpose a *nonsense*, as Wraithwhite, from his intercepted correspondence, had claimed? The classical world, the world of the Mediterranean, of Greece and Rome and North Africa and the Middle East, the world of Renaissance culture and art—how could they possibly be anachronistic when properly recontextualized for the 2020s? Therefore, how could the Institute be anything less than eternal, like Rome itself?

In his unstoppable narrative, Mario did not once mention Chatwin-Paine's notorious vices and faults, or the fact that his wages, perks, travel, car and food allowances, sundries, and housing—including an apartment near Gramercy Square in Manhattan and a two-bedroom suite on the top floor of Villa Nerone—cost the Institute nearly a million dollars per year.

None of these considerations had been worthy of remark? Daria had to wonder why. Was it because the president would continue to enjoy benefits thanks to a golden-handshake emeritus status? Or did it simply reflect the reality that, as Mario had said to her years ago, referring deprecatingly to her paltry wages, that, "Everyone earns six figures these days, the question is, are they high, medium, or low six figures?" As a society doctor and Ivy League professor, Mario Vinci probably cleared over a million a year. He lived in a high-rise Plexiglas bubble impenetrable even by machine gun fire or plastic explosives.

In contrast, the picture Mario painted of Charles Wraithwhite was strikingly somber, to the point of being difficult for Daria to believe. If Wraithwhite were such a disreputable character, why had he been hired and by whom? If he was known to have a cocaine habit and a drinking problem, and to have been caught dodging taxes and scamming colleagues, running up gambling debts, cheating on his exams in college, and being accused multiple times of sexual improprieties and assault on other young men who, like him, had a Raphael or Caravaggio smile, why had he been given the job?

Speaking of Caravaggio, hadn't the Baroque master, perhaps the greatest painter of the seventeenth century, been a slave driver, literally, and a rapist and murderer? Even by the abysmal standards of his day, Caravaggio had been the ultimate bad boy. Daria congratulated Mario for drawing the parallel with Wraithwhite. But was her brother aware that Caravaggio had actually committed homicide? And while she was at it, did he realize that Raphael was a *Renaissance* master and *not* from Rome's Baroque period?

Mario Vinci, MD, PhD, the heartless cardiologist, had signally failed to report to her anything about the ongoing cyber blackmail campaign, or the astonishing fact Daria had unearthed that it was Chatwin-Paine himself who had summoned the young Wraithwhite to Rome. The two men had known each other through mutual friends in New York City. They appeared, when the gloss and hair dye was rubbed off, to share many traits, habits, and sensibilities. Rumor had it they were or had been lovers, forming a triangle with Marco Torquato Scaramellato.

These reflections kept Daria entertained and occupied as she rode across Rome, then alighted from the streetcar and began climbing the curving, tree-lined streets from the Tiber flatlands toward the hilltop. Checking her watch, she wondered whether the meal she had ordered for Hugh Fowler had reached the porter's lodge at the Institute as requested— meaning about an hour ago—and whether, taken by surprise, Fowler would have fetched it, unwrapped the burrito, and found her handwritten note to him. She had dictated the words over the telephone to the manager of the Tex-Mex restaurant in Monteverde Vecchio, asking him to reread everything back to her aloud, twice, then a third time, making corrections.

Compliments of the American cop, the message began. *I hope it's spicy enough. Please be at the gate to the tunnel on the park side at 10 p.m. tonight. Don't let anyone see you. Destroy this message once you've read it. It's important.*

The note was to have been wrapped around the burrito under a layer of aluminum foil. She hoped the burrito's juices and the extra salsa had not leaked out and made the words illegible.

Stealthily approaching the path from the coiling road into the vacant lot's thick, dark vegetation, Daria marveled at the ingenuity of the boys from Brazil and their several female colleagues. The sex workers in this tony neighborhood had upgraded from the shabby tents and lean-tos of old. Now they had trailers and RVs, though most customers seemed to prefer a quick stand-up job out of doors, in the dark woodlands.

Along the crumbling sidewalk flanking the no-man's land, half a dozen smudge pots burned and smoked, the spluttering flames' chiaroscuro effect worthy of Rembrandt. The smudge pots were the preferred outdoor advertising of prostitutes everywhere in Italy of whatever gender. They had given sex workers the nickname *lucciole*. Fireflies. Daria paused and listened. It was a dark, quiet night by Roman standards and a little early for rush-hour business. Like mealtimes, sex times in

Rome began late, at about 9, with a peak from 10 to 1 in the morning. They lasted till dawn.

Passing through the woods undetected, she gripped the plastic bag in one hand and her service pistol in the other.

Reaching the three-way intersection, she switched on her headlamp and climbed the rest of the way to the pine tree snag. There she nested Scaramellato's tunic, just as Morbido had found it earlier that afternoon. Foscolo or his men would come upon it sooner or later, a discovery apt to lead to a predictably fake denouement.

Daria was about to head for the hole in the fence and enter the park when an intuitive sense of incompletion and missed opportunities caused her to halt. She checked her watch. It was too early to meet Fowler. She found the three-way intersection again and turned left this time, climbing up the switchbacks to the knoll, turning off her headlamp before leaving the cover of the trees. The lights in the windows of the Institute and its spotlit grounds were visible in the no-man's land beyond and below the forbidding, pockmarked city wall. As she had hoped, there, among the cardboard houses, stood the diminutive figure of an aged woman, surrounded by cats.

Fourteen

"**S**omehow, I did not think you would follow my advice, Signora Aurelia," Daria said. She had not meant to scold the cat lady but the words escaped her mouth before she could stop them. Daria hoped that Livia Emilia Aurelia realized how genuinely concerned Daria was for her safety.

Stepping slowly to the top of the knoll, Daria stood by the cat lady's side. Signora Aurelia did not turn or speak. Together in silence they watched the glowing city below, enchanted by the nighttime lighting, the swirling traffic along the Tiber, the sparkling fountains, jagged towers, and swelling, gilded cupolas and domes. As Daria's eyes adjusted to the darkness, she could see that the cat lady was smiling.

"Well," said Signora Aurelia after an interval of several minutes, "somehow, I thought you might be coming back up here tonight, Major Vinci. Somehow, I thought you might replace that smock where it was, behind the tree, as you just did, so that your friend from SISMI could find it and come to the same conclusions you have. But I regret to say, your friend and his men have come and gone and the tunic was not there during their search. You may need to give them a helping hand, a hint as to its location."

Chuckling almost inaudibly, Daria could not refrain from complimenting the cat lady again. "You are an extraordinarily observant and perspicacious individual, signora," she said.

"If you only knew the half of it," Aurelia retorted. "The things I see..."

"Such as?"

Aurelia stroked her sharking cats and glanced at the city walls bounding the Institute. She raised a small, tapered finger and wiggled it. "For instance, there's the man in black. He was up there again, beyond the parapet in the rose garden, a few minutes ago, pacing to and fro with his gardening clippers, in the dark! He seems particularly agitated these days."

"The man in black?"

"They call him the Black Widower, I'm told. He's a friend of the ambassador's and obviously very important and distinguished. He always seems to wear black, whether it is a gala concert as it was last night or the middle of August and as hot as blazes, with Rome emptied out and in the hands of the invading barbarians. That is why these city walls were built, as I'm sure you know. To keep the barbarians out. Tourism in the ancient world was recognized for what it is—a lethal blight." She sighed, then continued. "The man always wears black suits, mourning clothes, or outfits that are charcoal gray. Even his gardening gloves are black. He is irreproachably elegant in a sinister way, like an undertaker. I have seen him up there in the gardens for years. Years and years and years. And he has seen me over here on the knoll for years, we have stared at each other. He shakes his fist at me sometimes and curses my cats, then goes away. Sometimes I see him in the public park, at night, with the Brazilian transvestites, and then I understand why he wears black—so no one can see him. But he is silly. If he wore white no one would recognize him because he always wears black!" The woman cackled now. Daria could see she was getting excited.

"Aha," Daria said encouragingly, "this man in black, is he tall and thin and elderly?"

"He's younger than I am, but he's no spring chick," she answered. "He hates cats, he's been trying to get rid of us for years, but he won't succeed, will he, my darlings? We have powerful allies, don't we? The ambassador's wife is our friend, thank goodness, and so is Leonardo."

"Leonardo?"

"The head gardener."

"You mean Leonardo Leopardi?"

"Naturally. We call him Leo Leo, don't we, my dearies?"

Signora Aurelia, the cat lady of the knoll, was eternally grateful to Leo Leo for removing the poisoned food and the hideous animal traps the man in black or his minions—the under-gardeners and Signor Verdi, the custodian—set out, and for running interference between the hostile forces within the grounds of the villa and the pro-feline resistance forces on the knoll.

"On the other hand," the cat lady added philosophically, "to be fair, and to get back to your original question, I do not hold it against the man in black for bailing out as he did the other night and taking refuge in Leo Leo's shack, where the cats sometimes sleep. He chased them out and they came running down to momma. That's why I happened to look up and see him. My God that music was dreadful! It reminded me of the bombardments of 1942."

"How do you mean?" Daria asked, perplexed.

"Well, as that horrid howling and shrieking and clashing and banging went on, and my darlings were terrified and rushing to hide, I saw the man in black up there, behind the concert hall or theater or whatever it is. He walked away, from there to there, with his hands up covering his ears, and he went into the gardeners' shack and didn't come out for a good ten minutes, until the noise was almost over. Then I saw him tiptoeing back so no one would notice he'd been missing. Who can blame him? The composer and musicians are criminals, aren't they, my darlings? Each year at midsummer it's the same thing—they come and practice for days on end, playing the most hideous, nightmarish music, no matter who composed it, it is always awful, and my cats suffer horribly."

Daria showed Signora Aurelia the glowing screen of her smartphone. On it was a photo of Taylor Chatwin-Paine, downloaded from the Institute's website. "Is this the man in black?"

The woman looked, blinked, and said, "That is he."

Daria straightened up, pocketing her smartphone. "Is there any point in me repeating my injunction about staying away from the knoll for a time?"

"I doubt it," said the woman. "I'll see you in court one day if you think that might help my cats. Anything to save them."

Daria nodded, smiling to herself. "Just out of curiosity," she asked, "I suppose you must know Ambassador Bremach? That's who you were referring to a moment ago?"

"Oh yes," said the woman, smiling back. "I know his wife Priscilla better than I know Willem. She is a great lover of cats. She has adopted several from me and taken them to a lovely villa on the Riviera near Rapallo, where I am formally invited to visit one of these years or decades or centuries. Pinky and Willem have been essential in my struggle to preserve this strip of no-man's land and keep the nasty ornery man in black from realizing his nefarious plans." She laughed a coarse, full-throated Roman laugh.

"Well," Daria said, the light beginning to dawn, "in that case, I shall say goodbye the way the Ambassador does. Ta-ta!"

"Ta-ta!" laughed the cat lady.

They shook hands and parted, Daria shining her head-lamp onto the trail, making her way down the knoll, through the woods, and into the public park, the Giardini Gabriele d'Annunzio. She was no longer alone. Hidden in the dark laurel trees near the water fountain she saw and heard several pairs of grunting, shadowy figures. The air stank of cheap perfume and sexual lubricants, sweat, and semen. She could not imagine Taylor Chatwin-Paine would be foolish enough to patronize the sex workers now, with the Institute under surveillance. But satyriasis and patrician arrogance made men do stupid, risky things. Yes, men. By definition.

She checked her wristwatch. Hugh Fowler was late. Disappointment welled up and began to settle its dark wings around her. Guessing the Texan had failed to retrieve his burrito and therefore had not seen her note, she started home, then spotted the lanky figure of the painter slouching insouciantly across the park toward her. He tossed away a lit cigarette, then had a prolonged hacking and coughing fit. Before she could speak, Fowler said in his sticky Dallas drawl, "I got here early and decided to see what it was Charlie liked so much about the place at night. It's pretty cool, kind of like a scene from Dante's *Inferno*. Or maybe Fellini's *Satyricon*?"

Daria could not help smiling. She had been thinking the same thing. This was Satyr City, straight out of that surreal, 1960s movie by the Italian master. "Can we go back through the tunnels and talk in there?" she coaxed.

"If you want to get into the Institute without being seen," he remarked, "that's the only way. We're still on semi-lock-down, thanks to you and that dude with the jaw. Man, his head looks like a lantern, he's right out of central casting, a Mafia heavy. He even scared you away." Fowler chuckled and spat.

"Mmmm," Daria intoned, noncommittal. "I know what you mean, but I don't think Captain Foscolo is an actual Mafioso, you know, just very heavy."

Fowler laughed again. When he'd caught his breath, he said, "That burrito wasn't real Tex-Mex." Though not entirely satisfied, he sounded cheerful for the first time. "But it wasn't bad. Thanks for the extra hot sauce."

"Don't mention it."

"Yeah, it was, like, pretty cool of you."

Daria laughed quietly. They slipped past the water fountain, its gurgling and splashing covering some of the carnal moans and groaning imprecations of the satyrs. Descending the shallow brick staircase to the locked iron gate, her nostrils twitched. The air was acrid with the stench of urine. Fowler pulled a flashlight and a bottle of water from his pocket. Directing the beam on the lock and its long shackle, he poured the contents of the bottle over them, cursing and spitting in disgust. Then he opened the padlock and pushed the gate back. Daria switched her headlamp on. She followed him through.

"Not much difference once you're in here, day or night," Fowler said, closing the gate and replacing the padlock. He used gel disinfectant to clean off his hands, then spat again, this time on the walls of the tunnel. "Dark as hell. It's back to Dante's *Inferno*."

Daria was startled. That was exactly what she had been thinking and was about to say. Could it be that the scowling, brown-toothed Hugh Fowler of the filthy mouth and greasy hair had more to him than met the eye or ear?

"Before we go any further," Daria said, "let me show you this map, it's from a book about the archeology of this site." She brought up the PDF on her screen, found the map, and zoomed to about where they were, using her elegant fingertip and clear-polished nail to trace the position of a walled-up section of tunnel.

Fowler snickered. "Charlie beat you to it," he said. "He got that map months ago. Showed it to me and we had some fun poking around."

Daria was unable to hide her surprise. "Find anything?"

Nodding, Fowler pointed the beam of his flashlight at a fork in the tunnel. "Come on, I'll show you. Makes you wonder about the coincidence."

"Which?" she asked.

"The fact that Charlie found all this shit on them and then he goes and kills himself by accident with that fucking old revolver, it's really, like, incredible."

Daria made an empathetic sound. She was about to say, "This is Italy, anything can happen, everything does happen," but she restrained herself. After all, Wraithwhite was American and so was the Institute. Anything can happen and everything does—everywhere. Reaching into an inner pocket, she took out the digging tool she'd bought at the hardware store and held it up to her headlamp. Fowler glanced over but said nothing. They reached the fork in the tunnel and turned right, continuing down a smaller passage for fifty or sixty yards.

"You haven't been this way yet?" he asked.

Daria wasn't sure. "I might have, with the DIGOS team the night it happened, but I can't say for sure. It all looks the same. It'd be easy to get lost and get stuck in here. No one would find you."

"Yeah," he said, grinning, "that's why I like it. It's, like, being dead while you're still alive, right?"

"Right," she said, though she didn't know what he meant or if she agreed.

They stopped. The tunnel led nowhere. A discolored dusty brick wall rose from floor to ceiling in front of them. "This is one of the walls in that map," he said. "It must have been built a hundred years ago to keep the tunnel from collapsing or maybe for something else—or maybe it was rebuilt for something else is what I mean."

Daria shook her head. "I'm not sure I understand."

"You will, in a second," he said, grinning even wider than before. "Since you got that thing out in your hand, lend it to me for a second." He took the digging tool from her. It was a kind of chisel with an axe-like blade and a hook. With expert motions, Fowler used it to tap and wiggle out one of the bricks in the wall at the level of Daria's chest. "See, Charlie got here before you. Charlie may have been a jerk and was pretty fucking stupid to shoot himself, but he did figure out a bunch of shit and I'll bet that asshole Taylor is glad to be rid of him."

Grabbing the end of the brick with his long, bony fingers, Fowler pulled it out and laid it on the floor by his polka dot sneakers. Then he pulled out another two bricks and shined his flashlight through the gap. Daria peered in. At the back of a long, narrow chamber, she could make out stacks of long rectangular heavy-duty packing crates piled against the walls. The crates appeared to be made of wood. They were stenciled with large black lettering that she could not read. Taking off her headlamp and propping it against a brick in the hole, she set her smartphone camera on night photography, leaned it next to the headlamp, and took a series of flash photos. Then she tapped the photo gallery icon, opened the first image, and zoomed.

"The writing says NATO," Fowler remarked with triumph, not bothering to look at the screen. "Those are the kind of crates they used way back before we were born to ship guns and ammo in," he added. "I did a search on Google, looking for similar images with those letters and crates. You know what comes up?"

Daria shook her head, then said, "No, but I can guess."

"Go ahead."

"Stay Behind," she said softly, "Gladio."

"Pretty good," Fowler said. "Me and Charlie, we took photos, he even made a video, brought some lights in for that. What's written on the boxes is 'Stay Behind,' 'Schwert,' 'SDR-8,' 'Glaive,' and some other strange names—and 'Gladio' too, like you said." He recited from memory, then paused and chuckled. "See, I had no idea what it meant but Charlie did and he told me and the others in the Catacomb Club. Then we looked it up on the Internet. There's a shitload of stuff about it, the gladius short sword of the Roman Legion also used by gladiators, all that crap. No mention of the Institute anywhere, though. It's like they thought they knew everything and found all the hiding places with the weapons so they stopped looking."

"But they didn't find this one?" Daria said, wondering why the crates were lettered with so many different European names for the same secret operation—the creation of arms caches for "patriots" who would "stay behind" to fight the Communist invaders, presumably the Soviets, in the postwar period.

"Nope, they did not find this one," Fowler mused, interrupting her thoughts. "Maybe they forgot or maybe all the people died, I have no fucking idea. Maybe this was the last cache left and they just pretended it was all over and done with, because they wanted to hold some stuff back, just in case. That's what Charlie said."

"Charlie was a smart guy," Daria mused. "Did he think Taylor knew about it?"

Fowler shook his head, muttering, "He wasn't sure. He was trying to find out without giving anything away. That's what those stupid jelly beans and the little swords were about. Charlie said if Taylor knew about the caches then he'd get the

Gelli and Gladio message and would react, and Charlie would be able to watch and see what he did and maybe report him or blackmail him for a bunch of money, and bring the fucking Institute to its knees."

"What would Taylor supposedly have done once he got the message?"

"Fuck if I know," Fowler said. "He might've come down and tried to figure out if Charlie had found the cache. He might've tried to get people in to move the stuff out, through the park, maybe, I don't know. He might've tried to kill Charlie." He paused, then asked, "Who the fuck was this Gelli guy anyway and was he really a trustee of the Institute in the 1960s or '70s? I never bothered to read up on him. The swords and shit were enough for me."

"Who said Gelli was a trustee?"

"Charlie. The librarian backed him up."

"The librarian? You mean Signora Tomaselli?"

Fowler shook his head and laughed. "No, not her, she's Taylor's squeeze. I'm talking about Johanna Harrison, the assistant librarian, the hottie Taylor fired because she had figured things out and wouldn't let him fuck her anymore."

Daria frowned. Fowler's foul mouth astonished her sometimes. Worse, her father may have been a trustee at the time. Had he known Gelli? How could Roberto Vinci *not* have known Licio Gelli? Everyone who was anyone in Italy in those days knew Gelli, the way a Washington insider during the Trump Administration would know his gang of indicted criminals—Bannon, Flynn, Stone, each pardoned by the greatest American con man of the century. The Italians had done something eerily similar decades earlier, with an equally unsavory cast of characters. Taking a deep breath, Daria recited what she knew by heart about Gelli, giving Fowler the concise bio sketch.

Licio Gelli, the so-called Venerable Master, cofounded the secret Propaganda 2 Masonic lodge, a coven of Fascist coup plotters. In the 1970s and early '80s, he helped subvert NATO's Stay Behind scheme. Weaponry from the secret arms caches was rerouted to terrorists and the Mafia. The pinnacle of his career came when he masterminded the Bologna train station massacre that killed and wounded scores in the summer of 1980. An untouchable high-flying banker by profession, Gelli knowingly bankrupted a major Italian savings institution to throw investigators off his track, causing the ruin of thousands of investors. Gelli was a con man and a thoroughgoing old-school Fascist who got away with mass murder, terrorism, subversion, sedition, fraud, perjury, and more. Fleeing to Switzerland when he could no longer operate in Italy, he lived in luxury under house arrest to the ripe old age of ninety-four.

"So, who says crime doesn't pay?" Fowler asked sardonically.

"Sadly, sometimes it does," Daria admitted, feeling suddenly like a goody-goody prig, "no matter how hard some of us try to make it unprofitable."

Fowler made a face and shook his head, then ran his fingers up and back through his greasy mop of hair. "Man, this shit isn't my thing, it's, like, way too weird for me. All this old crap about communists and fascists and coups and guns—it's like one of those TV movies from way back, the shit you get for free on YouTube because no one watches it anymore."

Daria couldn't help laughing. "Except that Licio Gelli only died in 2015, and the case was only closed in 2020." She paused and became thoughtful again. "Does the story remind you of anything else, anything more recent, perhaps?"

Fowler smirked darkly and said, "Yeah, those shitheads storming the Capitol in D.C. Same kind of fucked-up mentality, a bunch of stupid, lunatic conspiracy fucks led by a psychopath."

"Exactly," Daria agreed. "Licio Gelli and Charlie Wraithwhite in their very different, unrelated ways were very savvy," she added, feeling very old and very square but unwilling and unable to use the kind of high-color vocabulary Fowler favored. "Let's put the bricks back into the wall for now. There's something else we need to do."

He grunted. "You going to tell that Mafioso dude Foscolo about this?"

Daria raised both eyebrows. "I might," she said. "Then again, I might not. I need to figure out a few more things myself." She paused and cleared her throat. The dust was starting to get to her. "But you shouldn't say that about him, it's dangerous, I don't think he's a Mafioso or a P2 type or anything like that, but he definitely has an agenda, so, just please be careful around him. Don't say anything to him, if you can avoid it. I'll do my best to make sure he doesn't try to lock you up."

"Lock me up for what?" Fowler blurted, angry and indignant. He slid the last brick into place, then whirled around. "I didn't do anything, I mean, okay, some shit and a few lines of coke when that asshole in the masks would bring it to us. The Russian roulette and the dares—that was Charlie's idea, not mine. He fucking wrecked everything. I could kill him if he wasn't already dead."

Daria laughed despite herself. "What dares?"

"That's what you do when you play fucking Russian roulette," he said dismissively. "You *dare* someone something and if they refuse to play because they're scared, they lose and have to do whatever you tell them. If they kill themselves playing, I guess they win some prize in hell." He laughed sardonically. "Charlie was always daring us to do shit, like climb on buildings and monuments and put up the decals and tag shit where Taylor would see it, or stuff those bags of beans and the swords into places. He kept telling us to be ready to act when the time came because something big was going to happen. Adele got scared once and wouldn't spin the thing on the revolver or pull the trigger. Charlie said she'd lost and had to sneak into Taylor's apartment and hide the beans and sword in his dresser drawer inside a pair of his boxer shorts." Fowler guffawed spastically and began to cough and spit. "What fucking blew me away is, Adele did it. I would have told Charlie to fuck himself."

Daria followed Fowler back to the main tunnel and around to the circular burial chamber. "Let's stop here," she said. "I have a theory and I need your help."

"My help? What can I do?"

Then Daria explained. She wanted to reenact the incident. They needed to light the olive oil lamps and place them exactly as they had been, then turn off their headlamps. First, she needed a prop from the gardener's shed.

After positioning the lamps as they had been the night of the shooting, Daria checked her watch. They climbed the steep staircase together to the shed. Fowler used his skeleton key to open the locked door. Once inside the shed, Daria chose a set of dark green coveralls hanging from a hook, slipped them on over her clothes, put on a pair of overshoes, then followed Fowler back down the staircase, checking the time as she went.

"Now, light the lamps," she said. Fowler took out his cigarette lighter. He flicked it with his nicotine-stained left thumb. Soon the oil lamps were twinkling the way Daria had seen them on the night of the shooting. "Please sit exactly where you were that night," she said. She watched as Fowler searched for several seconds, then plopped down on the dusty ground below one of the carved burial niches. "Now turn off your flashlight," she ordered. After Fowler had turned his lamp off, she did the same. "Let's wait for our eyes to adjust," she suggested, moving slowly to a position near the spot where Charles Wraithwhite's corpse had lain. A few feet behind her began the steep staircase to the gardener's shed. She looked at her watch again. "Ready?"

"Yeah, now what?"

"Can you see me?"

"No, too dark."

"What about here?"

"No, still too dark. I can hear you but, oh, okay, now I can tell you're moving around."

Daria smiled grimly. She thrust her arm out, holding her service pistol at about the height of where she guessed Wraithwhite's head had been. "Now?"

"Not really," Fowler said. "What are you doing?"

"That night, you were all high, smoking and drinking, right?"

"Right."

"The air was full of smoke?"

"Yeah, I couldn't see a fucking thing."

"Charlie was a lefty, wasn't he?"

"Yeah, I noticed it the first time we met because I'm left-handed and it's unusual. He was kind of ambidextrous, he could do a lot of shit with his right hand too but..."

"But not shoot himself?"

"I don't know," Fowler said. "What are you waiting for?"

Daria switched on her headlamp and stood still until she was sure Fowler had seen her striking a pose, her pistol extended. She checked her watch a final time. "Bang," she said.

"Holy fuck," Fowler exclaimed, getting to his feet.

"Yeah," Daria said. "Holy fuck."

Fifteen

After shaking out the gardener's coveralls and hanging them back on their hook, Daria knocked the dust off the overshoes, aligned them side by side, then paused and reconsidered. Reaching down, she turned one of the overshoes at a ninety-degree angle to where she had found it. Then she moved the coveralls one hook over to the wrong place.

"Let's give Leopardi a little thrill," she whispered to Fowler. "Word will get back to Chatwin-Paine eventually."

Tapping her half-parted lips, she wondered if a shooter had been hiding in the shed or the catacombs when the shot was fired. She wondered if the someone was Chatwin-Paine or an accomplice. She wondered what had happened to the coveralls plastered with Wraithwhite's brains and the gunpowder blowback from the revolver. Instinctively, she inspected the dozen coveralls hanging on hooks on three of the walls of the shed, pausing to hold up the pair of long black ones belonging to Chatwin-Paine.

"Are any of the under-gardeners tall?" she asked Fowler, whispering again.

He thought, nodded, and said, "Yeah, one of them is pretty tall for an Italian, over six feet. I'm not sure about his name. Enzo, maybe."

"Like Enzo Ferrari?"

"Yeah, that's it. Enzo something-or-other."

Daria pondered. Turning to Fowler, she said quietly that there was one more thing to do before heading home. She asked if he knew the "safe" route to walk from the gardener's shed to the back of the outdoor theater without being picked up by the security cameras—the route Aisha Williams had mapped out.

Showing his stained teeth, the painter grinned. A few seconds later he let himself out of the shed, walking away with practiced insouciance. Watching him go, she timed him. Four minutes later he reappeared. "Two minutes in each direction give or take," she whispered. "Plenty of time."

Fowler smiled but said nothing, studying her with something like admiration or awe or perhaps nascent sexual desire. "You're getting closer, right?"

"Right."

"Yeah, well, like, since you're here," he said with something bordering on reluctance, "and since I think you're wearing a white hat and you're not one of those motherfuckers, I have a couple of things for you to see up in my room, if you're not afraid of maybe getting caught by these asshole fascist types."

She pondered, perplexed, squinting at him in the semi-darkness, the beam of her headlamp playing on the walls. "That depends on what the things are," she said, echoing the cat lady.

He smiled wickedly. "You'll see, what've you got to lose?"

Returning to the circular chamber, they extinguished the oil lamps and followed the tunnels through the locked gates to the sub-basement of the Institute. Fowler left her there, going ahead to make sure the coast was clear. She knew the way to his room. If she took the back staircase and stayed to the left in the stairwell, there was little chance anyone would see her, unless Foscolo or his men happened to be patrolling in the stairwell itself.

"It's worth the risk," she muttered to herself, determined to get to the bottom of things.

Five minutes later, Daria nudged the painter's half-open door and slipped into the studio. It was inky with darkness. The orange tips of two cigarettes glowed on the outdoor terrace. She heard a murmuring of voices and stifled coughing.

Stepping out onto the terrace into a cloud of nicotine and alcohol fumes, Daria recognized the familiar gaunt features of Hugh Fowler. With one bony hand he was swirling a tumbler of something—whisky, she guessed, by the color of the liquid and the telltale smell. She turned to face the second silhouette. It belonged to a woman—a noticeably buxom woman. She also held a tumbler of liquor and a lit cigarette. The woman's right arm slowly raised the glass as her mouth—a large, wide mouth, Daria could see—actively drained its contents. Then the woman set the tumbler down on the floor of the balcony and cleared her throat.

"*Buona sera*, commissario," the woman said in near-native, unaccented Italian. Flicking her cigarette away, she extended a large, sinewy hand. As she and Daria shook, she switched to English and said, "I am Johanna Harrison, the former assistant librarian."

It was too dark for anyone to see Daria's eyebrows form the flying buttresses of perplexity. "You are the former employee involved in thorny personnel issues?" Daria asked, knowing the answer.

"I am," said Harrison tonelessly.

"You were made to sign a nondisclosure agreement on pain of—what?"

Harrison laughed softly. Her voice seemed unnaturally low—a contralto capable of female baritone falsetto, like the singer at the gala concert. It had the mottled timbre of the middle-aged heavy-smoking aficionado of whisky. Harrison covered her mouth and hacked. "On pain of a lawsuit," she said, "the loss of my monthly allowance—my hush money, you could call it—plus probable deportation, since Taylor seems to know everyone everywhere and makes astonishing things happen at the snap of his fingers." She laughed again, a bitter, sardonic laugh.

"Yet you aren't afraid to be here or speak to me?" Daria waited until Harrison had shaken her head and finished coughing.

"Who said I wasn't afraid?" she asked.

"Then I thank you doubly," Daria said, pausing to study the woman's features. "How did you know I wished to speak to you?"

The former librarian laughed a third time and tossed back her long hair. It was dark, probably once chestnut colored before dyeing, Daria could see, but there wasn't enough ambient light to be sure. "Let's say Hugh and some others I know had heard through the grapevine that you'd like to have a chat with me about Charlie and his research. After what happened, I was expecting someone from your office to reach out. The only one who called was Taylor. He phoned to tell me what had happened and to remind me of the NDA."

"What did he tell you had happened?"

"That Charlie had killed himself playing Russian roulette in the catacombs."

"That's it?"

"That's it."

Fowler cleared his throat and spat over the marble balustrade into the garden far below. Then he said, "After I got the message in the burrito, I offered to bring Jo in through the tunnels tonight, so she could meet you here. We figure if they took you off the case and are sending you to Venice, there must be a good reason. Like, they don't want you to find out what the fuck is really going on."

"That would be typical," Harrison added. "The things that go on here would make your hair stand on end. No one outside the Institute ever hears about them. Taylor and Patrizia Pizzicato quash and stifle with aplomb." She laughed, coughing harder than before.

Daria was unsure where to start. There were so many things she wanted to know. She asked Harrison if she could tell her concisely what she thought it was that Wraithwhite had stumbled upon, something that might have placed his life in danger. The former librarian glanced at Fowler, accepted another cigarette from him, lit up, and took a deep drag. He refilled her liquor glass and she drank down the contents and a promptly proffered refill.

"Want a shot?" Fowler asked Daria, tipping the bottle in her direction.

She shook her head. "Thanks, not now."

Harrison cleared her throat. "It sounds to me from what Hugh has said that you've already figured out what the crux of the problem is, from the standpoint of the Institute. Charles Wraithwhite had come across documentary material some time ago, possibly years ago, when he was researching a book about postwar Italy and the American-engineered electoral coup of 1948. That research led him to suspect the Institute's involvement with CIA-led special operations in the postwar period, plus the Vatican ratlines for smuggling Nazis and Fascists to Argentina and Brazil, and, most importantly, the Stay Behind program—Gladio—call it what you will."

Harrison began to explain that no one had ever been able to confirm the details or make the link between Stay Behind, the P2, Licio Gelli, domestic Italian terrorism, and the Institute of America in Rome during the Cold War period. Others had researched the subject long ago and come to dead ends. "I helped a historian about a decade ago who had been hired, like Charlie, to write a history of the Institute—a puff piece, naturally. When he pulled up the roots of the nettles, so to speak, he found a disturbing degree of, how shall I put it, coziness?" Harrison paused and took a drag and a sip. "Coziness, let's call it, between the Institute and the Fascist regime going all the way back to the 1920s and lasting through the war and afterwards—with the Christian Democrats. It was not the kind of historical background the Institute had wanted to hear about in their puff-piece, cof-fee-table fundraising book. So, they squelched and quashed the project.

"There was also the question of what the Institute was good for in the postwar period, what role it could play in what went from being a hot war against Mussolini and Hitler into a Cold War against Soviet Communism and the Italian Communist Party—the second biggest Communist party in Europe, after France. It made no sense to continue along the lines laid out by the founders in the 1800s. The board had long had difficulty finding worthy recipients of the Rome Award—they were remarkably mediocre, with few exceptions. After the war, the problem became acute. New York was the center of the creative world. Few artists or writers or architects of quality wanted to spend a year at the Club in Rome. That's what insiders started calling it. *The Club in Rome*. So, the insti-tution as a whole fell into the hands of the usual backstabbing, pretentious, persnickety academics on the one hand, and the ruthless cold warriors on the other."

Daria smiled wryly, interrupting. "Are you telling me that it really was a nest of spies, as the Italian Communists claimed?"

Harrison shook her head and let out a cloud of smoke. "It's clear many of those involved in running and funding the Institute, or sitting on the board of trustees, had a past in civilian or military intelligence, like Jefferson Page. He was OSS, COI, X-2, and all those other spy novel acronyms, posted in Latin America to watch Fascist and Nazi recruiting and shipping. Why be surprised? What good patriot didn't work for OSS and the others back then? It wasn't anything to be ashamed of. The nest of spies nonsense was not what was really going on. The real spooks worked out of the embassy and consulate, the way they always had. The Institute was about popular propaganda, soft power, setting up the CCF and courting the NCL, showing the Communists that America was the real role model, not the Soviets. If a spook or two blew through pretending to be residents or visiting scholars, or sat on the board, or used the Institute for CIA-sponsored cultural events, it made no real difference to basic operations. The CIA had money to burn back then. They funded half the cultural events, literary magazines, and mainstream publishers of the day in America and abroad. They underwrote the best painters and sculptors and writers and composers and musicians, and they did an outstanding job of it, if you ask me. It took decades for the story to break and the redacted truth to leak out. That was in the late 1960s. When the leak became a hemorrhage, Jefferson Page left his position at the Institute and returned to Washington, D.C."

Daria batted away the cigarette smoke. "Remind me what the NCL was, please," she said, "I haven't slept much in the last two or three days."

Harrison laughed her leathery laugh. "Of course. The Non-Communist Left," she said. "The CCF was the Conference for

Cultural Freedom. Jefferson Page practically ran the NCL and CCF European propaganda operations out of the Institute, from the get-go."

Daria tapped her lips thoughtfully. "Of course, of course," she mused. "The NCL and CCF, I have heard the acronyms used, but not in a long time." She paused to think, counting to a slow three. "Ms. Harrison, I find the history lesson fascinating, but somehow I don't think it was the apparent uselessness of the postwar Institute or the coziness with Mussolini or even the NCL and CCF or the CIA of the forties and fifties that led directly to the death of Charles Wraithwhite," she said. "I have to stick to the case at hand otherwise we'll get lost like the researchers you mentioned. I only have a few hours left to answer some crucial questions before I decide how to jump."

"I realize that," Harrison said dryly. "But I have risked a lot coming here to talk to you, so, please, try to comprehend the importance of what I'm saying as it relates to the case you're investigating." She paused for emphasis. "Here are several dots to connect that no one ever seems to think of connecting. They may somehow lead you to whoever killed Charlie, if he didn't do it himself." She paused again, took a deep breath, looked at Fowler, and continued. "Lift the lid on the cultural icons and acronyms that exist now, today—institutions that get millions of American taxpayer dollars—and who do you find at the beginning, at their founding? The answer is easy. You find the people Jefferson Page worked for during the war, plus some of the shadow leaders of the Marshall Plan—the behind-the-scenes folks no one has heard of and no one remembers. After Jefferson Page left the Institute in the sixties, he helped these future politicians and enlightened financiers to create the postwar cultural endowments we all know and some of us love. Page's protégé was a brilliant young art historian from Harvard named Taylor Chatwin-Paine. He was Page's anointed successor.

"So, back to your query about a nest of spies. The answer is no, they were not active spooks on the payroll of the CIA, and there was no nest of spies. These were the original cultural cold warriors. They won the Cold War for us. Everyone was looking for James Bond and the big bad CIA or FBI guys and they missed the really interesting show—culture! That's why the wall came down and the USSR fell apart. It wasn't the fear of nuclear Armageddon. It was Chevrolet convertibles and Coca-Cola and hotdogs and great painters and writers and comedians and composers touring France, Italy, and the other frontline countries with huge Communist parties—and Hollywood, of course."

"And the Institute played a role?"

"The Institute played an important role—yes, the Institute under Jefferson Page and under Chatwin-Paine at the beginning of his mandate. Not the Institute as it exists today. It has degenerated into a cocktail club for overpaid, underworked professors, as Charlie discovered. The Rome Award winners are a pretext to keep the Institute running. By and large, they are absolute nonentities—with the exception of Hugh, of course." Harrison smiled wryly, touching Fowler's cheek, the lit cigarette still between her fingers.

"Of course," Daria said.

Still smiling, Harrison pulled a smartphone from her pocket, entered a pin, and said, "Now that you have the background, I can give you what you really want. I have two SIM cards in this phone. On one of them Charlie installed a number to be used on the Signal Messenger app. He said if anything strange ever happened to him—like he went missing or died suddenly—I should use his SIM card to send a disappearing message with Signal then follow up with a phone call once the person sent a reply confirming receipt with the words, *It's hot in Suez.*"

"It's hot in Suez?" Daria repeated. "Is that something to do with shipping in the Suez Canal?"

"It's a wartime code," Harrison said, shaking her head, "something the French partisans or the OSS came up with. You can google it if you translate it into French. *Il fait chaud à Suez.*"

"Talking of Signal," Fowler chimed in, "if it's good enough for Snowden, it's good enough for me. That's what Charlie said."

Slumping from exhaustion, Daria pinched her aching temples for several seconds, blinked her dry eyes, and pointed to the glowing screen of Harrison's phone. "So, just to be clear, Charles Wraithwhite entrusted you with a smartphone chip with an address book on it and gave you instructions on how to use Signal and reach someone he trusted?"

"Correct," said Harrison. "There's only one number in the address book and no name associated with it. Charlie had me install the Signal app on my phone. He said to call that number and explain what happened to whoever answered, then delete Signal and destroy the SIM card, and throw the pieces in the fire once I'd gotten through."

"Extraordinary," Daria muttered. She sat up straighter than before, her tired mind racing. "Explain to the person who answered the phone speaking English or Italian?"

"Either English or Italian," Harrison said. "The person on the other end would understand both."

"And Charlie did not tell either of you who would answer or why the person should be informed?"

Fowler and Harrison looked at each other and shook their heads.

"To tell the truth," Harrison said in a hoarse whisper. "After what happened to Charlie, I hesitate to have anything more to do with any of this, so I didn't send a message or phone. What

I want is to give you the SIM card and take a long vacation to a distant land with no connectivity—that's why I took the risk of coming here tonight."

"That and so she could see me," Fowler said, trying to make it sound like a joke.

"That too," Harrison agreed, stroking Fowler's cheek again and smiling. "We want you to find out what happened but whatever you do, I want out."

Fowler spoke up. "See, Jo joined the Catacomb Club way back, before Charlie and his assholic pal with the masks came along and spoiled things."

Daria nodded slowly. "Ms. Harrison, may I ask you something personal probably unrelated to the above?"

"Of course," said the former librarian.

"Did Taylor Chatwin-Paine ever behave improperly toward you—as a woman, I mean?"

Harrison made a serious face then burst out laughing. "The pig? The goat? Surely you jest! Major Vinci, eighteen years ago, when I came to work at the Institute, I was an attractive young woman. I think I can assure you of that without being immodest. Taylor Chatwin-Paine tries his luck with every female he meets, at least once."

"With every male, too," Fowler said, "fucking pig asshole. He's the one who should've died down in the catacombs, not Charlie. He and Charlie and the asshole with the masks, they were a kind of threesome. Maybe that's what this shit is all about."

"To answer your question," Harrison segued, serious again, "the reason I was let go was I complained about repeated attempts at sexual harassment bordering on molestation and rape. Taylor still requires women to wear high heels, low-cut blouses, and short dresses—he came up with the uniform, and in my day, he regularly tried to inspect the contents. My gripes had nothing to do with the Institute's political dirty laundry or its iffy worthiness as an institution. I had a good, steady job and loved the place. I wasn't going to rock the boat. You might want to ask Patrizia what she thinks of signor presidente's attentions."

"The director has also been a victim?"

Harrison laughed savagely. "Yes, the doll who looks like an aging daytime TV hostess, a Berlusconi or Mafia moll. Then again, Patrizia doesn't seem to mind wearing the high heels and miniskirts. Maybe for her it's not harassment. I wouldn't know. She won't have anything to do with me."

Daria nodded, grimacing now. "Am I correct in thinking you know Ambassador Bremach?"

"You are correct," Harrison confirmed. "He has been a trustee for decades."

"He has," Daria agreed. "Have you two communicated about this affair?"

"We have," she answered.

Daria nodded again, this time with a wry smile. "That may explain a few things."

"I hope so," said Harrison pleasantly.

Daria turned to the painter, hesitated, then spoke pointedly. "One last question for you," she said. "Did you or Charlie ever explore the other secret hiding place, the one where they set up the radio transmitter during World War Two?"

The painter's hard-driven face was transformed. It beamed. He tossed his hair out of his eyes. "Hell, yes, it's way up above the elevator shaft, where the cable and motor house are. That was harder than the brick wall in the catacombs. We had to figure out how to get in without leaving traces the maintenance people could see. Who told you about it?"

"I guessed."

"Awesome," he said, "fuckin' awesome."

"What did you find?"

Fowler hesitated, glancing around, as if someone were listening or watching. "The same kind of stuff but smaller crates, handguns, small arms, hand grenades, ammo. No high explosives or long rifles or machine guns and bazookas and anti-tank shit, like the big crates underground."

Daria tried to hide her consternation. Those arms were still inside the Institute and catacombs and potentially still functional? Her mind raced. She had to wonder whether vestigial members of the P2 or some other domestic terror outfit remained operational, waiting to grab the arms, or if some family of organized criminals had access to them. Might they be the same coup plotters she and Ambassador Bremach had unmasked in Genoa?

Taking a long, slow, quiet breath through her flaring nostrils, Daria spoke as unconcernedly as she could manage. "Shall we go inside and turn on a light so you can see what you're doing with that chip, Ms. Harrison?"

Entering the painter's studio, Fowler turned on a reading lamp, pointing it at the floor to avoid casting shadows. Crouching, Harrison set to work removing the SIM card. Now Daria could confirm what she had suspected—the former assistant librarian was a tall, slim woman in her late forties, about Daria's own age. Harrison had the ravaged good looks of a former beauty. But her tousled dark hair was flecked with gray and her skin was withering under the influence of nicotine and what Daria guessed was an increasingly marginal lifestyle.

Extracting the chip with her blunt, nicotine-stained fingernails, Harrison asked for something to put the SIM card in. She watched Fowler ferret out a creased, dirty envelope with a letter inside. He removed the letter, balled it up, tossed it away, and handed over the envelope. Harrison slipped the chip into it and gave it to Daria.

Pondering for a moment, Daria took the chip out of the envelope and stared at it as she spoke. "Before I leave you tonight, allow me to insert this chip in my phone, and also to speculate aloud for a moment." She paused, glancing from one face to the other, then busied herself opening her phone, removing one of its two SIM cards, and inserting the one Wraithwhite had left. "Who could be at the other end of the telephone number?" she asked. "It would not be Taylor Chatwin-Paine or anyone at the Institute, I presume?" They both shook their heads and made scoffing sounds.

"No fucking way," Fowler blurted, tossing his hair back again. "All they want is for the boondoggle to continue another century. The last thing they'd want is for Charlie's research to go public."

"Did Wraithwhite have close friends or relatives or an associate or confederate in Rome or anywhere else—back in New York, for instance—that you know of?" Daria snapped her phone back together and powered it on.

"He had a ton of so-called friends," Fowler grumbled, "what kind of friends I don't know. Charlie ran with a crazy crowd, way crazier than we are. He liked the white horse and playing cards and roulette for real money."

"Russian roulette?"

"Yeah, but also the regular kind," Fowler said, making a spinning motion with his left hand. "He knew all these underground betting places and casinos everywhere."

"Literally or metaphorically underground?" Daria asked.

"Both," he said. "He *and* Taylor."

Harrison leaned toward Daria and said, "Charlie and Taylor met probably five or six years ago at a mutual friend's place in New York, about the time I was fired." She paused to smirk. "They had a lot in common," she added with a sardonic laugh.

"Do you know the mutual friend's name?"

"No," Harrison said. "Neither does Hugh. Charlie was very tight-lipped about everything. He only told you what he wanted to tell you, what he wanted you to know. Nothing else."

"So, no idea where Charlie met the masked man?"

They both shook their heads.

"Okay," said Daria, pocketing her phone and standing up. "What if the mutual friend was the masked man? What if the number is his number?"

"Tork?" asked Fowler.

"Yes, Torquato," Daria said.

Fowler and Harrison looked at each other and shrugged. They both coughed and wheezed. Finally, the painter snapped his fingers and said, "Yeah, Tork. It could be. Charlie did say something about telling him if anything weird happened. Now I remember. He said to give him the fucking flash drive. I, like, totally forgot." He laughed a goofy laugh and seemed genuinely embarrassed.

"What flash drive? Earlier today you said Charlie told you to never leave anything around, no paper trail, no flash drives."

Fowler stared at her and seemed to realize he may have said the wrong thing then and now. "Well," he mumbled, shuffling across the studio to a corner and coming back with a telescopic device that looked like a pole saw. "What the fuck, I guess I might as well give it to you, since that roundhead asshole in the mask has disappeared and I don't want to keep it with this Foscolo dude around, checking every fucking thing."

Extending the telescopic portion of the pole, Fowler used a lever to open a plier attachment on the tip of the device. Daria watched as the painter expertly guided the pliers upwards, to the narrow upper sill of the floor-to-ceiling windows. Grabbing something, he lowered the pole to the floor.

"Be my guest," he said, turning the plier attachment toward Daria. She plucked the flash drive out of the jaws of the pliers and examined it. "Yeah," said Fowler, smiling around his stained teeth, "I guess that's about all we can do for you tonight."

Sixteen

Daria had just finished gulping down the Italian equivalent of a banana smoothie, alternating swallows with gulps of sparkling water. She followed on with a double espresso and glanced down impatiently when her phone vibrated. It was Morbido.

"Not waking you?" he asked, knowing the answer. The app showed Daria as online. She snorted and held the phone up so he could hear the traffic whizzing past her table at the same dive of a café they had been to earlier near the Institute and city gate.

"I just dined on a delicious summer salad of baby vegetable everything and finally managed to clear the catacomb dust from my nose, throat, and lungs," she announced cheerfully, surprising herself. "Now I'm buzzing and overcaffeinated so I can't just give up and go to bed."

"You're keeping Spanish hours."

Checking her watch, she agreed. "This is a little late even for Rome. Are you back in Genoa by now?" she asked, knowing very well he wasn't.

She heard a guttural laugh as Morbido held up his phone and asked, "Where do you suppose *I* am? Sound familiar?"

Daria listened. "Very familiar, Anywhere Italy?"

"Try Ostiense," he growled. "The train station."

"You're still in Rome?"

Morbido explained what had happened. His 6 o'clock train had been an hour late to start, then two hours, then three, then it had rolled slowly to the next train station on the line—Roma Ostiense—stopping there for unexplained "technical difficulties." There it remained for two more hours until it was canceled.

"So, it's, what, almost 11:30 right now?" he asked. "I thought, why not check on my dear friend Major Vinci, see if she has left for Venice on the night train. Ha, ha, ha, ha, ha."

Daria snorted back, telling him she would be *driven* to the Lagoon City at 11 the next morning by armed, uniformed escorts with cuffs, straps, leashes, and butterfly nets. "To make sure I don't pretend to leave but actually stay in Rome, or turn around and come back," she growled. Then she took a deep breath and told Morbido what had transpired since she'd seen him that afternoon. The tale took her five galloping minutes to recount.

"Lordy lord," he muttered, suppressing a yawn. "Daria Through the Looking Glass. Things are getting curiouser and curiouser." It seemed to her that Morbido chuckled too long for comfort.

"So, what's up?" she asked. "What are you going to do?"

"I was going to ask if I could spend the night in one of the ten or twelve empty bedrooms at your mother's palatial apartment. But I suppose that's not in the cards, since you're out and unlikely to return home?"

Daria laughed. "I can send Mario a text message or wake him up with the landline and ask him to let you in. He'll be delighted! He thinks I'm upstairs asleep like a good little girl."

"Thanks," Morbido sighed. "Where are you anyway? Maybe I'll get a taxi and join you. The next train is at 6 in the morning. I'm going to be on it unless..."

"Unless what?"

Morbido said he didn't know. Then Daria told him she was at the same café where about ten hours earlier he had devoured six panini in less than half an hour.

"I wouldn't mind a porchetta sandwich right now," he grunted, interrupting. "I'll be there in twenty minutes. Order for me? Three. One each, porchetta, mortadella, and prosciutto crudo with mozzarella."

"No," she cut him off. "I have a better plan. Your predicament is pure serendipity."

Explaining what she had in mind, Daria told him he was perfectly placed right where he was. She needed him. He should meet her at midnight at the outdoor ice cream parlor on the west side of Piazzale Ostiense, kitty-corner to the Porta di San Paolo city gate, the one right on the edge of the Parco della Resistenza, not a quarter mile from the Ostiense train station where he'd been marooned.

"I know it well," Morbido said suspiciously. "I think it closes at midnight these days and I'm hungry now. So, I'll head over and get something to chew on while I wait for you. Then what?"

"Then we'll see if he shows up, or if my educated guess is off the mark and I get in trouble and demoted again."

"Who?"

"I'll give you one guess."

"Scaramellato?"

There was laughter in Daria's answer. "Bravo, you see, you did deserve your promotion."

As she waited to pay the tab, she told Morbido her plan, starting with the honeypot she had just set out for the Candy Man.

Before leaving Hugh Fowler's painting studio, she explained, Daria had sent an encrypted disappearing voice message to the number on Wraithwhite's SIM card, on the assumption it was Marco Torquato Scaramellato's number. Who else could it belong to? The recipient of the message had thirty minutes to listen to it before it fizzled into the ether. She had stated the following, without ever mentioning Scaramellato's or her own name. She replayed it aloud to Morbido, then forwarded to him the copy she'd made.

It's hot in Suez, repeat, it's hot in Suez. This disappearing voice message has an expiry time of thirty minutes.

First, if the recipient of this message cooperates, he will be protected and might escape prosecution.

Second, if he does not cooperate, there is no telling what might happen to him. Because if the sender of this message has figured things out, others will do so soon. Therefore, the recipient's usefulness is already over for those he has been conspiring with.

Why? Because if he really has destroyed the coveralls as ordered, and if he has left the soiled tunic hidden behind the dead tree on the knoll as instructed, then he may well be in the clear with the authorities. Maybe. But then so would the actual assassin. The only conclusion the authorities could draw would be that Wraithwhite had accidentally shot himself. This leaves the recipient of this message unneeded by his co-conspirators and unprotected from them.

Third, he should come alone and meet the sender of this message tonight at precisely 12:30 a.m. Place: The Porta di San Paolo, TBC upon reply to this message starting with the words "The Eagle has landed."

Fourth, only a fool would have destroyed the coveralls and the recipient of this message is not a fool. Therefore, he

should bring the duffle bag with the coveralls in it and be pre-
pared to tell everything from start to finish.

Fifth, the sender of this message will deliver into the hands
of the recipient the flash drive containing the kompromat. The
contents have been copied and are being analyzed. In case
of need, the recipient of this message will be able to use the
flash drive as a bargaining chip against whoever might seek
to harm him, until the authorities have neutralized all threat-
ening co-conspirators. The tunic the recipient of this message
wore in the catacombs and which proves he did not fire the
shot will also be restored to him, together with a copy of the
laboratory analyses proving this fact.

Sixth and finally, the recipient must realize by now that
everyone knows he was the accomplice to a murder and that
he smuggled out the coveralls at the behest of the assassin
of Charles Wraithwhite. If apprehended, he could be extra-
dited to the U.S. where capital punishment for such a crime
might apply. In Italy, he will spend the rest of his productive
life behind bars, unless he comes clean, turns state's evidence,
and cuts a plea bargain deal.

This first meeting with the sender of this message is the
start of his new relationship with the authorities. His assis-
tance is needed to lure the assassin or assassins of Charles
Wraithwhite into the open. He is accustomed to doing deals
in the business world. This is a deal he cannot afford to
decline.

Five minutes later, the recipient had answered with a disappearing message of his own—a text message this time.

The Eagle has landed.
The sidewalk on the south side of the Porta di San Paolo,
flanking the Protestant Cemetery and Pyramid of Cestius.

"My God!" Morbido exclaimed, huffing and puffing as he trotted across what sounded like a busy traffic circle, clutching his phone. "And what am I supposed to do?"

"Tail us, give me some backup, make sure Foscolo isn't onto him, or whoever was in on this with Scaramellato. Be prepared for anything. The person might be armed. If it is Scaramellato who shows up, he's going to be pretty mad when he discovers I don't have the tunic and have no intention of giving him the flash drive. I haven't had time to read anything on it let alone copy it."

"Is that how they got the malware onto the Institute's computer system?"

"Maybe."

"You know for a fact they told him to destroy the coveralls?"

"Of course not," she laughed, checking her watch and jumping to her feet. "I've got to run to make it on time. See you in a few."

Speeding downhill and across town in a taxicab headed for Via Marmorata, Daria ran a series of simulations through her feverish, caffeinated mind. What if the telephone number had not been Scaramellato's but rather someone else's—someone working with Wikileaks, for instance? Wraithwhite was known to be an admirer of Julian Assange and Edward Snowden. What if it corresponded to one of the co-conspirators who had hoodwinked Wraithwhite and wanted him dead and would now want Scaramellato out of the way? A professional killer? If so, she had given him advance warning.

Daria clutched the armrest as the taxi slalomed down a succession of narrow cobbled curving streets, sliding across the streetcar tracks on Viale di Trastevere and swerving to avoid potholes big enough to swallow a Fiat. It bounded toward the Tiber embankments where dozens of night owls flapped wing in wing, partying along the parapets as if Rome had morphed into Barcelona or Paris.

She reran in her mind the cat lady's words about the man in black and the head gardener, Leonardo Leopardi, recalling the gardener's shed and the coveralls and the steep staircase from the shed into the circular chamber. She wondered how anyone other than Taylor Chatwin-Paine could have put on the coveralls, descended into the catacombs, fired the shot, climbed back up to the shed, removed the coveralls, given them to an accomplice, then returned unnoticed to the back of the outdoor theater while the concert was ending.

But what if he had no accomplice and had simply hung up the coveralls, knowing they would be laundered the following day? Had anyone thought to check for blood, brains, and gunpowder on the coveralls hanging in the shed? She had not. She cursed herself now and was flooded by dark thoughts and self-recrimination.

What if her thesis was completely wrong? Scaramellato had the keys to the padlocks and came and went through the tunnels as he liked. He could have arrived early with an accomplice who hid in a tunnel and crept up at the last minute to fire the shot. In that case, the assassin would have dropped the gun that fired the shot so that it would be found near the body. Then he would have taken away the unfired gun Wraithwhite had been playing Russian roulette with. Then what?

Come to think of it, whoever fired the shot—assuming it wasn't Wraithwhite himself—would have had to do that: first shoot the gun, then drop the gun, then pick up the other gun Wraithwhite held in his hand but never fired.

Then how would the assassin get the unfired gun from the catacombs back into the drawer in the third-floor room? Unless the assassin was Taylor Chatwin-Paine, who was the only person at the Institute other than Wraithwhite with a key and the ability to come and go unnoticed.

Unless there was a third identical handgun and perhaps a third copy of the key. Had Wraithwhite or Scaramellato or Taylor Chatwin-Paine managed somehow to make a duplicate of the impossible-to-copy, century-old key to the third-floor room? How could Scaramellato or an accomplice get in and out of the Institute in time to escape after killing Wraithwhite and before the alarm had been raised?

Daria shook her head, trying to stop the buzzing sensation in her ears. There were too many factors to process. She had not slept enough to think straight. The coffee had been a mistake. She was no longer a teenager, though she continued to behave like one much of the time—impulsively, irresponsibly, recklessly.

Seized by something like panic, she asked herself why she was doing this at all. Certainly, it was not because she wanted to save the Institute or protect its reputation. Was it because her father had been a longtime supporter and trustee those many decades ago? She felt no loyalty whatsoever to Taylor Chatwin-Paine, on the contrary. The loathsome Black Widower had tried but failed to molest her when she was what, fourteen or fifteen years old? Why had she never told anyone? Because no one did back then, in the bad old days. Pigs and goats and rapists got away with everything including incest, most of the time. Luckily, she had not allowed Chatwin-Paine's groping to reach an advanced stage of violence. She had done damage to his private parts with a swift, well-aimed kick, the kick that had led her to practice kickboxing for a decade afterwards. Chatwin-Paine had never dared touch her again. And she had erased the incident from her memory. Until a few days ago. Until the death of Wraithwhite and that ghoulish, famished, vampire look in Chatwin-Paine's eyes when he glanced at her twinkling toenails on the staircase into the catacombs.

She shook her head in fury and groaned from frustration, the taxi driver's eyes on her in the rearview mirror.

What if her irresistible desire to pursue the case to its end had nothing to do with Taylor Chatwin-Paine or her father or brother or the Institute itself? What if it was an instinctive response to a tease, a snapping at bait, the work of her diabolical godfather? Had Willem Bremach foxed her again, baiting and luring her by pretending to warn her off the investigation while feeding her clues and sending people her way? The cat lady? The former assistant librarian, Harrison? Who else?

By the time the cab had dropped her on the west end of the Parco della Resistenza, near the monumental Fascist-era post office, she had convinced herself that the best way out of this ungodly mess was to get in touch with Foscolo immediately, tell him about the planned meeting with Scaramellato, hand over everything, and head to Venice with a clean conscience and a light heart. But as she reached for her smartphone her resolution failed her. The notion evaporated as quickly as it had arrived.

Sneaking up stealthily behind Morbido as he gobbled a sandwich and guzzled mineral water at a table edging a scruffy park, Daria laid her hand on his right shoulder and whispered in his ear, "It's hot in Suez." He shot to his feet, knocking the table over as he reached for the gun in his shoulder holster. Luckily, catching sight of her, he did not unsheathe his pistol. The handful of late-night customers turned toward the commotion, staring. Several laughed out loud self-consciously before turning back to their ice creams, sandwiches, and beer.

"Not funny," Morbido grumbled, "you've ruined my digestion again."

"What if I'd been Scaramellato or someone worse?" she asked. "By the way, you're demoted for something else too."

"What?"

"*Serendipity*. That's what I said on the phone. But no such thing exists. Before you called, I checked and saw your train was canceled. I knew you'd be stuck in the Ostiense Station. I knew you'd call me sooner or later. I was going to phone you anyway to check up. So, I set up the appointment with Scaramellato at the Porta di San Paolo, knowing you'd be in the area, though God knows if he'll actually show up. We have no guarantee that's his telephone number. What if it's a Mafia hitman? So much for serendipity."

Morbido stared at her, his face a blotchy greenish purple in the fluorescent light. "You are a harsh taskmaster, Major Vinci. I'm not sure I can forgive you for this one."

Daria sat next to him and laughed as she spoke. "Now that I think about it, I'd better demote myself too. Serendipity *does* exist."

Morbido watched her, his eyes narrowing. "I'm too tired for this."

"No, listen. There are two things that are really seren-dipitous in what's going on—serendipitous or just plain good luck. The first is, Scaramellato or whoever answered agreed to meet at the Porta di San Paolo city gate and you happened to be nearby because the train broke down. The second is, the Vinci family tomb is in the Protestant Cemetery, alias the 'Non-Catholic Cemetery,' across the street from us." She pointed.

"I don't get it. My condolences once again, by the way. I admired your mother. She certainly had pluck. But I still don't get what you're driving at."

Daria nodded. "My dearly departed mother was Protestant and my father was an atheist or said he was. He believed in Freemasonry and the law, not the church."

"Freemasonry? Was he a member of the P2?"

Daria's expression changed. "He might've been, I'd never

considered it." She reflected, then shook her head. "I doubt it. His lodge wasn't secret, for one thing. Most of all, he hated and feared Fascism and Fascists as much as he feared and hated the Soviets and their pseudo-Communism."

"*Pseudo-Communism?*" Morbido scoffed. "Okay, I know that was a dig at my redshirt father. I'll let it pass. I still don't get what you're talking about. The fact that your family's tomb is over there and we are here is coincidence, not serendipity, unless you planned that too, for some reason, and in that case, it is neither coincidence nor serendipity but another diabolical conspiracy I don't understand."

"Never mind," Daria laughed, her voice cheerful. She glanced at her watch, eager for the action to begin. "Midnight. I listen to the bells. Ha, ha, ha, Osvaldo, have you noticed that the church bells no longer ring after 10 o'clock? Not even in Rome."

"Daria? Are you all right?"

"Absolutely. I'm right on time, I got here early. Now, finish your sandwich if you can and let's take a walk. He might arrive early too."

"He might already have spotted us," Morbido muttered, "after that scene you made."

"I hope so," she chortled. "I did it on purpose. Scaramellato doesn't know us. He'll be looking for a lone female—he's heard my voice message, right? He won't be looking for an unusual middle-aged couple consisting of a willowy, tall woman and a large, shall I say, robust, man, having a playful argument?"

Morbido shook his jowls. "Ambassador Bremach is right," he muttered. "You'll be a lieutenant colonel soon, then a general, and God knows what else after that—a dictator. You were born to be cruel."

"It's all in the line of duty," she remarked, standing up and beckoning. "Where's your suitcase?"

"What suitcase? Everything I need fits in my pockets. You ought to learn to travel light, commissario." Morbido snickered. "You never know what might happen."

Seventeen

Fifteen minutes elapsed in what felt to Daria like fifteen seconds. She and Morbido strode side by side up and down the ill-lit, potholed alleys of the Parco della Resistenza, a park dedicated to the memory of the heroes of the Italian Resistance. The condition of the site spoke volumes about the current state of indifference among Italians to the women and men who risked their lives to defeat Mussolini and Hitler.

Along the rough quadrangle's northeastern edge, the female fireflies and requisite bands of boys from Brazil were carrying on a brisk trade. Techno rap blared from a car stereo. Daria glanced away. Her thoughts were elsewhere. The logistics and logic were not in her favor. She wished she had at least half a dozen backup officers scattered around the neighborhood covering for them. "Foolhardy" was the operative word regarding this improvised honeypot trap. It played in her mind on a loop, the proverbial scratched record, a metaphor comprehensible only to those like her raised in the days of predigital devices and vinyl.

"So, you think you've baited him," Morbido panted, trying to keep up with Daria's relentless pace. "But what if he or they are luring you? These are not unpracticed people."

"And we are?"

"That's not what I'm saying. What if he comes with reinforcements? What if he's already cooperating with Foscolo? Then they've just gotten you to trip yourself up and land in their hands and give them the precious, unfindable flash drive and tunic. You'll be the one with the target on your head."

"I think I already have a bull's eye painted on each temple."

Morbido was not listening. "Or what if Chatwin-Paine has called on his old pals, whoever they are, and told them he needs help with tenacious investigators who risk damaging international relations if they're not halted, ruining the perception of a strategic ally and fellow NATO member by revealing the predictably typical Italian kind of anarchistic chaos and sedition? Yet another arms cache, after all these years, a coven of hardcore extremists, and so on?"

"Those are a lot of what-ifs," Daria agreed. She knew he was right to worry. But what good would it do to admit her fears to him?

Checking her watch again, she saw the time for action had come. "Stay on this side, under cover of the trees and parked cars. He and I will walk past the cemetery, then probably head toward Monte Testaccio."

"Why don't you parlay behind those oleanders? The shrubs will give you cover."

"That is an excellent idea," she said. Waving at Morbido as if he were a boyfriend and not a stolid colleague, Daria skipped away across the wide street, dodging an oncoming streetcar, pausing to wave again, then merged with the shadows of the tall, crenelated ancient Roman city gate. From there she crept stealthily onto the chiaroscuro sidewalk, kicking away piles of pungent litter as she went. Slowing her pace and glancing around, her right hand in her pocket, she felt her index finger curl around the trigger of her service revolver.

Seconds later, she spotted a man stepping from a corner of the hulking brick gateway, pretending to zip up his pants. He was medium height but had the triangular build of an athlete. A crop of short black hair stood up like a rooster's crest on his round head. It was a very round head. Daria was struck by the contrast of the triangular torso and the roundhead circle topped by a bristling brush. The man's eyes flashed. They seemed to be made of obsidian. The man wore sporty casual khaki-colored clothes and rubber-soled gymnast shoes. He carried a compact matching sports duffle bag. Overstuffed, it bulged, the zipper apparently caught in a fold of dark green cloth that was hanging out of it.

"Such a beautiful summer evening," Daria said aloud, speaking to no one in particular. "The breeze is so clean and fresh, nothing like the air of the catacombs."

The man sized her up as they walked together in silence down Via Marmorata. Towering above and behind them was the whitish ancient marble Pyramid of Caius Cestius, the most impressive funeral monument in the city—as long as you disqualified the immense Castel Sant'Angelo and gigantic Mausoleum of Augustus.

"The dust is highly unpleasant in the catacombs, signora, I agree," said the man. "I always wear a mask when underground and so, too, perhaps, should you." Clearly well educated, he spoke with a rich Roman accent in a tuneful tenor voice.

From these two short sentences, Daria felt the full force of Scaramellato's cocky gallantry. Might he be the proverbial scholar and gentleman—an unlikely Mob lawyer?

"Two masks are unquestionably better than one," she remarked as they turned left on Via Caio Cestio, following the

Protestant Cemetery's tall perimeter wall. Its scabrous, puckered pink plaster cried out for repair. "Have you ever been inside?" she asked provocatively. "It's beautiful, like a park."

"Remarkable," he agreed. "Shelley's tomb in particular is very moving." Then he recited the famous inscription on the poet's tomb, speaking in flawless American, or was it Canadian, English.

> Nothing of him that doth fade,
> But doth suffer a sea-change
> Into something rich and strange.

Daria waited a beat, impressed. "It is wonderfully lyrical," she said. "Still, I prefer Keats's inscription. *Here lies One Whose Name was writ in Water*. It's easier to remember."

"Ah, but it is a terrible way to die—drowning."

Daria assented. "Something tells me it's rarely pleasant to die."

"Possibly," he mused, "one thing is certain, sooner or later we'll all find out."

"With luck, it'll be later," she said.

"What might be worse than death is a lifetime in solitary confinement," he added thoughtfully. "I would prefer death, but not by drowning."

"A bullet to the head, perhaps?"

"Why not? It's instantaneous, messy but then the mess is left to others to clean up, isn't it?" Sounding like one of Dumas's Three Musketeers, Scaramellato laughed a light, histrionic d'Artagnan laugh. "Pity we can't go in and have a chat among the tombs of the poets," Daria mused aloud. "Isn't your nickname Torq as in Torquato?"

"Excellent!" he exclaimed. "Torquato is my middle name, not my nickname. Shall I recite my favorite lines from *Jerusalem Liberated*?"

"Please don't," Daria said. "Better stick to the Romantics." She paused and glanced around. No one appeared to be following them. "Let's stand behind those oleanders or find a bench in the slightly less poetic Parco Cestio around the corner," she suggested.

"Oh dear, must we?" Scaramellato asked, making a face. He stopped where the sidewalk veered through several clumps of dark-leaved, thirsty shrubbery. The cemetery's perimeter wall was only about four feet high but topped by a series of tall, narrow decorative crenellations, like the top of a medieval castle. "You seem a sporty type, Major Vinci," he quipped. "A pole vaulter you were, once upon a time, perhaps? What say we hop over that wall and find some real privacy? I'll give you a leg up if you need one."

Turning from Scaramellato to face the wall, Daria said, "What about the security cameras?"

"But there are none, not along here. They've set them up by the poets' tombs and of course in the vicinity of the dearly departed Andrea Camilleri, who understood the Sicilian soul so well. Look for yourself," he said, spreading his arms. Daria's eyes followed his hands to the left and right as he motioned and added, "Nothing, no security devices."

"Guard dogs?"

"Oh no, nothing remotely like that," he laughed. "Haven't you ever been in at night? I thought every good Roman broke in at least once in his life, or her life. For a lark. Just as we used to in Paris, at Père-Lachaise Cemetery, when I was a young exchange student at the Sorbonne. Then Jim Morrison died and the movie came out and ruined everything. We wound up with twenty-four seven security guards, cameras, razor wire, Dobermans, the whole nine yards. Perhaps the same will happen here now with Camilleri? So far, things are still, how shall I put it, dead quiet?" Scaramellato laughed and pivoted away, a crooked smile on his lips.

Before Daria could reply, he looped the strap of the duffle bag diagonally across his powerful torso and sprinted to the wall, leaping up and pulling himself to the top between the serried crenellations. A moment later he lifted his left leg, stepped over the top of the castellated wall, turned, and beckoned to her. "Give me your hand," he said in a stage whisper. "I'll haul you up."

Daria blinked, unable to hide her surprise and consternation. She felt her face flush with sudden heat. The dim streetlights cast long, unhelpful shadows. She wondered where Morbido was. Could he see Scaramellato on the wall and guess what was about to happen?

"Stand back out of the way," she said, running and jumping up in the same place he had. She hoisted herself to the top, wiggled between the crenellations, and dropped silently into the cemetery on the other side. For half a second, Daria wondered if she had just made a strategic error and if, from his position atop the wall, Scaramellato might simply drop back outside and run away. But why would he? A moment later he laughed pleasantly as if the caper were a harmless dare, then jumped down onto the path below. Dusting off his clothes and hands, he made a sweeping motion and said, "After you, signora."

A wavering, purplish, sepia-hued square of light seeped into the graveyard from the Piazzale on the southeast side of the pyramid and the street opposite it, where they had come in. But Daria did not need light. She knew exactly where she was. She had been to this graveyard a hundred times over the years. Scaramellato also seemed to know it well. Bent low, he scooted along a looping path, avoiding John Keats's tomb and the security cameras trained on it. Daria followed, running in a stoop.

Zigzagging down to the grassy moat fronting the monumental pyramid, Scaramellato took refuge behind the broken marble foundations of some long-ago Roman building abutting the ancient city wall of Emperor Aurelian.

"We ought to be safe here," he said when Daria caught up with him. "At least for a few minutes. Long enough to come to terms."

Catching her breath, she bent one knee on the grass in the dark lee of the ruined foundation walls, trying to decide which way to run if she had to escape. "I need to let my people know I'm here, so they don't force their way in," she whispered, tapping an encrypted message to Morbido, telling him to wait out of sight on the street side of the cemetery wall. "Now," she said, her voice steely. "Down to business."

Wordlessly, Scaramellato unslung the bulging duffle bag and dropped it into the grass at her feet. "The business," he whispered, "is messy, like a bullet to the head. Just so you know, the multiple-point disappearing bluff voice message you sent me includes several errors which may or may not have been intentional. First of all, I was not the accomplice to anyone. I was working with Charles Wraithwhite, negotiating a lucrative deal with the Institute."

"For the purchase of nonfungible tokens and kompromat?" Daria interrupted ironically. "Photographs of compromising jelly bean bags and plastic swords—and documents relating to... what? The P2, Gladio? Gelli?"

"Very good," said Scaramellato with a crocodile smile. "The negotiations required us to meet in the catacombs. The tunnels and chamber were the only places Charlie and the other club members felt safe talking to me. They also happened to house the materiel and were where the P2 held meetings once upon a time. So, Major Vinci, ask yourself this: what interest would I have in killing Charlie or helping anyone kill him?"

"Who gave you the coveralls and why did you take them away and hide your tunic?"

Scaramellato smiled again. The half moon of his thick lips revealed his shiny, small, square white teeth. They seemed all the shinier and squarer because his head was so astonishingly round. "This is what happened," he said. Then he told her. He had arrived as usual through the tunnels and found the Catacomb Club in session. They were smoking hash and drinking. He joined in but had difficulty hearing their words because the burial chamber vibrated and shook and echoed with music coming from above. It was also hard to see from the smoke. Wraithwhite had already told him via Signal that something big was about to break, that he had them where he wanted them—*them* meaning the Institute and Taylor Chatwin-Paine. Wraithwhite and the others began playing the ritual game of Russian roulette, handing the old Smith & Wesson revolver around, spinning the cylinder and clicking the trigger. He, Scaramellato, had taken his turn, confident the cartridge was a blank or a dud and knowing the odds were always with him no matter what. Leaning forward and passing the gun to Wraithwhite, the moment the weapon had changed hands, Scaramellato had leaned back into his habitual funeral niche. Then he was deafened and blinded by a blast. He saw Wraithwhite flung over violently.

"I wasn't sure what had happened, whether the gun had gone off by mistake, whether Charlie had pulled the trigger early by mistake, whether someone else had fired from inches away from his head—nothing was clear to me. One of the oil lamps had fallen over. The woman named Adele was screaming and writhing and holding the side of her face and her arm and shoulder. The others were screaming too. Everyone panicked. They got up and ran. I roused myself and forced myself to stay calm. I decided to look around before leaving, to see if Charlie was still alive, for one thing. I switched on my headlamp. There he was, deader than dead, half of his head blown off. The gun was lying in the dust next to him. I was confused. Then I sensed a presence hovering at the edge of the burial chamber. I could make out movement but could see nothing distinctly. I held my breath. A shadow seemed to be climbing the staircase and then it disappeared. I turned off my light, waited, and followed. At the top of the stairs, the door to the shed was ajar. I looked through the crack but it was too dark to see who was there. I heard clothes being taken off then shoes being kicked out of the way. Then the door from the shed to the outside opened a crack. In the streak of light, I saw a tall man dressed in black. He slipped away and shut the door behind him. That's when I decided to go out that way myself and try to disappear in the crowd at the concert then somehow get off the property unseen. When I stepped all the way into the shed, I tripped over something piled on the floor. I stooped. It was a pair of coveralls. They had fallen to the ground off a hook. Then I understood. So, I picked them up and stuffed them in my bag. They barely fit into it. I decided it was too risky to go out from above. So, I went back down to the burial chamber and out through the tunnels. I had just made it into the park when I saw the swirling lights of the ambulance entering the grounds of the Institute and knew the police would follow." He paused and stared directly at Daria.

"Then you stripped off the tunic and hid it behind the tree," Daria interjected, picking up where he had left off, "and you ran back down through the woods past the prostitutes to the street, where you had parked your car."

"My motorcycle," he corrected.

"Why did you leave the tunic behind?"

He pointed at the duffle bag. "I had two masks and the coveralls in the bag and the tunic wouldn't fit. I thought, I can come back for it. If they find it, they will quickly determine that whoever was wearing it didn't shoot the gun. Don't forget, Major Vinci, I am a criminal lawyer."

She was about to say, *and the lawyer of criminals*, but restrained herself.

Daria tapped her lips. "Okay," she said, buying time. "Two things right away and then we discuss terms. One, who introduced you to Wraithwhite and, two, can you ID the tall man in black who stepped out of the shed?"

Before he could answer, she saw Scaramellato turn and stiffen. He pointed, cursing under his breath. A flashlight or smartphone had lit up on top of the castellated perimeter wall, at a point near where they had entered.

"Who is it?" he asked, hoarse.

"Not my people," she growled.

"Goddammit," he cursed in a whisper. "I should've known."

Without waiting for her to answer, Scaramellato bounded through the darkness toward the near corner of the pyramid. He reached it where it joined the tall brick city wall and formed a steep crook invisible from nearly all other standpoints in the cemetery. Edging his way up the first twenty or thirty feet like a skilled free-climber, Scaramellato reached the top, pulling himself up the last few feet of wall using the dense, dangling caper bushes sprouting from crevices in the bricks. Daria watched in awe. Clambering onto the pyramid's steep marble cladding, he became visible in the bright streetlights shining up from Piazzale Ostiense.

"Stop!" shouted a raspy voice from the overlook facing the pyramid. "Police!"

Two other voices shouted. "He's armed!" yelled one. "Drop it!" roared another.

A shot rang out. Daria was unsure who had fired or where it had come from. Then a hailstorm of bullets broke and flew over her head at Scaramellato. Teetering along the pyramid's smooth white marble surface, he took a hit, screamed and twirled then fell, tumbling outside the city walls and down the far flank of the pyramid into Piazzale Ostiense. One of the policemen rushed to the bottom of the pyramid and tried to scale it but slid back down to the moat several times before giving up and running away, following the other two officers already running toward the perimeter wall. All three scrambled over.

Not waiting to see what might happen next, Daria lifted the duffle bag and moved swiftly and silently in a stoop, heading south by southwest. She dashed up between the trees and shrubs on the sloping ground toward a clump of cypresses leaning against the city wall. Passing from there into a forest of mossy, lichen-mottled tombs, she threaded her way toward the ruined tower behind Shelley's grave. Then she remembered the security cameras and veered away, running down the gravel path flanking the Aurelian Wall until she found the familiar alleyway sloping to the right toward her family tomb. Ducking behind a massive boulder topped by a cross, she forced open the tangle of shrubs covering the Vinci family plot. Tucking the duffle bag into the greenery, hoping it could not be seen, she burrowed down through the branches, hiding herself behind a low hedge. Shutting her eyelids tight, she tried to control her breathing and think straight. Reciting her trusty mantra—*calm, quiet, methodical*—she regained composure a few minutes later.

What to do? Wait overnight? Send Morbido another message? Tell him to get away, to take the early train to Genoa before they nabbed him? Tell the cemetery guard when the time came in the morning that she was waiting for her brother to arrive with their mother's urn? Or hope the police would give up looking for her so she could climb back out?

Were they looking for her? Did they know she had been with Scaramellato? She contemplated phoning Foscolo and turning herself in. But events made the decision for her.

Eighteen

Even an untrained ear can distinguish the many different sirens of Rome. A trained one can identify the specific components of the continuous cacophony of acoustic alarms, a contemporary soundscape worthy of Maestro Katzenbaum. Lying on her side behind the hedges encircling her family's tomb, Daria listened, her heart pounding. She quickly realized that what she heard was not the Italian state-controlled gas or water companies' shrieking emergency intervention squads, or the Ministry of the Interior's belligerently bleating national Polizia di Stato, or the apocalyptic wailing of the Ministry of Defense's munitions and bomb removal squads, or the brusque, bombastic riot control police, or the screaming customs and tax enforcement authority, or even the whining municipal police or the roaring, ripping, eardrum-rending Carabinieri. What she heard were the benign though terrifying fire brigade and ambulance sirens, specifically a siren on an ambulance from a public hospital. She knew the firehouse was only two blocks away, on the corner of Via Marmorata and Via Galvani. The nearest public hospital was farther upstream, a mile on the Tiber Island.

Cupping her hand to shield the screen of her glowing smartphone, she read Morbido's latest encrypted message. *Arriving w fire truck and ambulance. Stay put.*

Several considerations struck her simultaneously. Why were there no police sirens? Surely, the raspy voice she had heard belonged to Captain Foscolo? He was SISMI, the military intelligence unit, but was working with DIGOS, part of the Polizia di Stato. Where had he and his men gone? Had he seen her earlier on Via Marmorata with Scaramellato or intercepted her theoretically unbreakable Signal messages to Scaramellato or had he simply guessed she was with the fugitive? Did Foscolo know about the coveralls and the duffle bag and if so, how did he find out?

No, she decided, shaking her head. She could not stay put. Listening carefully to the noises from beyond the cemetery's wall and orienting her footsteps to the full-throated commands of the firefighters and ambulance crew on the city street, she crawled out from hiding and wended her way among the tombs to the base of the perimeter wall, twenty or thirty yards southwest of the graveyard's main entrance. In the flickering light of a distant streetlamp, she saw the top of a fire ladder progressively rising up over the wall. Moments later, the shiny silver-helmeted head of a fireman appeared. He pivoted, looking like an extraterrestrial, grabbed something from behind, then heaved and tipped another, shorter ladder over the wall onto Daria's side. She rushed to it and, before the extraterrestrial could climb over and down, shouted at him. "Wait, I'm coming up. Go back down. This is Major Daria Vinci of DIGOS."

Up she scampered in three seconds. Lifting her legs high one by one to crest the wall and then climbing down a ladder on the far side certainly beat jumping. It was definitely an easier way to get over, she decided. Holding up her ID like an amulet, she advanced on the group of astonished firefighters. They stepped back as she thanked them and shouted an order in passing. "There's no point going in. The victim fell from the pyramid into Piazzale Ostiense, not into the cemetery. Get back into your rigs and drive around as fast as you can. He may still be alive."

Emerging from the shadows as the firefighters and ambulance crew pulled noisily away, Osvaldo Morbido pursed his thick lips and studied Daria's face. "Never a dull moment," he remarked. "Not around you."

She shook her head in consternation. "I fear he's dead," she whispered, waving at the pyramid. "Let's move before you-know-who shows up."

"Why would he?"

"Search me, but he will. He was here, I'm sure it was his voice. He may have fired the first shot."

They turned right on the first paved road, heading the back way to Via Marmorata as fast as Morbido's overburdened legs would carry him. The street did a dog's leg between industrial sheds topped by rusted iron roofs and surrounded by potholed, sprawling parking lots. Daria saw a streetcar flash past at the end of the road, a hundred yards ahead, beyond the dark clustering trees of the Parco Cestio.

"There's a taxi rank at the train station," she said in a hoarse whisper.

Morbido shook his head. "I already called a limo. It's waiting on the corner."

Daria's smile spread but faded fast. Stepping off the sidewalk on Via Marmorata by the idling Uber came Captain Foscolo. His congenital lapidary expression was as hard and pale and pitted as the Pyramid of Cestius. Saluting them as they approached, he stared menacingly at Daria, then spoke in his raspy, rusty basso voice.

"May I ask what you are doing here, Major Vinci?"

She waited a beat, cocking her head to one side. "You may ask, Captain Foscolo. This is a free country, despite what some say. By the same token, and before I consider whether I will answer, will you kindly tell me what *you* are doing here and why you are accosting us in this manner?"

Foscolo glowered, avoiding Morbido's eye as he spoke. "I am following up a lead," he said.

"Well, that's helpful, isn't it?" Daria ironized.

"The meter's running," Morbido growled. "Do you mind stepping aside?" Before Foscolo could move or answer, Morbido elbowed him out of the way and strode to the Uber limo. He pulled open a door and waited for Daria to get in.

"Allow me to pacify and tranquilize our esteemed colleague," Daria said with venomous calm. "Let's get this in the right order. First, Captain Morbido's 6 o'clock train was canceled, at the Ostiense Station, around midnight. Osvaldo, please show Captain Foscolo your ticket," she ordered.

"It's electronic," Morbido growled.

"Then show him your screen. We're wasting time."

Morbido complied. Foscolo glanced at the smartphone, expressionless and silent.

"For your information," snarled Morbido, "not that I am in any way obliged or even inclined to share anything with you, I just happened to be strolling by. I heard shots, fired, no doubt, by some reckless troublemakers larking around the cemetery or by a bunch of trigger-happy greenhorn cops who should probably be suspended or fired or jailed."

Daria segued, "So, you see, Captain Morbido here did the responsible thing. He called the fire brigade and an ambulance, asking them to phone the authorities. As to my presence,

I had come down to keep him company while he waited for the next train. Captain Morbido, show Captain Foscolo the receipt for your sandwich and mineral water, please, from the café on the corner, over there." Daria pointed. The café was closed by now. But Foscolo clearly knew the place and also knew they had been there earlier.

The SISMI officer's stone face quaked with anger. "Is this a farce?"

Daria's laugh was mirthless. "Not in the least," she snapped, putting steel into her words. "Since you have not been forthcoming with us, I will make inquiries to ascertain what investigative lead you are supposedly following up at 2 a.m. on Via Marmorata, when a shooting has just occurred in the cemetery a few hundred yards away. For now, excuse us, if you will. We must be off. I have a great deal to do before leaving for Venice tomorrow morning."

"This morning," Morbido corrected. "At 11 o'clock on the dot."

"You will hear from me," promised Foscolo, pale with rage.

"I think you will hear from me before I hear from you, captain. It is certain you will be hearing from your superiors. Now, good night. I hope you haven't killed him. That will cause a monumental mess no one can cover up, not even SISMI."

The three officers saluted each other stiffly. Daria and Morbido got into the waiting car and the driver floored it, burning rubber.

"Take it easy," Daria barked. "We don't want trouble with the police."

"Never again," Morbido muttered. He let out a long, hissing breath as the limo sped toward the Tiber. "Don't ever invite me to Venice, I'm not coming."

Daria chortled. She let down the window and drank in the night air. "Of course, you will, Osvaldo. Your wife will force you to, if I lean on her."

Morbido shook his head incredulously, his purple-rimmed, bloodshot eyes grappling to focus on Daria's maddening, inscrutable smile. "Franca is Genoese for ten generations, she practically remembers the wars when we, the Repubblica di Genova, trounced la Serenissima Repubblica di Venezia. She hates Venice in her soul."

"Nonsense," Daria interrupted. "Franca adores squid ink risotto, she told me so herself years ago. You can have a second honeymoon."

She observed Morbido. Brooding now and sullen from exhaustion, he stared out of the taxi's open window at the nighttime scene, the glowing monuments, and soaring sil- houettes of columns and tombs and tumbledown temples. They meant nothing to him, a Genoese. But Daria knew she would miss them, miss the craziness, the noise, the higgledy- piggledy mess, the dented, flawed, tarnished humanity of Rome.

Speeding north by northwest on the riverside boulevard heading toward the Vinci family apartment, they made good time.

"Foscolo didn't swallow it," Morbido mumbled. "What did you do with the duffle bag, by the way? That's why he looked you up and down. He's not interested in feminine beauty."

"I hid it," she sighed. "We'll get it tomorrow. I mean, later this morning." Yawning, she glanced at her watch. It was just after 2. That left her about nine hours before the DIGOS driver arrived. She wondered if Scaramellato could possibly have survived. He had been shot at least once then fallen. The slide down the Ostiense side of the pyramid and the fall of thirty or forty feet into the Piazzale below would be enough to break anyone's neck. Another thought assailed her: had Foscolo and his men violated the protocols and conventions on the use of deadly force? They would claim it was Scaramellato who had fired first—that they were in mortal danger and had merely responded with appropriate force. Who would challenge them? Who *could* challenge them? Only she could. But she herself wasn't sure if Scaramellato had been armed or tried to scare them off with a warning shot. Tragically, the world would be glad to be rid of Marco Torquato Scaramellato—at least the sunny side of the world.

"They've watched too many American cop shows," Morbido remarked, as if reading her mind. "Bang, bang, you're dead."

Daria nodded. She was too tired to speak or think straight. "Ask yourself this," she said, yawning again and struggling to get the words out. "Why would Foscolo want Scaramellato dead?"

"First I'd ask myself how Foscolo knew the guy was going to show up where he did and why he wasn't surprised to see the two of us afterwards. They must've been tailing him. How did they know he was involved with Charles Wraithwhite? The real problem is we don't know what Foscolo knows. He doesn't share."

"Neither do we," she muttered, shaken by a deep, uncontrollable yawn. "Maybe Foscolo thinks Scaramellato killed Wraithwhite."

"Foscolo seems to want to think Wraithwhite killed himself, despite evidence to the contrary."

"Exactly."

"Exactly what?"

"It's inconvenient if Wraithwhite didn't kill himself by mistake playing Russian roulette. But if someone killed him, the preferred candidate would be Scaramellato. If Foscolo doesn't know about the coveralls and hasn't found Scaramellato's tunic in the woods, he might legitimately say he suspected Scaramellato did it."

Shaking her head and yawning again, Daria tapped her lips and closed her eyes and said she needed a ten-minute catnap before she could do or say anything else. If they got to bed by 2:30 or 2:45 they could get a couple of hours of shuteye before he had to catch his train, she mused aloud.

"We'll cross that bridge when we come to it," he mumbled, yawning violently. Daria's yawns had spread their contagion.

"That bridge might prove to be the famous Ponte Rotto or Pons Aemilius, alias the Broken Bridge," she joked. "We passed it a few minutes ago. It collapsed centuries ago, a thousand years ago, two thousand years ago, who knows? And it still hasn't been repaired. It's Rome. It's Italy. Read Plutarch or Livy, they'll put you to sleep."

But Morbido said nothing in reply. His head had lolled forward. He was already sleeping.

Nineteen

"**G**uess who's coming to breakfast?" Daria ironized as Mario wandered into the kitchen at 5:35 a.m. Blinking at her, he stared bleary eyed, yawned, and shook his head. "I don't do jokes this early," he mumbled. "Coffee."

"Not a joke," Daria said. "Osvaldo's train was canceled. He's sleeping in Davide's old bedroom. I'd better wake him up or he'll miss his train to Genoa."

Mario grunted, stared at the small Bialetti for two, then took down the big, aluminum family-sized stovetop espresso maker, unscrewed it, grimaced at the corrosion inside, began scouring, gave up, and filled the bottom of the machine with water from the tap. Daria made to leave the kitchen but paused instead, watching in fascination as Mario bustled in his robe and slippers between the cupboards, fridge, sink, stovetop, and table, laying out three settings, a sugar bowl, a jug of milk, a bottle of mineral water, and an old tin box stuffed with tasteless cookies. His mannerisms, the way he shuffled and arranged things, his choice of breakfast items, the expressions on his craggy, groggy, worry-worn face—the face of some-one's cantankerous grandfather—were eerily like those of their mother. Barbie. The Barracuda.

Daria glanced up at the tall glass-fronted cabinets on the wall. The funerary urn sat on top of them, near the kitchen door. She and her brothers had not been able to agree on a better place for it. Pointing up, she waited for Mario to notice. He didn't.

"I'm taking it to the cemetery this morning," she said. "As soon as I've cleaned up and breakfasted and finished the last-minute packing."

Mario thrust his lips forward and down like an aged silver-back gorilla or a petulant child. "I'll go with you," he offered at last. "I'll drive us. Then I have to pack. We're leaving for New York."

"You and Taylor?"

"Yes," Mario said, concentrating on getting each tiny spoonful of powdery coffee into the basket of the espresso machine. "This afternoon."

Daria tapped her lips in consternation, trying not to scowl or shake her head or scold. She took another tack. "I've got to get into the graveyard the minute it opens—before it opens," she said, "and get out again, fast."

He nodded. "Your car comes when? Ten?"

"Eleven," she said. "I've never heard of anything so outrageous and idiotic. Then again, if you're eager to be rid of an inconvenient investigator I suppose you're willing to be outrageous and idiotic."

Mario shook his head. "You think I have something to do with this," he said. "You're wrong. Though admittedly your taking charge of the case looks bad."

"Conflict of interest?"

"Multiple," he said.

"Captain Foscolo already sang that song to me," she remarked.

"Well, perhaps Captain Foscolo is right."

"Perhaps."

She returned to her bedroom, took a final look at the screen of her laptop, confirming that the contents of the flash drive had now been copied for a third time—first onto the hard drive, a second time onto an external hard disk, and a third and final time onto another flash drive she had inserted into a USB port. The kompromat. The skinny on the Institute, plus the malware. All in one convenient location. She would give the copied flash drive to Morbido for safekeeping. Just in case.

Glancing around the bedroom, trying to summon feelings of nostalgia, Daria made an effort to remember what it had looked like when she was a child or an adolescent. There was not a trace of her girlhood to be seen. The moment she had rebelled and left for America, aged twenty-one, her mother had removed all her belongings, brought in the painters and decorators, and henceforth refused to refer to the room by its former longtime designation, Daria's Nest.

Would she miss it? Would she miss the apartment or living in Rome? Of course. In all probability, her brothers would outvote her and sell the place, cashing in and cutting the last tenuous connections they had with the city of their birth and their father's ancestors. They certainly did not need the money, unless "need" could be construed to mean desire. Did they desire another luxury car or perhaps a condominium somewhere in Florida or southern California for one of their offspring, Daria's many caring nieces and nephews who went out of their way *not* to stay in touch? Divided six ways, after the sale, she would be left with resources enough to buy a broom closet or a one-car garage in some godforsaken spot in Italy.

Emerging from the bedroom into the premodern bathroom, she let the hot water run into the clubfooted tub-shower, massaging and relaxing her neck muscles. There was too much going on to process. Her two-hour catnap had recharged her batteries—but only partway. A fast charge. Would it be enough to get her through the morning? As to the afternoon, all bets were off.

Shaved and perfumed and dusted with talcum powder, Osvaldo Morbido appeared at the breakfast table, dwarfing it to Alice in Wonderland or Lilliputian proportions. He looked almost presentable despite his rumpled unlaundered clothes and dusty leather shoes. Perched opposite Daria, his neckless head pivoted to right and left, like the turret of a tank, as he scanned the apartment for Mario. She could see Morbido was relieved that her brother had already breakfasted and left. But Morbido remained wary.

"When does the cemetery open?" he whispered, gulping a cup of sugary tar while crunching down a handful of cookies.

"You'll be on your train by then," she mused. "We'll drop you at Ostiense."

Morbido shook his jowls. "No," he said. "You need me. I'll take a later train." He paused, glanced around, and asked conspiratorially, "At this point, what does it matter if I'm twelve or eighteen or twenty hours late getting back to Genoa?"

Daria laughed quietly. She leaned in and whispered back, pointing at her mother's funerary urn. "Remember, Mario doesn't know a thing about what's going on. Just play along. We'll leave the urn with him at the cemetery and take a taxi the rest of the way to the station, once we have the duffle bag."

Morbido winked one bulging, bloodshot, bovine eye. "I stuffed a bunch of crinkled-up newspaper into the satchel you gave me," he whispered back. "And I found some plastic flowers in the hanging closet, so I put them in too."

"Brilliant!" she exclaimed in a hushed voice. "I'll get another bunch of them from the living room. Disgusting, hideous things. The maid put them around everywhere."

"No one will know the satchel is empty," Morbido continued. "Are you sure Scaramellato's duffle bag will fit inside it?"

Daria assured him it would, as long as he got rid of the flowers and balled-up newspaper.

They left the kitchen moments later and in silence followed the dour Mario downstairs to the garage in the basement under the courtyard.

Shoehorning himself into the rear seat of the electric SUV, Morbido's body spilled sideways, his back pressed against his door and window. He watched Daria settle into the front seat, the funerary urn on her lap.

"Their first reaction will be to not let us in," she said to Mario, pursing her lips. "Please allow me to do the talking. When we get there, you carry the urn, Mario. Wait with it at the cemetery office and bring the caretaker or gravedigger with you to meet us at the grave site. They'll need to open that rusty grate and the lock on the tomb. I don't have the keys and I don't suppose you do either?" Mario shook his head, accelerating silently into the street, south through the city's dense, meandering, cacophonous morning traffic. "Osvaldo and I will go straight to the tomb and clear away the dead branches and leaves," Daria added in what she hoped was a reverential, mournful tone. "We've brought some flowers, those horrible plastic things Maria Pia left. Later we can buy live plants and pay to have fresh flowers brought regularly."

"All right," Mario muttered, yawning. He seemed uninterested. "If worse comes to worst and they won't let us inside, you can take a taxi and I'll wait with the urn until things open."

"Good idea," Daria said. She glanced at Morbido. Both kept straight faces.

They rode for ten minutes in stilted silence. When the traffic bottlenecked near the Vatican expressway underpass, Daria reached into her purse and extracted a compact swirling police emergency roof light mounted on a suction cup. Switching it on, she reached outside and slapped it onto the roof of the SUV, then waved her right arm to attract attention. "Drive around them, go down the other side of the street," she ordered Mario.

"Are you mad?" he asked. "I'll do no such thing."

"Yes, you will," she barked. "If you don't, I will take over and drive or Osvaldo will. We have no time to lose."

Trembling with suppressed rage, Mario gritted his teeth, put on his emergency flashers, and timidly pulled the car out of the traffic jam, flashing his headlights as he drove slowly the wrong way down the riverside boulevard.

"Excellent," Daria remarked. "Now step on it. We'll make a policeman of you yet."

"I am shocked and dismayed," he spluttered. "You are abusing your privileges and making me an accomplice or an accessory."

"Believe me," she said. "If you knew what the stakes really are…"

"Well, what are they?"

"Just drive," she snapped. "One day, if I feel you're worthy of trust, I might let you know."

At the Protestant Cemetery, as she had predicted, several patrol cars had slalomed to a stop and were parked at odd angles in front of the gates. A police barrier had been erected around the access route for hearses. She recognized several of the officers on duty. Standing among them was the affable elderly Roman man in charge of maintaining the site. He had been shaken out of bed earlier than usual, she guessed. He seemed flustered and was flapping his hands and arms and pacing back and forth like a crazed penguin. Striding toward Daria when he recognized her, he thrust out his hand, and his face was transformed by solicitude and a practiced simulacrum of grief.

Leaving Mario to glower at the wheel, with the urn still sitting on the front passenger seat, Daria and Morbido approached the cemetery manager. Flashing their IDs at the patrolmen, they explained in a few words that they needed to get into the grounds for purely personal but very urgent reasons. She pointed at the plastic flowers sticking out of the satchel Morbido clutched, then she turned and waved at the urn on the seat of the car, visible through the open passenger door. The procedure was highly irregular and exceptional, she realized, she said apologetically. But since the graveyard was already open for reasons about which they had heard through the grapevine, they hoped the helpful authorities would accede to their wishes, given her precipitous transfer and promotion to vice questor. Before they could answer or deny admittance, Daria signaled vigorously to her brother. Reluctantly, Mario got out of the car, picked the urn off the passenger seat, and joined them by the gate.

"No need to accompany us," she told the manager breezily. "Our tomb has been here for nearly thirty years. We know very well where it is, don't we, Mario? Captain Morbido and I will go ahead and give it a good cleaning. Mario, please wait here with the manager and then bring along the caretaker and gravedigger so we can open the lock." She beckoned to Morbido. They walked briskly through the main gate and down the graveled lanes. "That's the closest he's been to our mother since infancy," she muttered once they were out of earshot.

Moments later when they reached the tomb, Daria began flailing her arms like a grounded helicopter, removing fallen leaves and dead branches from the surface and surroundings

of the elaborate Vinci family tomb. She made a show of preparing things for the arrival of the urn, all the while scanning
the alleyways around them, glancing up to check for drones or
cameras, and talking a mile a minute without saying anything.

Bent double and reaching under the hedges and shrubbery, Morbido finished emptying the plastic flowers and
wadded-up newspapers from the satchel. Then he pulled the
coveralls from the hidden duffle bag and began to cram them
into the empty satchel when Sergeant Eugenio Pompelmo
caught sight of them and ambled over from his post by the
Aurelian Wall. Stopping short, he saluted, glanced at the tomb
and flowers, seemed to remember something, and mumbled,
"My condolences, Major Vinci, I had forgotten about the loss
of your mother. What a strange coincidence to find you here
this morning." He seemed genuinely puzzled.

Smiling sorrowfully, Daria glanced at Pompelmo. "Eugenio!
What in heavens are you doing here?" she asked. Out of the
corner of her eye, she watched Morbido finish pulling the
straps around the satchel then buckle it closed.

"Searching the cemetery," Pompelmo said.

"For what?"

"I'm not supposed to say," he remarked, glancing around.

"Oh, come now, since when do we keep secrets from each
other?"

Pompelmo looked around again, then whispered, "A
person, perhaps wounded or dead, and a duffel bag."

"How odd," she remarked, turning to shout at Morbido.
"Osvaldo, didn't you find a duffel bag in the bushes over
there?"

Morbido's panicked look quivered across his features as
he pivoted and spluttered. "Why, yes, I did see a duffel bag,
over there, I think." He pointed to a tomb twenty or thirty
feet away. "Take a look, Pompelmo, it was a green duffel bag,

if memory serves. Behind that tomb that looks like a boulder with a cross on top."

The sergeant trotted away and began beating the bushes behind a massive faux boulder surmounted by a crucifix. Cursing under his breath, Morbido stuffed the scattered newspapers into the duffle bag, zipped it up hastily, checked to see if Pompelmo was looking, then threw the bag as far as he could away from himself in the opposite direction. He hissed at Daria under his breath, "You *are* mad, your brother is right!"

Daria laughed. "Eugenio," she called to the sergeant, "Osvaldo was wrong, that bag he saw is over there." She waited until Pompelmo returned from the far side of the boulder, then pointed. "I think it's by that tomb, over there." The sergeant stalked away toward it. "More to the right, yes, in that direction." Daria winked at Morbido, then whispered, "Grab the satchel and follow me out, if you see Foscolo don't stop, don't argue, don't give him that bag, it's your private property, you're traveling to Genoa with it."

With a cry of triumph, Pompelmo lunged into the shrubhery and stepped back holding up Scaramellato's duffel bag by the shoulder strap. His smile spread from ear to ear. "Thanks!" he exclaimed.

"I'm so happy we could help," Daria said. "Listen, my brother will be here in a minute with my mother's urn. Do us a favor, Eugenio, and wait for him, would you? You know Mario. He might need your help. Osvaldo and I have to run. He has a train to Genoa and I am going to Venice and we're both late." She smiled wickedly. "It's been a pleasure working with you," she added, saluting and striding off. Stopping short, she walked back to where Sergeant Pompelmo was standing and said, "My best to Captain Foscolo, by the way. I was almost forgetting. Please be sure to tell him that Scaramellato was unarmed and could not have fired the first shot or any shot.

Who was in the Piazzale anyway, Eugenio? Or hidden and waiting in the cemetery? Was it you?"

Pompelmo flushed red and stared at Daria with his mouth gaping open. He licked his lips. "It wasn't me," he stuttered, "I swear. It was a SISMI guy, two of them, I don't know what their names are. They were beyond the wall, in the Piazzale. If someone else was in the cemetery, I don't know about it."

"Don't worry," Daria said. "I'll find out. Good luck to you, Eugenio. Just remember, stuff happens. Beware your colleagues."

"Sì, commissario," he said, standing to attention and saluting.

As they rode in the taxi toward Piazza del Cinquecento and the Termini train station, Daria took a deep breath and let it out slowly, her nostrils flaring. She watched Morbido mop his brow for the third or fourth time in the last ten minutes.

They had left the cemetery hurriedly, almost jogging, barely pausing to remove the swirling police light from the roof of the SUV and shouting their goodbyes and apologies to Mario. He did not seem surprised or unhappy to see them go. On the contrary.

Afterwards, rushing down the Via Caio Cestio in the direction of the Tiber, Daria and Morbido had circled left toward the Ostiense taxi rank and, flashing their IDs, had jumped the queue. Much to the irritation of the cabbie, she had barked out the address of the lab, slapped the swirling light on the roof of his car, and ordered him to get them there yesterday. "Lean on your horn," she had commanded, "flash your headlights, get us through the red lights and traffic." Then she had sat back and slapped Morbido on his elephantine thigh. "We got him!" she had gloated.

Watching her warily with bloodshot eyes, Morbido shook his head and checked his watch. They were almost at the station by now. "I'll have a couple of hours to kill before the train," he sighed. "Time enough to buy Franca a little souvenir and get myself a nice picnic for the ride."

"Does Franca still collect those little pewter spoons with tourist sights painted on them?" Daria asked, laughing. Morbido blushed with embarrassment.

"I'm afraid so," he admitted. "She has about a hundred of them."

"That's how I'll get her to Venice!" Daria exclaimed, snapping her fingers.

"You're diabolical," Morbido groaned. He handed her the satchel and watched as she unbuckled it and undid the straps. Reaching in, she carefully removed the green coveralls. As she did, a glove fell out of one of the pockets. She caught it, holding it up with her fingernails. It was an ultrathin ribbed latex gardening glove. Black, not green.

"Well, well, well," she whispered, "as Ambassador Riemach might say, this is most interesting." Forcing the glove and coveralls back into the satchel, she told the taxi driver she was getting out at the next corner. "The second stop is Termini, where you drop the captain," she added, handing over a twenty-euro bill. "Keep the change," she remarked, reaching up and prying off the swirling roof light. "Ta, ta, Osvaldo," she said. "Keep me posted and I'll do the same. If you're afraid of getting into a gondola, we can use the police cruiser. Franca will love it."

Jumping out and slamming the car door, Daria sprinted the remaining block to the lab. "More than urgentissimo," she said to the receptionist at the counter, handing over the satchel. "Mind the gloves, too, inside the pockets of the coveralls. This time I'm looking not just for gunpowder, blood, brains, and bone on the outsides, but also genetic material on the inside of the clothing, meaning hair, flakes of skin—whatever it might be. Run a match with the database. Keep the clothing here, send me an email with the report, print it out, then print out the report for the analysis of the tunic from yesterday. Someone will be by later to pick everything up. That person will identify himself or herself by saying 'Daria sent me.'"

As she left the premises, the words *the tunic from yesterday* rang and echoed in her mind's ear. Could it be? Only yesterday?

She was still mulling over the chronology of recent days when she stepped inside a corner café, drank down a caffè americano made from a double espresso, and wolfed two slices of olive oil–daubed pizza bianca. Checking her messages, she wondered if she could make it to the Institute and back to her mother's apartment in time and if she should bother. They would figure things out and get him—get *them*—sooner or later. She had an hour and a half left before the DIGOS driver arrived. The taxi ride from the lab to the Institute would consume at least twenty-five minutes, ditto from there to the apartment. That gave her maybe half an hour to track down Taylor Chatwin-Paine and say her farewells. The prospect was irresistible. Once again, she trotted to the nearest taxi stand, jumped the queue, slapped the roof light in place, and barked her orders to the cabbie.

Twenty

This message will self-destruct... Daria said to herself. She knew it would not fizzle in five seconds in the style of *Mission Impossible*. Rather, she would program the app to vaporize the messages precisely thirty minutes after Willem Bremach had opened them and begun listening. Thirty minutes should be plenty. She would time herself as she spoke at her smartphone. She was getting good at this. That was the beauty of the Signal app's disappearing message function. You no longer needed to be a spy to operate like one.

Daria was glad the swirling light on the roof of the taxi did not include a siren, though she wondered what it might sound like if it did—the bomb squad's siren, perhaps? That would be appropriate. If her calculations were correct, she had about fifteen minutes left to cross town and climb the hill—plenty of leeway for her to text headquarters then leave a longish voice memo for *Sua Eccellenza, l'Ambasciatore* Bremach. Watching the merry-go-round of traffic beyond her window, she spoke slowly and clearly, trying her best to be logical, precise, and concise.

Dear Willem, she began, checking her watch, *I trust you and Priscilla made it home safely and found the cats in good health. The felines of Rome are certainly well cared for, at least those living in and around the Institute. Their caretaker is charming, witty, and almost as observant as you. I wonder what her real job was for those many years at the ministry. Never mind. One day you'll tell me.*

I also wonder what Johanna Harrison might have done once upon a time to supplement her meager stipend from the Institute. Was she on the payroll at Langley or merely a some-time informant? Again, no matter. She has done her duty admirably. I thank you for making that happen.

In approximately ten minutes, I will say hello and good-bye to our mutual friend, the president. He will be surprised to learn that his six-foot-something under-gardener's coveralls are currently being analyzed externally for the usual telltale signs, and inside for the genetic material we might hope and expect to find in the case of a shooting death. A long, silvery patrician hair, for instance, or a few flakes of Pilgrim skin? He is a direct descendant of the Great White Fathers, is he not? Certainly, there must be a chromosome or three of Thomas Paine left in him. It will be very easy to make a match when the time comes. Something tells me he's already in our database. In fact, I know for a fact that he is.

What will really surprise him will be the discovery of his very own black gardening gloves stuffed into the pockets of the coveralls and presumably imbued with gunpowder. Will he be able to spin some story about that? Blame the murder on the under-gardener, for instance? Or on a coven of neo-Com-munist conspirators? We shall see. I think it might be difficult for my higher-ups and those in that other admirable branch of intelligence to turn the other cheek or sweep this under the proverbial carpet. Plausible deniability—that's the term they prefer these days Stateside, isn't it? Granted, this is not the storming of the Capitol, but it is almost as undeniable and in its own way nearly as egregious. Wasn't there some other, less violent, more elegant way to be rid of Charles Wraithwhite? Why didn't he just buy him off? Rage? Jealousy? Greed?

Before I forget, the coveralls and the reports on them and the gloves and, separately, the tunic that our friend Torq wore, await friendly hands at the lab. You know which—the one near Termini. The overflow lab. Tell them Daria sent you—you or whomever. So, yes, you're right, several sets of unauthorized eyes have already seen the evidence and the reports. Security has been compromised in the name of speed but also to ensure nondeniability, in case deniability appeared to be an option in the minds of certain parties—Taylor, the vice questor, Rossi at SISMI?

The details regarding the untimely demise of Charles Wraithwhite and Marco Torquato Scaramellato will have to wait until you and Pinky visit Venice—unless you know them already.

Now, for the juicy stuff you have been waiting for. Momentarily and under separate cover, I will be sending you a PDF of a historic archeological survey map of the Institute's site. I have done my best to place the red X in the right spot, but I marked up the map last night at about 3 in the morning in my bedroom and I have not had much sleep in the last seventy-two hours. Our good Captain Foscolo or his replacement, should Foscolo's head have rolled already, will know where to look. Here's a hint: go down the dead-end tunnel with the brick reinforcement wall at the back, on the right-hand side. Several bricks are loose, at about chest or head height for the average person. Beyond the wall, in the chamber, is part one of what Foscolo and others—including, I am guessing, you—have been looking for all these months and years.

The second part of the cache is easier: ask Taylor or the cus-todian or anyone else working at the Institute where the radio transmitter was hidden in the glory days of the war. Perhaps you already know. How silly of me. Of course, you know!

Please be sure to congratulate our other mutual friend, the brigadier general, Foscolo's superior, for his choice of the sterling captain to take my place and ensure Taylor would go scot-free and the P2/Gelli connection be hushed up. What a pity Captain Foscolo did not find the arms caches first, or the cover-alls and gloves, for that matter, or the tunic Torquato wore. For the gallant captain's benefit, I have put the soiled and rather smelly garment back where it was found, in the trees below the Institute, at the end of the middle path from the three-way intersection in the woods, in case anyone asks you for directions. Thanks again to the keeper of the cats! Her hints were precious.

The brigadier general will want to note that at least one eyewitness who is still alive knows Torquato was unarmed and did not fire a shot, and more than one witness can swear that the first gunshot did not originate from the pyramid but rather from the Piazzale or perhaps from elsewhere inside the cemetery. Yes. Definitely at least one came from inside the cemetery. Go figure. How else could Taylor get the authorities to execute an unarmed man fleeing in the darkness? So, they authentically thought Scaramellato was shooting at them?

Now, honestly, Willem, who was it down there in Piazzale Ostiense or in the cemetery, and who would have done such a thing? Why would Captain Foscolo and his men return fire with what sounded like fifteen rounds each in a matter of seconds after a single shot was fired, a shot that was not aimed at them? Why would anyone want to bring down Marco Torquato Scaramellato? Personally, I cannot imagine. Can you?

Please note that this message really will disappear half an hour after you start listening to it. I do hope I've made myself

*clear. You should have time to listen twice before my words
evaporate.*

*As ever, I am unsure whether to thank you or curse you
for your puzzling intervention—your encouraging discourage-
ment. If only Priscilla knew the truth about you. Perhaps one
day I will tell her. Yes. One day I will. A gondola ride would
be the perfect venue, don't you think? Just she and I. In the
meantime, take care, don't go anywhere I won't be able to
follow, and see you soon in Venice. Ta-ta, as you like to say. Mi
raccomando!*

*Oh, and, how could I forget? I happen to have a flash
drive with the kompromat and malware on it—Foscolo missed
that, too. I think I might keep it hidden somewhere. A kind
of insurance policy, you know. There are two copies of it, in
case anything should happen to me. I am not quite ready
to self-destruct like this message. If I do, those copies will be
instantaneously placed in several pairs of safe hands that no
one, not even our friend the brigadier general, can reach. And
then all hell really will break loose. Ta-ta...*

As Daria was signing off, the taxi slid to a halt in front of
the wrought-iron gates of the Institute. Daria pointed to the
roof light and ordered the taxi to wait, then walked calmly to
the security checkpoint, smoothing the wrinkles in her clothing as she went.

The guard on duty at the porter's lodge confirmed what
she suspected. First, the security lockdown had been lifted,
because "the authorities," meaning Captain Foscolo, had confirmed that Wraithwhite's death had been accidental. Second,
Adele Selmer had not recovered yet and was still in the hospital. Her future looked bleak and brain dead.

Hearing about Adele, Daria's mood shifted from triumphal vindication to sadness, then anger. She steeled herself
for what was to come.

"You will find il signor presidente in the rose garden," the guard answered her query while glancing at a bank of security cameras and pointing at one of them.

Nodding back, Daria began crossing the grounds. Then she turned around and asked the guard, "The president leaves this evening, is that correct?"

"Sì, commissario. With your brother, Dr. Vinci."

As Daria approached the rose garden, Taylor Chatwin-Paine did not see her. He went on deadheading and pruning the Institute's prize-winning tea roses with uncanny precision. Wielding his clippers with his right hand, he gently steadied the targeted branch with the index finger, forefinger, and thumb of his left hand, snipping each stem at a forty-five-degree angle, a fraction of an inch above the joint where a new bud would form. Daria watched in silence for a full minute before stepping up from behind and leaning on the marble balustrade a few yards in front of him. She drank in the vista.

"Daria!" he chirped, looking up from the flowerbed and smiling. "How kind of you to see me off. I thought you were already in Venice."

She shook her head but did not turn to face him. "I wouldn't have missed it for the world," she said, taking a deep breath.

"A rose is a rose is a Daria Vinci," he joked, snipping off a perfect yellow bloom and handing it to her. "Lemon Spice," he said. "Out of date, no longer a prize winner, but, still, one of my old favorites. It does smell extraordinarily of sweet Meyer lemons and spices. Some say cinnamon, others insist on allspice. So much depends on the soil, the air, the sun."

Daria's face was a mask as she accepted the rose and sniffed it reluctantly. "I had forgotten you were so passionate about roses. About roses, too, I should say."

"About many things," he agreed, apparently catching her meaning. "And you? What are you passionate about?"

"I'm single-minded and very boring," she mused, shaking her head. "A prig and a prude, some might say. The only thing that rings my bell is justice. The law. The quaint notion that we are all equal before the law and must follow it and answer for our crimes when we break it, even if we're the president of a country—or an institute. I suppose it's something I inherited from my father."

"Quite possibly," he said, dusting down his black coveralls and peeling off his matching gardening gloves.

"New gloves?" she asked, pointing. "Pity you lost the other pair. Perhaps the authorities will return them to you? The lab has done its work by now, I'm guessing. Many low-security correctional facilities I am familiar with have fine gardens you might thoroughly enjoy. If not, I'm confident you will prevail upon the lucky governor of your prison to let you create and plant a new rose garden somewhere."

Chatwin-Paine chuckled and shook his head in mock astonishment. "What a card you turned out to be, Daria," he said. "A carbon copy of your mother, physically, but with your father's temperament and personality. So serious. An avenging angel. If he were still alive, Roberto would be proud of you." He glanced around, as if expecting someone to rescue him. "Mario tells me the two of you installed Barbie's urn this morning at our beautiful cemetery. A delightful spot you have there. One of the best. I was present when your mother chose it. I might add that our association made it possible for her to acquire it, as you doubtless know."

"I thank you for that," Daria remarked. "Actually, I had no idea you managed that deal. But I should have known. The keeper of the keys, the president of the ghouls."

Chatwin-Paine laughed heartily, then became serious. "Yes indeed, Daria, it was wise of you to take care of things at the cemetery this morning, I suppose. You might get very busy in Venice and not return to Rome for quite some time. Vice questor? At last!"

Daria tapped her lips, her sardonic smile widening. "You know, Taylor, once upon a time, a man in your position might decide to fall on his sword. It would make life so much easier for so many people." She spoke slowly, savoring the view, sniffing the Lemon Spice rose and waiting for the meaning of her words to sink in.

Chatwin-Paine waited several beats. Then he cleared his throat and said, "Or he might take ship to America or Australia and disappear—once upon a time. Nowadays there are airplanes." The quip rang hollow.

Daria did not laugh. "Nowadays, there's such a thing as extradition and it works both ways. Let's do the numbers, Mr. President. Beyond Charles Wraithwhite and the unfortunate Marco Torquato Scaramellato, there's also Adele Selmer. She may never wake up. It wasn't just those chips of stone that struck her in the temple, as you know. It was the ricocheting round you fired from Jefferson Page's old revolver. I'm told the flattened bullet was only extracted from her brain yesterday evening. Adele continues to hemorrhage. By my count, that makes three birds with one stone—one of them intentional and direct, the other two collateral, or, perhaps I'm wrong, it's two with one stone, and one collateral?"

"Aha," Chatwin-Paine said, "the trick is to find the proof!" He smiled around his long white teeth. But his usual bantering cockiness was beginning to fade.

"There's enough to lock you up several times over," she remarked. "If you don't believe me, it doesn't matter. You'll find out soon enough. Willem can bring you up to date. Or Foscolo. Or Rossi. Or I might give myself a treat and do it myself, right now." She glanced at her watch and nodded with approval. "Yes, I think I will. There's enough time—just."

As if conjured by a genie, a notification appeared on her smartphone screen, accompanied by a ping and a bleep. Unlocking her phone, she tapped the email, then opened the PDF attachment from the lab. The subject line read *Urgentissimo: Preliminary Findings.* Daria's smile widened perceptibly. Speaking out loud and enunciating with emphasis, she read the single-paragraph synopsis to Taylor Chatwin-Paine.

"Gunpowder, blood, brain, and bone matter are evident on the exterior of the black gardening gloves and dark green coveralls. Strands of unusually long silvery white hair from a male Caucasian subject aged approximately seventy-five to eighty-five have been found inside the coveralls. Flakes of skin from the same subject were found inside the gloves. DNA sequencing and matching is under way." Daria paused and stared at Chatwin-Paine with a mixture of hatred and pity in her flashing green eyes. "I wonder, were you thinking of the Vietcong as you pulled the trigger, Lieutenant Chatwin-Paine?"

The president of the Institute of America in Rome stepped forward out of the rose garden and onto the terrace, visibly shaken. His face had turned a paler shade of white. He blinked several times but said nothing. Then he raised his eyebrows, shook his head, and spoke decisively. "You surprise me, Daria. Doesn't this kind of reckless conjecture go against every law on the books?"

Daria nodded speculatively, then spoke again. "I surprise myself," she said. She paused to sniff at the rose again. "Okay, let's do the numbers one more time. You're almost eighty. You'll have the best legal team available and you'll probably get them on the Institute's nickel, knowing you. The U.S. authorities won't seek the death penalty, not for you, not at your age and with your background. But you will discover what it means to be a felon and a jailbird for the rest of your days." Daria waited. She glanced at her watch.

"What about the materiel?" he asked, his voice fading.

Daria laughed mirthlessly, her upper lip curling. "Foscolo will know how to dispose of it with utmost discretion. If not Foscolo, someone else, perhaps Rossi himself. Naturally, if you make noise and trouble, your beloved Institute will be dragged through the mud and, God forbid, may well be sued out of existence, and it will do you no good at all. Frankly, I'm not sure I would care one way or the other. Do you care, in your heart of hearts?"

Chatwin-Paine grimaced and leaned on the balustrade to steady himself. "Yes, of course I care," he objected. "I have spent a lifetime working on behalf of the Institute, on behalf of my country. How could I not care?"

Shrugging, Daria was about to say something about malign narcissists and the fate that generally awaited them but decided to stay on message instead. She checked her watch, shut her eyes then opened them, and took another deep breath. "Do you have anything more to say for yourself?" she asked.

Chatwin-Paine straightened up. He cleared his throat. "Yes, naturally I do. Shall I tell you the tale from the start? It won't take long. I suppose you know there were three short-lived presidents of the Institute between the end of Page's watch and the beginning of mine? They were difficult years. There's not much documentation on what went on. That's when Licio Gelli became a trustee and his friends were regular guests at Villa Nerone."

"That would explain the mixed provenance of the munitions cases? The reason they came from Belgium, France, Germany, and so forth, and at so late a date, when everyone thought Gladio was being wound down?"

Chatwin-Paine seemed surprised. "Yes, well, I suppose so. I had not really thought of that." He paused and licked his lips.

"The crates are marked not only 'Gladio' and 'Stay Behind,' but also 'SDR-8,' 'Schwert,' 'Glaive,' and so forth," Daria explained, the words hammering out of her mouth. "The leavings, the dregs, the detritus of Stay Behind, once Gelli and his pals had undermined and gutted it?"

"Yes, possibly," he agreed. "At any rate, as I was saying, they were ugly times, in retrospect. The Years of Lead. Kidnappings and kneecappings and murders everywhere. The Communists came close to seizing power from the Christian Democrats. The Soviets were outperforming us across the globe. Vietnam and the assassinations of JFK and Robert Kennedy and Martin Luther King had brought disgrace on the image of the country. You're too young to remember."

Daria nodded. "I only skimmed the kompromat on the flash drive," she volunteered. "There are thousands of pages and documents. Some go into the Gelli period at the Institute."

"Yes," agreed Taylor reluctantly. "Charles Wraithwhite was remarkably gifted. A handsome young rogue too. Thoroughly corrupt, unscrupulous, lawless, reckless, and venal."

"You had a lot in common," Daria remarked, her tone tinged with sarcasm. "Was he also a serial molester like you?"

Chatwin-Paine shook his head then sighed. "I thought we'd moved on from that eons ago, Daria. You were a saucy little thing. So tall and pretty and all grown-up and as curious as a cat, so like your mother it gave me the shivers."

"I see," she said, no longer attempting to disguise the sarcasm. "So, it was my fault? A fourteen-year-old?"

"Surely you were seventeen or eighteen," he insisted. "At least that's what you claimed. Let's not exaggerate. Admittedly, I behaved badly."

"*Badly?*" she scoffed. "You were a swine. A criminal. Today you would go to jail for that or at the very least lose your job and be a pariah."

"Yes, perhaps you're right," he mused. "But it was so long ago." He glanced at the view then began again. "To get back to the Institute, I only found out about the arms caches years after taking over. Page wrote me a compromising letter laying out everything he knew. I was foolish to preserve that letter. Charles Wraithwhite found it in the archives. What was I to do? Expose the Institute to shame and degradation and blackmail or lawsuits and perhaps bankruptcy and closure?"

"So, you kicked the can down the road?"

"Yes, of course. Wouldn't you? The arms were safely underground. No one knew they were still there and if they did, they couldn't access them anyway. Over the years, a few pious academic or journalistic asses came sniffing around. I had to put a stop to that. I pulled the plug on the projects they had undertaken in Rome and sent them packing. Then this damn seven-figure legacy tied to the restoration of the third-floor room came along and I could no longer control the board. They've been working up to a palace coup for years. Your blessed brother was dogged, in that galling way of his, like your father. Blundering on no matter what the cost. It clearly runs in the family."

Daria waited before answering. The time had come. She wanted closure. He was stalling. "Indulge me, Taylor," she said. "Indulge yourself. You deserve it. Sit back and listen and give yourself one last round of applause.

"You must have been very proud to have planned the perfect murder. It almost worked. First, you introduce your old friend, the fixer Marco Torquato Scaramellato, to the irresistible little daredevil Charles Wraithwhite, your boy toy from New York, who has inconveniently decided to stick it to you. Charlie wants money, lots of money. He also earnestly wants to take you and the Institute down. Because he has uncovered enough to outrage even him.

"Charlie doesn't know that Torq is your double agent, your source inside the Catacomb Club. Torq tells you exactly what Charlie is up to, what he has discovered, how, where he is, when, with whom, why. But you are double-dealing your double agent. You don't tell Torq what you're really planning. You think that when Charlie is found dead, the victim of a tragic accident, the house of cards he and Torq have built to ruin and disgrace you will come tumbling down and disappear. After all, you have as much dirt on Torq as he has on you. He will have no idea you have engineered the death of Charlie Wraithwhite. Or will he? Has he figured it out? Doubts arise and assail you after you've committed the crime. Now you need to get rid of Torq too. But how?"

Chatwin-Paine grunted and glanced at her from the corner of his eye. "Preposterous," he remarked. "But do go on with your colorful conjecture, Daria. I'm flattered you have spent so much time thinking about me and my supposed conspiracy."

Daria shrugged off his words and continued, slowly but with increasing confidence. "I puzzled at first over why anyone would try to kill Charles Wraithwhite on the night of the gala. I puzzled over why the Catacomb Club would agree to meet that evening. Eventually it became clear. Fowler and his friends were not going to attend the concert in any case. They had decided to boycott everything the Institute organized and show their dislike and contempt for you.

"You knew that from the inside information you had from Torq. So, following your instructions, all Torq had to do was insist that Charlie hold a club gathering that evening, so that he—Torq—could reveal crucial discoveries and plans and prepare the acolytes for action. Torq cut the cocaine and heroin with Quaaludes and made sure the hash was extremely high grade—Fowler confirmed as much and so did the coroner's analysis. You didn't tell Torq why he should do any of this, and he didn't ask, did he? You did not tell him you were going to sneak down while the music was blaring and blow out Charlie's brains. How could Torq, or Charlie for that matter, have suspected you were capable of such a thing?

"Dressed in your black tux, with those dark green coveralls and black gloves, you knew no one would see you and if they did see something or someone moving around, they would never be able to identify that someone as you. You had already hidden the revolver in your black coveralls in the shed. You made sure the cartridge was fresh. You made sure the gun was in perfect working order. You made sure it was one of Jefferson's pair of vintage revolvers, not a more modern revolver from the Stay Behind caches. You would fire the shot, drop the gun into the dust and leave it behind, then pick up the unfired gun Charlie had been holding and pocket it. Fingerprints wouldn't be an issue—you wore gloves and if any prints were left on the gun, they would have come from the Catacomb Club members' handling of it at some point in the past. So, once you'd shot Charlie, you would wait in the dark for a few crucial minutes, until the club members had scattered. Then you would calmly climb up the stairs to the gardener's shed, take off the contaminated under-gardener's coveralls, the ones belonging to the tall young man named Enzo. You would transfer the unfired revolver Charlie had had into your tux pocket and walk back unseen by security cameras to the rear of the outdoor theater. Then, in the confusion at the end of the concert, you would slip upstairs to the third-floor room and replace the unfired revolver in the box in the drawer. That was your first mistake. Why didn't you put the unfired revolver in the glass display case on the wall?"

Chatwin-Paine's Adam's apple bobbed visibly. He thrust his lips out. "Go on," he said in a choked, petulant voice. "I am more and more astonished and intrigued by your imagination."

Daria laughed. She sniffed the rose he had given her but grimaced. "Let's see. What were your mistakes? No—*mistake* isn't the right word. What you didn't *foresee* was the ricocheting bullet that almost killed Adele Selmer, and the immediate reaction by a certain visiting police officer who happened to be seated right above the circular chamber and heard the shot fired. Things happened too fast—much faster than you'd planned. The first real mistake you made was you didn't imagine someone might wonder why a man as short as Charlie Wraithwhite would choose a revolver from a glass case way up on the wall and leave behind an identical one in a box he could easily have opened. The night of the murder, I checked the chairs and furniture in the room and asked Verdi, the custodian. They had not been moved. Charlie could not have reached that display case on the wall without climbing on a chair.

"So, I wondered, did someone else get him the gun? It might have been one of the other Catacomb Club members. It might've been Torq. But that seemed unlikely. Only Charlie had the key to the room. Charlie and you. He wouldn't have given the key to anyone else, not even Marco Torquato Scaramellato, and he would not have risked letting Torq wander around the Institute unaccompanied.

"You also didn't foresee your blunder in hastily hanging up the coveralls in the shed. You assumed they would be taken away and laundered the following morning, early, so no trace of the crime would remain. But maybe because of the darkness, or maybe because you rushed and didn't pay attention to this smallest of details, you mistakenly hooked them in the wrong place, on the wrong nail. They fell off. You also stumbled and kicked the overshoes by mistake, so they were no longer aligned. Your head gardener noticed. He is a very observant gentleman.

"A few minutes after you had murdered Charlie Wraith-white, your faithful fixer Marco Torquato Scaramellato, who was panicking, climbed up the staircase into the gardener's shed behind you, trying to figure out who had been in the circular chamber. He wanted to get out of the Institute from above ground. But he tripped over the coveralls on the floor. He picked them up and saw they were soiled with blood and brains, put two and two together, and decided to take them with him, moving another set of coveralls to the nail he thought was the right nail, so no one would notice. But it was the wrong nail again. The head gardener noticed. Then the following day or perhaps that same evening, Torq made the fatal error of telling you what he'd seen and done. Was that foolish of him?

"I thought, at first, Torq was lying to me about the entire episode of the coveralls and shed, that he was your accomplice not only in your double dealings with Charlie, but also in the murder. Then I realized he must be telling the truth—not a thing Torq was in the habit of doing. He was afraid of you. He had guessed what you had done and what you were up to and he knew he was outgunned by you and your friends. You had the unwitting authorities on your side and other potentates in the know—your old friends from the P2, perhaps, or SISMI and the Company? I realized too late Torq was in earnest. If I'd known, I could have saved him. By then you had decided to eliminate the last person who might blackmail and incriminate you—your friend the fixer, Marco Torquato Scaramellato.

"Was it you who fired the shot from Piazzale Ostiense when Torq was scrambling over the pyramid? Or were you not actually in the Piazzale but waiting in the cemetery already? I had forgotten until the evening of the gala that you are also the honorary president of the Italian-American Association for the Preservation of the Protestant Cemetery of Rome. Such a fine long name your association has! You have the keys to the gates to the cemetery. You know how to disarm the security cameras. Yes, it makes perfect sense. It must have been you, unless you also purchased the services of Captain Rocco Foscolo. But why would Foscolo put his career and possibly his life in jeopardy? No, I think not. I think it was you. You were the only one who would know where to find Torq after the shooting in the catacombs. You had his phone number. You had his address. You were the only one who could order him to meet me last night at the city gate and climb into the cemetery and lure me to follow him in. Were you planning to shoot both of us dead? Or just Torq? Leaving me in that case up to my neck in trouble, ready to be demoted again or drummed out of the corps. Congratulations, Taylor. Well done. You only made those very few small mistakes and miscalculations."

Checking her wristwatch one final time, Daria threw the rose over the balustrade, turned away, and walked across the garden toward the gate before Chatwin-Paine could answer. She had done her bit. She had covered her back. The rest would work itself out.

* * *

Forty minutes later, at precisely 11 a.m., Daria stepped out of the front entrance to her family's apartment building carrying two suitcases and one hanging bag. The driver of the DIGOS car rushed up the stairs to assist her. "Make sure my trunk follows," she said, getting into the back seat and slamming the car door before he could do it for her.

"Sì, vice questore," the driver barked, saluting and rushing to and fro.

"Please," she added, "turn off the radio and your smartphone and refrain from conversing with anyone. I intend to sleep until we get there."

As the car merged with traffic, Daria propped herself in a corner, shut her eyes, and woke up exactly six hours and eight minutes later to the sound of seagulls and the shouts of a passing gondolier.

FINIS